THE SHADOW

A BERRY SPRINGS NOVEL

AMANDA MCKINNEY

HH TISEVICH

Paperback ISBN 978-1-7324635-6-1
eBook ISBN 978-1-7324635-5-4

Editor(s): Nancy Brown
Jennifer Graybeal

https://www.amandamckinneyauthor.com

DEDICATION

For Mama

ALSO BY AMANDA

BESTSELLING STEELE SHADOWS SERIES:

Cabin 1 (Steele Shadows Security)

Cabin 2 (Steele Shadows Security)

Cabin 3 (Steele Shadows Security)

Phoenix (Steele Shadows Rising)

Jagger (Steele Shadows Investigations)

Ryder (Steele Shadows Investigations)

Her Mercenary (Steele Shadows Mercenaries)

BESTSELLING DARK ROMANTIC SUSPENSE SERIES:

Rattlesnake Road

Redemption Road

AWARD-WINNING ROMANTIC SUSPENSE SERIES:

The Woods (A Berry Springs Novel)

The Lake (A Berry Springs Novel)

The Storm (A Berry Springs Novel)

The Fog (A Berry Springs Novel)

The Creek (A Berry Springs Novel)

The Shadow (A Berry Springs Novel)

The Cave (A Berry Springs Novel)

The Viper

Devil's Gold (A Black Rose Mystery, Book 1)

Hatchet Hollow (A Black Rose Mystery, Book 2)

Tomb's Tale (A Black Rose Mystery Book 3)

Evil Eye (A Black Rose Mystery Book 4)

Sinister Secrets (A Black Rose Mystery Book 5)

And many more to come...

LET'S CONNECT!

Text **AMANDABOOKS to 66866** to sign up
for Amanda's Newsletter and get the latest
on new releases, promos, and freebies! Or, sign up below.

https://www.amandamckinneyauthor.com

THE SHADOW

A gruesome murder linking to a famous painting sends FBI Criminal Profiler Eli Archer down a path of lies, deceit... and infatuation.

Eli Archer has been called many things at the Bureau, but carefree and light-hearted aren't two of them. As one of the FBI's top criminal profilers, Eli spends his days inside the minds of sadistic serial killers, and he's got the brooding eyes and permanently packed suitcase to prove it. Days, murderers, and dead bodies blend together until he gets a call about a homicide that's shockingly similar to a case that haunts him. He catches the next flight to the small, southern town of Berry Springs even though there's no way the cases are connected because he already caught the killer... unless he didn't.

Payton Chase grew up in a family rich in money, dysfunction, and secrets, leaving her with a mountain of cash and emotional brick wall to match. Determined to gain independence from her past, Payton buries herself in work, chasing her dream of becoming a network news anchor. When a young woman is found tortured to death, Payton is certain that this is the opportunity to catapult her into the spotlight... she just has to figure out how to work with the secretive—and incredibly sexy—federal agent who's on the case.

As Payton's and Eli's chemistry steams hotter than the heat wave blazing through the mountains, another victim is found that looks eerily like Payton, and Eli fears she may just get her lead story... with her name as the headline.

1

$\mathcal{E}$LI SWATTED AT the mosquito buzzing incessantly around his head. It had been a while since he'd had the pleasure of being in the presence of so many aggressive blood-suckers. Then again, he'd never been this deep in the Ozark Mountains at dusk—in the middle of the damn summer.

The humidity was suffocating, like being in a sauna with ten middle-aged country-clubbers just off of a round of golf. Although this was no country club. Country clubs didn't come with mutilated corpses.

He ignored the bead of sweat that trickled down his back as he paced the small clearing at the base of the mountain. Nothing but miles and miles of woods surrounded him, thick and wilting. He'd chucked his suit jacket the moment he'd stepped out of the postage stamp-sized building they called an airport and the heat had hit him like a slap in the face. Berry Springs was in the middle of a brutal heat wave, typical for August, according to the local weatherman. He'd rolled up the sleeves of his blue button-up, but the fabric was still sticking to him like papier-mâché.

His black slacks and black wingtips were already dusty. He'd worked plenty of homicide cases in the Deep South in the summer, but this scorcher was unprecedented—about as unprecedented as the amount of time the BSPD lieutenant was making him wait.

Normally, he'd be inclined to say a big "screw you" and hightail it out of there—God knows he had a million other things that needed his undivided attention at that moment —but hell on earth couldn't keep him from visiting this particular crime scene. The moment he'd received the call from the Police Chief David McCord, he booked the next flight out.

They had to have something wrong. There was no way the cases were connected... right?

Eli circled his rental car for what seemed like the hundredth time. A normal person would be sitting in the driver's seat with the AC on blast, but he had too much energy to sit. His mind was racing already, wondering what hell lay before him on this mountain. The directions had been shoddy, but homicide scenes in the middle of the woods usually were. He'd driven straight from the airport and the road he had to take to get to the specified meeting spot was more like a jogging trail... and his rental had the scratch marks to prove it. Not that he gave a shit. The red, eco-friendly sardine box they'd rented him had about as much power, speed, and agility as an eighty-year-old hooker on a Sunday morning. The damn thing belonged on a toy train track leading matchbox cars around a bunch of preschoolers—not that he knew much about that... toys, or children for that matter.

God, he was hot.

He glanced up at the sky where beams of red and orange

fused together, fading into the mountains. He guessed they had about an hour before they lost the light.

He was just about to head into the woods by himself when he heard the low rumble of an engine in the distance.

Finally.

A blacked-out truck bumped over the ruts and rolled to a stop behind his rental.

"Sorry 'bout the wait." The moment the lieutenant stepped out of the door, he sized Eli up, no doubt noticing the wrinkled button-up and dusty shoes. Hell, the guy was lucky Eli hadn't stripped down to his boxer briefs. In training, they'd been told to always wear a full suit—jacket and tie—during initial meetings. First impressions weren't just everything, they were the first pissing match with local authorities. Suits projected professionalism, and in some cases, intimidation.

But Eli didn't give a shit. Never had. And as one of the top criminal profilers at the FBI, he didn't need to.

Next out of the truck came a tall, jacked-up dude with short, buzzed hair wearing a perfectly-starched uniform. A newbie, by all counts. But, the guy had a look of steel in his eyes and the squared shoulders of pent-up testosterone that reminded Eli of a loose cannon. Note to self.

"Lieutenant Quinn Colson, nice to see you," they shook hands. "And this is Officer Owen Grayson, former search and rescue swimmer with the Coast Guard." Well that explained the brick wall demeanor.

"Agent Eli Archer." Another handshake.

"Special Agent," Quinn corrected. "Thanks for coming out so quick." He grabbed a bag from the back of his truck. "After we saw her, we were directed to you immediately." He paused. "Your reputation at the BAU precedes you. Hopefully you're as good as they say you are."

Eli stared back. He hoped he was, too.

"Anyway, sorry about the wait. We had a domestic on the way out. My officer needed a hand."

"Not a problem." Eli knew all about the lack of resources and staff in small-town police departments, but the lieutenant was here now, and he wanted to get a move on.

"Call me Quinn."

"Head's up." Grayson launched a yellow spray can and Quinn caught it mid-air. "You're gonna want to spray this on." He handed Eli a can of DEET, and instantly became his best friend.

"Thanks." He shook, sprayed. "Aggressive bastards."

Grayson snorted.

"How far out is the scene?"

"'Bout a quarter mile through the woods. Bugs'll get worse. Especially at dusk, and we're not too far from the lake."

Lucky him.

Quinn sprayed down his T-shirt, tactical pants, and ATAC boots—attire much more equipped to handle a hike through the mountains—and Grayson followed suit. After Eli grabbed his bag from the car, they fell into step together, descending into the woods, which were darkening with each passing minute. He made a mental note to come back out at first light.

"Has the scene been released yet?"

"A few hours ago."

Dammit.

"Run me through everything again." Although he'd read the report in addition to the phone call with the chief of police, he still always made a point to get the story from as many people as possible. Perception was a huge hurdle when hearing a story second-hand. Small details that one person missed would be exaggerated by another. Biases—whether realized or not—were always injected into a replay of events. Especially in small towns.

"Vic's name is Mary Freeman." The buzz of the heat bugs was so loud around them, Quinn raised his voice. "Twenty-three, single, works as a tech at the local vet's office. Animal lover, apparently. Straight A's in high school, member of FFA. All around good girl, or so her friends and family say. Rents an apartment with a girl she works with."

"Roommate's name?"

"Cami Whittle. Works the front desk at the vet clinic. Same age, best friends since babies."

"Cami got an alibi?"

"Iron-clad. She was working the overnight shift at the clinic. Went in at four, was there until five the next morning. When she got home and realized Mary wasn't there, and hadn't appeared to sleep in her bed, she called everyone she knew asking if they'd seen her. Nothing turned up. She finally called us around noon, 'bout four hours before Mary's body was found."

"Mary's folks live here?" Eli stepped over a rotted, fallen log crawling with ants.

Quinn nodded, swatting a fly. "Raise chickens. Homebodies. Church-goers. Donate half their income to the church. Typical Berry Springs family. Not much to talk about. Mom says she talked to her at seven-fifteen yesterday morning, while Mary was on her way to work. Folks at the vet says she left when her shift ended at four o'clock."

Exactly twenty-four hours unaccounted for—a lifetime in a homicide.

"Did her co-workers know where she was going when she left? Any plans for the evening?"

"No. One thinks she remembers her saying she needed

to go to the grocery store at some point, although that was it."

"You check the store cameras?"

"Yes—nothing."

Eli knew that BSPD still didn't have any solid leads, let alone a suspect. According to the thin file, they'd checked Mary's email, bank account, and had already received the phone dump for her cell. No secret internet love luring her to meet. No communication with anyone from her past that raised a red flag. No angry emails or text messages. No suspicious calls to, or from, unidentified numbers. Mary Freeman had no crazy boyfriends, past or present, wasn't into drugs or alcohol, and walked the straight line as far as anyone was concerned. Mary Freeman didn't live a high-risk life. It was as if she'd disappeared into the thin air... and then been guided into the deepest depths of hell.

Just like the other two.

The chief had been quick to call him in, chomping at the bit for Eli's help to solve the case, although Eli got the feeling it wasn't to help the grieving family get justice, it was to keep him from looking bad. One day down, and not one solid lead.

Nothing, nada. Zip. Thin air.

Just like the other two.

Quinn continued. "The owner of the land found her yesterday afternoon. Man named Gary Powell. Called dispatch about sixteen hundred. We were out here maybe twenty minutes later and closed off the scene immediately." He paused, shaking his head. "I've got to be honest with you, I haven't seen anything like this in my career."

Eli wished he could say the same.

"You saw the pictures, right?"

Eli nodded. They were burned into his brain.

"Sick son of a bitch, man. There's the start to your criminal profile right there. Anyone who could do that to a woman... a girl... shit, anyone."

Sick son of a bitch. Unfortunately, Quinn couldn't be more wrong. But there'd be time to discuss that. For now, he wanted to start from square one and check out the crime scene.

"Take me through when you arrived on scene."

"It was obvious she was fresh—"

"How so?"

"A few things, her clothes weren't dirty, soiled, wet. Hell, they looked like they'd just come out of the dryer. She was dressed in scrubs—blue—the kind they issue at the vet's office. Her skin was pale, grey, but not scavenged, which made me think she'd been recently dumped." He paused. "She looked good, so to speak, considering the heat."

Eli nodded. Heat sped up decomposition significantly, especially this firebox.

"I checked her neck for a pulse, anyway. And that's when I noticed the burn marks on her arms. Before I even kneeled. Cigarette burns."

"How are you sure?"

"I actually wasn't at first. Owen was."

Eli glanced at the mountain of a man walking next to him who had been silent so far. The guy carried a certain edge—akin to most military guys, in his experience—that made Eli a bit uneasy.

"I've seen more female victims with cigarette burns on their bodies than I can count overseas." Owen said. "It's a very common branding practice with gangs, terrorist groups. Sometimes the burns are symbols, like branding a cow, other times it's plain torture."

He believed that. Burning a woman with a cigarette in

violent cases was common. It almost always signified the man exuding dominance over the female.

"In this case, there's no pattern to the burns indicating a symbol of any kind."

Eli watched him while he talked. Wasn't a big talker, but confident, smart, with eyes that said he'd seen a hell of a lot. Eli guessed he had some sort of special ops in his background.

Quinn nodded. "I had a hunch it was foul play at that point but when I noticed the slices on her wrist..." He paused and shook his head again. "I thought maybe it was suicide. She burns herself—I've seen that before—all leading up to the grand finale of ending her own life. Finally, one day just did it. Something she'd probably been contemplating a long time. But, there was no blood on the ground around her. Nothing. Not a single drop. No way in hell she cut herself that deep then walked out into the woods."

"You canvass the area?"

Quinn nodded. "Walked almost a mile radius around this spot. Got nothing. No blood, no drag marks, tracks, nothing. Called in our K9 trackers, too. Nothing."

Eli looked down at the ground where his shoes were crunching against dust-covered rocks. The environment was perfect for finding trace evidence—dry as a bone, and low winds over the last few days. He narrowed his eyes and looked around the dense forest as Quinn continued.

"I didn't see her face initially, her head was cocked to the side with her hair covering it, but when I noticed the matted blood, I turned her chin." Pause. "The face was unrecogniz-able." Something in his tone had shifted now. Deeper, darker. "Mary had been beaten so badly I wouldn't have even been able to tell if it was someone I'd talked to the day before." Another pause. "Then, I noticed the eyes."

Eli looked over and watched the six-foot-two lieutenant shudder. He knew exactly what that moment was like. He knew exactly the gut squeezing moment of looking at two hollow holes in a woman's head where her eyes had been ripped out. He'd seen it twice now.

"At that point, I backed away and waited for Jess."

"Jess?"

"The medical examiner. Oh, that reminds me, I chatted with her on the way over. She's expecting you after this. Anyway, at that point the team started slowly moving in and we started taking pictures." He looked over at him. "I read Miller's file."

Eli felt his body begin to tense.

"I spoke with the warden where Miller's locked up, too. No way he could've gotten out, killed Mary, then snuck back in prison…"

The lieutenant trailed off, leaving the implication hanging in the air like a dead weight—a weight that had settled onto his shoulders since the moment he'd received the call about the mutilated twenty-three-year-old.

Grayson pointed ahead. "It's just past that thicket of bushes."

Eli looked around as they walked through the thick underbrush. He'd expected a clearing, maybe a biking trail at the very least. As if reading his thoughts, Quinn said—

"Whoever dumped her had to carry her body out this far, so he's got to be strong."

"Not necessarily. The strength could've been drug induced."

"Considered that too, but that's a long damn walk."

"He'd have to have parked somewhere, too. You're sure you didn't see any tire tracks."

"I'm sure. But that doesn't mean there aren't any. There's plenty of places around here. The entire mountain's covered in hiking and biking trails, which makes it surprising that no one saw him."

It made it risky, too.

"I'm guessing he dropped her during the night, or early morning."

"The ME give a TOD?"

"Her estimate at the scene was that Mary had been dead less than twenty-four hours. We haven't received Jess's full report, yet. She might have it completed by the time you get there. Here we are."

Quinn motioned to a small patch of ground beneath an oak tree. The grass was bent from where the body had laid. Bent grass, nothing else—no blood or bodily fluids from the beginning stages of decomposition, nothing. He kneeled down, peering at the patch of dirt as his mind reeled.

Why here?

Why that day?

Why her?

Everything had a purpose, a reason. Everything added together, and it was his job to put together the psychological piece of the puzzle that would lead back to the suspect.

It was his job to predict the killer's next steps. His job to prevent another victim from turning cold.

A few minutes ticked in silence as they surveyed the scene.

"So, what's your take so far? A copycat?" Grayson asked, getting straight to the point.

A copycat killer was the obvious go-to, but the ball in Quinn's gut was telling him there was much more to this than a copycat. When he didn't respond, Quinn said, "I'd like to read your report on Miller. If it is a copycat, that'll give us a few things to go on."

Eli tore his gaze away from the tree he'd been analyzing and turned to the lieutenant. "I'd like to talk to the ME first, then I'll have more of an idea of what we're looking it."

Quinn shifted his weight, an impatient tick Eli had seen plenty times before when officers expected him to immediately draw a full picture of their suspect for him.

He glanced up at the thick canopy of trees absorbing the last of the day's light. "I'll have something for you first thing tomorrow morning."

Quinn nodded as his cell phone rang. He stepped away and answered as Eli did a three-sixty scan of the woods. Miles and miles of dense forest, miles and miles of secrets.

Quinn clicked off the phone and nodded at Grayson, "We've got to get on..." He turned to Eli.

"You go," Eli urged. "I know my way back." He looked over his shoulder in the direction of the clearing where they'd parked. He needed to get back soon, too. He had about a hundred calls to make, and return. This was going to cause a media firestorm. Careers would be destroyed, fingers pointed.

Plenty of fingers pointed directly at him.

Quinn glanced up at the sky. "You've got about thirty minutes until these woods'll be black as ink. You got a light?"

Eli nodded to his bag.

"Alright then, I'll talk to you first thing tomorrow morning."

As Eli watched Quinn and Grayson disappear into the woods, the words, *copycat* echoed through his head.

No, this was no copycat. Arnie Miller, sentenced to life

without parole for the first-degree murders of Courtney Howard and Pam Robertson, didn't inspire someone else to imitate him and kill another innocent woman by extreme torture and mutilation.

Why?

Because Arnie Miller didn't do it in the first place.

2

*P*AYTON CLENCHED HER jaw and glanced impatiently at the clock on the wall.

7:07 p.m.

It had only been three minutes since she'd last looked. Only *three* minutes.

Good *Lord...*

She inhaled deeply and mindlessly lifted the Styrofoam cup filled with a drop of the seven-dollar bottle of champagne the station had purchased for Bob Seams's retirement party. Bob had been the lead cameraman at NAR News since it opened its doors thirty years earlier. With a bald head and distended belly, Bob was the type of guy that spoke a little too closely, let his eyes linger a bit too long, and habitually made off-hand, borderline sexually offensive comments that left her feeling like she needed to hit the showers.

She sipped and forced herself to swallow the room temperature bubbly. Although the air conditioner had been on blast all day, the relentless heat wave Berry Springs was in the middle of permeated through the windows like an unstoppable force. That, combined with the number of bodies packed into the conference room, made the already small space seem suffocating. Chairs were haphazardly scattered about, balloons bobbed on the floors. The long table was covered with empty pizza boxes and cupcakes topped with gravestones that read *stick a fork in him, he's done*. A catchy little number that the front desk receptionist, Bonnie, had handmade and made sure everyone knew it—ten times. Payton wished she could be that impressed with herself on a daily basis.

A cloud of discount perfume stung her nose as Lanie Peabody, the lead evening news anchor breezed past her without so much of a glance. Payton watched her saunter over to the producer, Kip Feldman, and whisper something in his ear, her caked-on makeup looking robotic against his flushed skin. Both flicked a glance at Payton before smiling. Payton fought an eye-roll and kept her gaze locked on them until they looked away. *Yeah, I saw that.* She didn't know what the hell Lanie's problem was with her, and frankly, she didn't care. She assumed it had something to do with the fact that Lanie knew Payton wanted her job, or maybe because Payton was the only one to stand up to the narcissistic Barbie doll. Or, maybe it was because Payton had finally earned her investigative journalism stripes after helping track down a psychotic murderer months earlier. Either way, Payton wasn't going to waste her time worrying about Lanie Peabody... hell, the egotistical anchor had nothing on the women Payton grew up around.

Her gaze shifted to the window, and she imagined hurling herself out.

Next-in-line evening news anchor plummets to her death after an evening of cheap champagne and under-cooked chocolate cupcakes.

No, that wouldn't work. She couldn't go out like that. Maybe if the cupcakes were strawberry...

Laughter rang out, pulling her out of her half-baked escape plan. One second longer and she would've answered a fake phone call... some sort of family emergency. Not that anyone in her family would call her for an emergency. They had a paid staff to handle those inconveniences.

She forced a smile. If she had to do one more fake laugh, her head would explode. Although, no one knew that, of course. Payton had perfected her fake laugh by the age of five.

She'd learned from the best—her stepmother.

She turned just in time to see Bonnie grab the microphone from the portable karaoke machine. When the beginning beats of Queen's "Another One Bites The Dust" hit the air, she set down her cup.

That was it. She had to get the hell out of there. She had somewhere much more important to be.

She glanced around the room filled with people who say they're committed to delivering late breaking news to the Ozarks, but not a single person knew about the murdered woman found on Summit Mountain... and Payton was determined to keep it that way. Until she got first shot at the story, at least. By the time word was out, she'd have the exclusives. The story would be hers and she'd finally have enough clout to ask to be the on-air reporter for the story, not just the writer behind the scenes. Lanie would have a conniption.

It would be Payton's first step to becoming a network news anchor. Her first big step toward accomplishing her dream.

She grabbed her purse.

"Oh, my *God.* Can you *believe* Bonnie?" Gia Taylor, part-time public relations for the station, full-time friend, whispered over her shoulder. Wearing a form-fitting navy blue suit, Gia hiked her hip onto the table, her blonde, perfectly curled hair spilling over her shoulders. Although Payton and Gia were like oil and water, they'd been best friends through elementary and junior high, until Payton's parents had shipped her off to a boarding school a thousand miles away. They'd seamlessly picked up where they'd left off when Payton returned to Berry Springs, with Gia continuing to be the ultimate girl's-girl, and Payton being the token introvert, workaholic of the group.

Payton wasn't exactly sure when the tides had turned, but over the last few months, it was like she'd become the station's pet project to loosen up and break out of her "antisocial shell"—so they'd said. When she'd first accepted the position almost a year earlier, people left her alone—exactly what she wanted. NAR News was just a small stepping stone to leave Berry Springs for good, her first move of what promised to be many until she finally earned her stripes and became a network news anchor.

Sure, she worked too much—make that all the time—but it was because she loved it. She loved to work, but more than that, she loved the independence it provided.

Gia leaned in closer. "So, a few of us are gonna head to Frank's after, if you're interested."

Payton glanced at Bob swaying back and forth, the bottom button of his shirt dangerously close to popping open. "If *a few of us* include *that,* I'm out."

Gia grinned. "Bob's not invited."

"In that case, I might consider it."

"No, she won't." Jax, the sports reporter and former baseball star chugged the rest of his champagne and tossed it in the wastebasket. "Pay here never leaves her house, or her desk for that matter." He looked at her. "I'm telling you, Payton, you need to get out there more if you're going to get anywhere in your career."

Like she'd never heard that before.

He winked, and for the hundredth time Payton wondered why she wasn't attracted to him. *Dear God,* maybe she'd officially lost all traces of her sexuality. In a panic, she immediately began ticking off the months since she'd last had sex, when—

"You never close your eyes anymooooore when I kiss...." Bob extended his hand and swayed over to her while That Lovin' Feeling started up in the background.

Purse in hand, she turned her back to the sweat-slicked cameraman with his navel on full display. "Welp, that'll do it. I'm outta here. See y'all."

Gia laughed and maneuvered in between her and the unsteady drunk and said, "I'll shoot you a text when we get there, just in case."

Payton mouthed *thank you,* then was out the front door quicker than you could say *get-that-man-a-cab... and a new shirt.*

The heat hit her like a brick wall as she stepped into the parking lot. Dusk was on the horizon, but so far, the waning light did nothing to ease the humidity.

She pulled her phone from her pocket—7:10 p.m.
Dammit.

She was ten minutes late for her meeting.

Payton broke out in a jog, her high heels clicking on the hot payment as she skillfully dodged the cracks. She slid behind the wheel of her sports car, a sheen of sweat instantly coating her skin as she closed the door, sinking into the black interior that felt like two-hundred degrees.

She cranked the AC and clicked open a new text—

I'm sorry I'm running a bit late. Is now still a good time?

She nervously chewed her lower lip as she waited... and waited. Finally—

Sure. Come on by.

She blew out a breath.

Thanks. See you in five.

As Payton pulled out of the parking lot, her stomach tickled with nerves. A renewed energy had her thumbs tapping the steering wheel as she drove into the mountains.

This was going to be the case that made her career.

This was going to be the case to change her life.

3

*E*LI TOOK ONE last look around the trees where Mary's body was found. The sun was far behind the mountains now and the dim glow of twilight settled between the trees.

He closed his eyes and flexed his fingers, slowly pacing the grounds.

Inhale, exhale.

Another few deep breaths, then he slipped into a dream-like state that made him one of the best criminal profilers in the country. His mind, body, and spirit left the present moment, as Mary's final moments settled around him.

He let his ears guide him, taking him deeper and deeper into his out-of-body experience, imagining what Mary's killer had heard when he'd dumped the body. The wind blowing through the dry leaves, the deep thrum of the bugs, birds, squirrels skirting from branch to branch. Scavengers out looking for their next meal. A coyote howling in the distance. The forest at night—a seductive keeper of secrets, unable to speak. Forever silenced, luring evil of all kinds to lurk behind its shadows seeking the illusion of cover. The silence, stillness of nature desecrated by evil.

His pulse started to pick up as he traced his finger along the jagged scales of the tree trunk.

"You'll tell me," he whispered, eyes still closed, feeling the bark beneath his fingers. He inhaled deeply, and the images began to flash behind his lids.

She fought me, and I liked it.

With every struggle I stabbed my cigarette into her arm, over, over, and over again. Listened to her scream until she no longer cared. Until the tears dried in her eyes, the hope, long gone. The fight she had in her replaced by panic, fear. It was just the beginning, little did she know. Next, I moved to the tire iron. I broke her nose first, watching the blood spurt out of her face, she started wailing again. Then, I used my fists, dislocating her jaw. Her face became distorted, I liked that. She's disoriented now, so I moved onto the eyes. I'd never seen pain like this, I liked it. She started vomiting now, pleading for her life. Not yet. Not yet. Then for the finale, I beat her until she was almost unconscious, then carefully cut out her eyes and listened to the screams, until I sliced her wrists and watch her slowly bleed out.

A bead of sweat rolled down Eli's squeezed face as he gripped the tree, and swallowed the knot in his throat.

He saw her. Behind his closed eyes he saw Mary Freeman's mutilated body being carried through the woods and dumped underneath the oak tree.

His heart was racing, but he didn't notice. He was too far in now.

A warm breeze prickled his skin, pulling him from his trance. His eyes opened and he slowly lifted his gaze to the darkness that was beginning to surround him.

He wasn't alone.

Snick.

His hand slid to his sidearm as he turned.

"Who're you?"

"Eli Archer, FBI."

The man stepped out of the shadows, and Eli zeroed in on the bulge of a firearm underneath a faded blue T-shirt that clung tightly to a wide chest and biceps covered in tattoos. Eli wasn't the only one packing.

"Badge," the man demanded, and then it hit him. The man was defensive and protecting something—his land.

"Gary Powell?" Eli asked.

A quick nod.

Eli relaxed his stance, reached into his pocket and flipped open his badge.

Gary stepped closer, the hot air slowly deflating from his puffed-up chest.

"Didn't realize they'd call in the feds."

By his tone, Eli had no doubt Gary Powell wasn't a fan of "the feds," as was the case with most small-town cowboys.

"You found the body, is that correct?"

Twilight shadowed the man's features, but Eli guessed Gary was pushing fifty, and based on the number of wrinkles, he'd spent most of those years in the sun. Bugs zipped around him but he didn't seem to notice, didn't seem to care.

"Yeah, I found her," the landowner said moments before spitting a string of tobacco on the ground. "Was out looking for coyote tracks. Bastard's killing my chickens. Almost damn stepped on her."

Eli watched him closely as he spoke, almost emotionless about the young woman found murdered on his land, speaking of her as if she was no more of a rotting deer carcass.

"And when did you call it in?"

"Immediately." He tapped his pocket. "Always carry my phone."

"And gun?"

"That's right." He said with a touch of attitude.

"You get a lot of coyotes around here?"

Gary snorted. "Less since I've been hunting 'em."

"How long have you owned this land?"

"Inherited it. Been in my family for seventy years."

"So you know it well, then."

"Like I know my own hand."

"See anyone last night?"

"No."

"Lights? In the woods?"

"No."

"Cars? Trucks on the road? Perhaps ones you hadn't noticed before?"

"No. I've been through all this already with the lieutenant, I'm guessin' you know that, though."

"I just got into town, so I don't know much, yet. Hoping you could help me out."

"Well, that's it, then. I just told you what I know."

A moment of silence settled between them as they stared at each other.

Gary broke first. "I'll tell ya one thing, I don't want a bunch of people tromping around on my land. I won't have it. Told the lieutenant that too."

"I get that, Mr. Powell, but Mary Freeman's parents probably feel differently. I'm sure you get that, too. You know them?"

There was a flicker in the man's eyes before he said, "Know them like I know anyone else in town."

"Meaning, you consider them friends, or...?"

"Meaning I see them around from time to time and

that's it. Anyway," His tone lifted. "I don't want the news folks and people out here. Just do your business and go on."

The cue was as subtle as a lead balloon.

Eli nodded. "Thank you for your time, Mr. Powell, and while I can't promise that others won't come onto your land, I can promise that I will. I'll be back because I came to Berry Springs to help find the person responsible for taking Mary Freeman's life." He pulled his card from his pocket. "Please call me if you think of anything else."

With that, he turned and walked away. As he made his way through the woods, two things bothered him about Gary Powell. One, why hadn't Quinn told Eli the landowner was less than cooperative? And two, what the hell was he hiding on his land?

4

$\mathcal{E}$LI SLOWED HIS pace as he saw the beam of a single flashlight bouncing off the trees in the distance, heading straight toward him. It was almost completely dark, with just enough light to see about a yard ahead. Who the hell would walk around the vicinity of a gruesome murder, *alone,* after dusk?

By the sporadic flashes of light, he could tell that whoever it was, they weren't bee-lining it to a certain location, they were looking around, obviously taking their time. On a leisurely hike, perhaps?

Yeah, right.

Maybe it was Lieutenant Colson? Grayson coming back for a second look? The scene had been released, so technically, it could be anyone from the public, although he doubted whoever it was would appreciate the welcoming committee. Gary Powell kept a close eye on his land, that much was obvious.

Then, he heard the voice...

"*Yeah... Yes. No, I didn't tell him. Okay, yes, of course. Okay, bye.*"

It was a woman.

A *woman* walking around the middle of the woods, at night... alone.

Who the hell was this genius? For a split second he considered calling Quinn and having him send an officer out to talk some sense into this mindless creature. Whoever this fearless bonehead was, she was using a serious lack of judgment that could put her in harm's way. Eli had investigated way too many homicides where a woman's lack of good judgment landed her in the morgue. Stupid, stupid. Anger began to bubble up...

And then he saw her.

He stopped, stared a moment, then quickly slid behind a tree—he wasn't sure why—and continued to watch her. She stepped fully into view, and his thoughts dissolved like vapor. She wore a white blouse that pulled tightly across a pair of breasts that not even the dim light could conceal. The shimmery shirt was tucked into a skin-tight black pencil skirt that hugged her hips and thighs before cutting off just at the knee. On her feet—*God help him*—a rugged pair of ATAC boots.

She had long, auburn hair that was pulled back in a slick ponytail, highlighting a long, thin neck where his gaze lingered a bit too long on that little spot just below the ear. A pair of earrings—rocks, more like—twinkled like the intensity of her gaze as she slowly swept her flashlight along the trees and ground. Her face masked in concentration, she bit the corner of her bottom lip, full and painted the kind of red that was meant to catch a man's eye. The kind of red that made a man wonder what kind of panties she wore... the kind of red that brought men to their knees.

The kind that would taunt a serial killer a mile away.

That thought pulled him out of his lustful daze... what the hell was she doing out here?

He narrowed his eyes as she edged closer. The woman had no clue he was there. He could be Mary's killer for Christ's sake, out looking for his next victim. She was the kind of woman that was an agent's worst nightmare. The type of woman to jog with earbuds in, removing one of her most valuable senses. The type to never lock her doors. The type of woman so oblivious, so *it-could-never-happen-to-me* that she ignored all common sense.

He sized her up—early twenties, she was short, five-two at best, one-twenty, give or take a few with those curves. Expensive clothes, well-maintained. Obviously from money. Her body had the lines of someone who worked out, and the expression on her face had the fire of someone who was too fearless for their own good.

He heard her phone buzz, but she ignored it. She was completely lost in her search. For what, he wondered? A trip to the emergency room courtesy of Mary Freeman's killer? Not on his watch.

It was time to teach this broad a lesson.

Eli slinked back behind the tree, planning to wait until she was right next to him to casually step out of the shadows. He'd scare her, but that was exactly the point. Mean? Maybe. Lifesaving? Possibly.

There was a break in her steps, and he frowned, listening. A second ticked by, then a full minute of silence. Where the hell did she go?

He peered around the edge of the tree trunk—nothing.

What the hell?

He turned back and was face to face with the barrel of a SIG P938, with a bejeweled handle.

Fire as red as her lips blazed from deep blue eyes.

"Get your hands up."

He cocked a brow.

"I said, get your hands up."

He fought the smirk that was pulling at the corner of his lip, and just for fun, went along with it. What the hell was she going to do? Shoot him? He slowly raised his hands.

"Okay..." she said, and he watched her brain race to figure out what to do next. "What're you doing watching me from behind a damn tree?"

"Getting my ass handed to me, apparently."

Her eyebrows tipped up and the tension in her shoulder relaxed, tilting her gun in the slightest way, giving away the fact she was dropping her guard. It was a small shift in demeanor, but a mistake nonetheless.

"Name?"

"James Williams, ma'am."

"Mr. Williams, I'll ask again..."

Her aim was shifting, her elbow relaxing.

"What were you doing watching me from behind a tree?"

"My dog ran off and I've been out looking for him since the sun went down. Since I got home from work. Damn golden retriever. Natural wanderers they are." He added a southern accent. Everyone trusts southerners.

She inhaled and nodded. "Okay. Well, this isn't a good place to be right now. I can call animal control and they'll look—"

He lunged forward, dislodging the gun from her hand, spun her around and pinned her against the tree as smoothly as a warm hug.

She didn't scream, didn't squeal. Her nostrils flared as she turned her head.

"Ma'am, my name is Eli Archer and I'm with the FBI. Consider that a free lesson in self-defense."

He watched her eyes slowly widen.

"You shouldn't be in these woods right now." He released her and stepped back, fully prepared for the swing that missed his jaw by a half-inch. The woman was a pistol.

Her chest heaved with anger. "I should have you arrested!"

"You should thank me."

"*Thank* you?"

"Yeah. The moment I told you my fake name, you relaxed. Why? Because James is the number one most common name in the United States and almost everyone knows someone with that name, so it immediately relaxed you. You felt like you knew me, although didn't realize it. Your aim wavered the moment the words came out of my mouth." Her face dropped in embarrassment, but she quickly hid it, jutting out her chin in defiance. He also noticed her grip tightening around the gun she'd picked up off the ground—good. He was getting through to her. She was listening. Maybe she wasn't a blunt instrument as he'd first thought. He continued, "But it wasn't until I played the victim card, and threw in a nice puppy that you relaxed enough for me to take you down. Never trust anyone. Never sneak up on someone. Walk away. Or, better yet, stay home." He cocked his head. "You get points for seeing me, though. Got that one past me. Nice work."

Her face scrunched in... disgust, was it? "*Nice work?* You're a condescending prick, you know that?"

He couldn't fight the grin this time. "Been called worse."

She heaved out a breath. "If your name isn't James Williams, then at this point I shouldn't believe you're with the FBI, either. So show me your badge."

He flipped it open as she cautiously leaned forward and read every single damn word on it. Finally, she nodded, in approval.

"Special Agent Eli Archer, then."

"Eli."

"I'm assuming you're here about Mary Freeman, then?" She slid her gun into an ankle holster hidden in her boots. Nice.

"Who's Mary Freeman?"

She rolled her eyes.

Okay, so word was getting out. "What's your name?"

She hesitated, then said, "Payton Chase."

"Miss Chase, what are you doing out here past dark? Alone?"

"Exact same thing you are. I wanted to check out the crime scene of a murder victim. They released it this afternoon."

He looked her up and down. No way in hell was this woman a cop. "What business are you in?"

"I'm a journalist."

That explained it—the lack of judgment. Greed clouding all common sense. Anything to get a good story. He absolutely despised journalists.

"You're going to find Mary's killer, huh?" Condescending? Yep.

"I have the utmost faith in BSPD," she said, mimicking his tone.

"Then let them handle it."

"My job is to cover the news, and this is going to be a huge story when people find out."

"*When* people find out?"

"That's right."

"Word's not out?"

"Not yet. That's why I came now, *at dark,* because it will be out. Soon. Nothing's a secret in this small town and they'll be looking for answers." She looked him up and down in a way that was meant to be intimidating but instead sent a shot of sexual awareness through his body. "And I'm going to give it to them."

"Are you now?"

"That's right."

"If word's not out, how did you hear about it, then?"

"Connections."

Connections—he wondered exactly *how* Payton Chase got those *connections.* One wink of those baby-blues, one swipe of her tongue over those red lips would send any man into a babbling state of admissions. He hoped that was all she'd done. He'd heard stories of much, much more morally depraved acts journalists had done to get an exclusive.

But something told him that one who carried a SIG wouldn't be one of those women.

"Do you have any leads?" She squared her shoulders, eyeing him like he was eyeing her now. Like two people trying to figure each other out. When he didn't answer, she said, "Not that you would share with me, anyway, huh?" The roll of her eyes and attitude in her voice told him she was still pissed about his lesson in self-defense. She looked past him, shrugged. "Well, I guess I'll just have to walk around these woods until I find something, then. In the dark. *Aloooone.*" She rolled her eyes again, then shoved her hands on her curvy hips and blew out a breath.

She was baiting him. She was using the first thing she'd learned about him—that he didn't like her out there—to get what she wanted. No, not a blunt instrument at all. Payton was smart.

Smarter than he'd given her credit for, and that knocked

him off balance. His instincts were never wrong about people. His job—and lives—depended on it.

"I'll tell you what," he said. "I'll walk you to the scene if you'll tell me what you know about the vic."

"I'll tell *you* what. I'll tell you what I know about the vic, if you tell me what you know about the case so far."

"You know I can't get into the details, Miss Chase." That was the second time he'd called her by her last name, and she didn't flinch, even though she was young. She was used to it. Yes, this woman was definitely from money. "But I *can* make sure no one else is waiting for you behind a tree."

Her big, blue eyes met his, with an expression that told him there was one hell of a story behind why she carried a gun.

"Deal," she said.

Smart. He glanced at his watch before clicking on his flashlight. This little detour was going to make him late to meet with the medical examiner, but he had her number and address. He'd find a way to meet her no matter what.

They fell into step together. Night had officially fallen, and again, he found himself unbelieving that this woman was fearless—*crazy*—enough to go out to a crime scene after dark, alone.

"You obviously came straight from the airport?" She glanced at his clothes in a way that had him straightening.

"I did."

"You live in Virginia?"

"I do."

"How long have you been an agent?"

"I've been with the FBI sixteen years."

She gaped at him. "Sixteen years?" She stared at him trying to do the quick math to guess his age. "You must've entered the academy right out of college?"

"What makes you say that?"

"You don't look that old." She smirked.

"Thanks, I guess? And, yes, that's right." He wanted to ask how old she was but that would be easy enough to find out—but there was no question he had over a decade on her.

"Did you get accepted into the academy right off the bat?"

"Pushed a pencil for a while, then yes."

"I hear training's hell?"

"For some." He looked at her. "And if you're working on the opener of your next column, there's plenty of information on the 'net."

"Geez, just making conversation."

"The deal was to tell me about Mary Freeman."

She glanced thoughtfully up at the sky, and with a somewhat sarcastic tone, she said to the trees, "True to certain stereotypes, Special Agent Eli Archer kept information close to his chest, not unlike the blue Gucci button-up saturated with sweat after an evening hiking around a crime scene. Heat, or nerves, I wondered as I walked beside him..."

Amusement had him fighting a smirk. She'd moved on to attempting to flirt the information out of him. Well, two could play at this game.

"Boring."

"Boring?"

"Boring. I wouldn't read it."

"Well, yeah, 'cause you live it."

"No, there needs to be more of a grab in the opening line like, 'The air around me was an inky-black, heavy with humidity, and the unmistakable stench of death... not unlike the future of a fearless journalist who crossed dangerous lines for her next big story."

She raised her eyebrows. "That's dark, Agent Archer. And a clever maneuver from the original subject—you."

"You're not here to write about me, Miss Chase, you're here to get your next big story."

"People love to hear stories about special agents. Why do you think *James Bond* is such a successful franchise?"

"Because they prefer make-believe to the real story."

She nodded, and a moment of understanding slid between them. "That's my job. To tell the real story, without all the fancy—or fake—bells and whistles."

"Then you can start by telling me about Mary Freeman."

"Honestly, I don't know her. She's an only child, born and raised here, a few years younger than me. Shy type."

"How do you know this?"

She cocked her eyebrow. "I'm a journalist, or haven't you caught that already?" She laughed. "Anyway, the obvious isn't there. No crazy boyfriends, nothing like that. She was a virgin, you know."

"How the hell do you know that?"

"I will not reveal my sources."

"You're friends with the roommate."

An innocent shrug.

"What else did Miss Cami Whittle have to say?"

"As I said, I will not reveal my sources."

"You need to work on your poker face."

"You need to work on your people skills, Mr. 'here's your free lesson'…"

Wasn't the first time he'd heard that.

"Well, a poker face doesn't really matter if you have an ace in the hole."

He narrowed his eyes and glanced at her.

She smirked, enjoying that she had something to share. Yes, worst poker face ever. "Have you found her car, yet?"

"That's something you'll need to pull from the PD."

"They haven't. I know where it is."

"You do?"

"She drives a white four-door Camry. It's parked at Hank's Hardware, just off Main Street."

How the hell did a journalist find Mary's car before the police? Didn't bode well for the local PD. He stared at her and waited out the silence.

Her smile grew. "Okay, fine. When I met with my source, right before coming here, she'd tried to flick on the porch light, but it was out. Made a comment that it had recently gone out, along with the kitchen light, and that she'd felt bad because she'd griped to Mary about it. I guess that was the last thing they'd talked about. So, anyway, what's a nice girl like Mary going to do? Oh, I don't know, probably stop by the hardware store on the way home. So I drove by...and bingo."

Smart. "Have you called it in?"

"Yes, just seconds ago. I was on the phone with them right before I pulled my gun on you." She chewed on her lower lip. "So, Mary Freeman's last stop was to the hardware store. Someone took her from there."

"Not necessarily. She could've gotten in with someone." He started to pull his phone from his pocket—

"No cameras. Hank doesn't have any."

Dammit. Of course, small-town Hank from Hank's Hardware doesn't have security cameras. But that doesn't mean there weren't dozens around the area. Would be hours and hours of combing through footage.

"What can you tell me about the murder? What shape was she in?"

Eli had perfected the art of body language to not give

anything away, but something must've flashed in his eyes, because she said—

"It was bad, wasn't it?"

A second slid passed as her gaze bored into him.

"Eli, I know."

He studied her, her eyes round, with the slightest bit of fear. "I know she was beaten, badly... and I know about the eyes."

He shook his head and looked away, lips pressed in a thin line. Damn small towns.

They walked a few more steps.

"You know about the painting, right? About Theo LaRouche?" She asked.

Like the back of his hand.

"You do, right?" She asked again.

He cast her a side-long glance. "A bit, but nothing like someone born and raised in Berry Springs. Tell me."

"Legend is that Theo was born in France, then his mother snuck him onto a ship to come here. He was raised in these mountains, specifically Berry Springs, before it was even established. He began painting when he was young. His paintings resemble the post-impressionism movement. Long strokes, blurred lines, muted colors. Story has it that his mother began selling his paintings to put food on the table, and little by little word-of-mouth spread about his talent. Have you seen his paintings?"

Every single one. "A few."

"Haunting aren't they?"

To say the least.

"His dad died when he was just a baby. Rumor has it his mother was schizophrenic, and I think it's safe to assume some of that passed onto him."

"Tends to happen when you try to gouge your own eyes out."

"So you do know about him. Have you seen the painting?"

"Of the young, red-haired woman with black holes instead of eyes?"

"Yeah. Creepiest thing I've ever seen in my life. There's always a sicko that dresses up like that for Halloween. They sell masks of the face—pale, gaunt, blacked-out eyes. Terrifying." She shuddered. They walked a moment in silence. "Rumor is Theo had no siblings or kids; there's no family left except for distant relatives who live in France. Is that right?"

He glanced at her. "How do you know all this?"

"It's one of Berry Springs's legends. Hell, his original work sells for hundreds of thousands of dollars. The woman with no eyes—"

"*Sans Couer.*"

"Sans... what?"

"*Sans Couer.* That's the name of the painting. It's French for soulless."

"Soulless," she whispered. "I read that one sold for close to a million dollars. It was his most expensive painting. A French businessman bought it. Do you know who?"

"It was donated to a museum in France."

"Wow. What about all the others?"

"All over the world. Some are in museums, some sold in private auctions. Distant cousins got their hands on a few and sold them. Very difficult to trace. Although, there aren't that many. Twenty-two paintings, total. He took over a year to paint a single picture, and would burn the ones he didn't like. Only eleven paintings are accounted for."

"You mean to tell me there's eleven paintings out there somewhere?"

"Yes."

"I read that the reason he tried to cut out his own eyes was because he thought his paintings were so terrible that he shouldn't try to paint anymore."

"Tortured soul."

They meditated on that, then she looked at him. "Do you think there's a link?"

"A link between a man that's been dead for a hundred years and Mary Freeman?"

She shrugged. "Worth checking into. Into the specific painting, at least."

Payton had no idea how much he'd already checked into it.

She continued, "Especially with the festival tomorrow night..."

"Festival?"

"Yeah. Summit Mountain Art Festival. It's our little, big deal. Artists and craftsmen come from all over the state."

His back straightened with this new news. "*Tomorrow* night?"

"Yep. Down Mainstreet, in the next town over. A big parade kicks things off. Vendor tents, food carts, music, free painting and pottery demos, you name it. People dress up and everything." Her mouth dropped. "There's always a few people who dress up as the eyeless woman in LaRouche's painting. *Eli...*"

Yeah, he didn't think the timing of Mary's murder was a coincidence, anymore. Too many coincidences were beginning to muddle together into one incoherent story.

"We've got to..." she quickly caught herself. "I mean, you've got to check it out. Who knows, maybe some of

LaRouche's paintings will be there." She said it joking, but they both let the comment linger. Then, she inhaled and said, "So, that's what I have to share—the car, and my thoughts about the painting. Now, you answer me one question. How many suspects are you looking at?"

His attention was pulled to something skittering up the tree next to them. His hand itched to grab his weapon as he scanned the darkness. He wouldn't be so jumpy if it were only him... but she was there now...

"You'll have to ask your connection at the department."

"But, *you're* here. They wouldn't have called you if this wasn't connected to another homicide."

"They don't know if it is connected."

"And that's why you're here, to determine that... are there others, Eli?"

He pushed through a patch of shrubs and shined his flashlight on the small patch of grass where Mary Freeman's body had been disposed. "Here's your crime scene, Miss Chase."

Her eyes widened as she looked down at the grass, forgetting her Spanish Inquisition. Then, her face hardened as she went into investigative journalist mode. He watched her scan the area, the bushes, the trees, her flashlight fading into darkness. He kept his eyes peeled, and ears open for any sounds around them, half-expecting the gracious landlord to make another welcome visit.

She moved slowly, steadily, as she studied the scene, careful to stay off the grass. Not wanting to destroy any missed evidence? No, it was a matter of respect to her— respect for the dead. She kneeled down and he couldn't help but notice the way the skirt pulled against her thighs, weaving up to a tiny waist. He hadn't seen curves like that since his drive into the mountains.

She looked over her shoulder. "Thanks for the escort, Agent Archer. I know my way back."

She couldn't be serious.

"I don't want to keep you."

He stared at her for a moment. The woman wanted him to *leave* her there? He fought an internal battle—to stay uninvited, or leave her to her own fate.

He'd do neither. "Be smart, Miss Chase," he said as he turned away.

"Eli?"

He stopped, keeping his back to her.

"Thank you for the lesson. I seriously mean that."

Eli descended into the darkness, then settled in behind a tree to make sure Payton Chase arrived safely back to her vehicle.

$\mathcal{I}$T WAS 8:45 p.m. by the time Eli parked next to the small wooden sign that read *County Coroner*.

A short, stalky redhead with an armful of folders was locking the front door. She turned, her green eyes twinkling in his headlight beams.

He pulled the keys from the ignition and pushed out of the car.

"Dr. Heathrow, Eli Archer."

Her eyebrows slid up. "I was worried you weren't coming." She gave him the once-over before unlocking the door and stepping back inside. "Flight delayed?" She clicked the lights and set the stack of folders on a desk.

"No, I stopped by the crime scene on my way in."

Eli scanned the building, always surprised how similar they all looked. Not much decor needed to impress dead bodies. This one had a small office with a desk, filing cabinets and a cramped seating area to the side. A window looked into the lab where multiple silver tables sat in front of a wall of refrigerated boxes.

The morgue. The coldest place on earth.

Her face squeezed with intensity. "I didn't realize you were going to the crime scene. Anything else turn up?"

"Not that I know of. I'd like to see the official autopsy report on Miss Freeman, if you don't mind."

"Of course not. I've printed it out for you to review. I'm going to take another look tomorrow morning before I release her to the family, though, just FYI." She pulled a folder from the top of the stack and handed it to him, but kept her grip as he tried to pull it from her hands.

He met her gaze, her eyes deep with sorrow. "I'm going to be honest, Agent Archer. This was a tough one for me. Someone really took their time with her." She released the folder.

Her and two others. "Care to give me the Cliffs Notes?"

"I'll give you whatever I can, whenever you need it, to help you find this psycho." Her steady voice wavered with anger.

Eli cocked his head. "You knew her. You knew Mary."

"We grew up on the same street."

"I'm sorry."

"Me, too." She inhaled deeply. "I'm assuming you've already seen the pictures and have spoken with Quinn, right?"

"Right."

"Okay." She paused. "I've seen a lot, Agent Archer... but the torture of this one..." She took a deep breath to steady herself and grabbed a notebook from her desk. After clearing her throat and squaring her shoulders, she continued. "The official cause of death was cardiac arrest due to blood loss. The victim had roughly three-inch lacerations along her wrists, severing the ulnar artery in each wrist. She died approximately twenty minutes after her wrists had been severed."

Her eyes met his, ice-cold, then shifted back down to the paper. "She was devoid of approximately 75% of her blood by the time she was dumped. The remaining blood pooled along her right side, which, as I understand it, was how she was found. She was on her side." She paused. "There were multiple tool marks along her orbital bone. My guess is he used a knife to remove each eyeball." It wasn't often he watched a medical examiner get grossed out. "But that's not all. A part of her lid, on her left eye, was still intact... and there were tiny microscopic lacerations in it. Also, just below the eyebrow. Like pin pricks."

"Pin pricks?"

"Yes."

They stared at each other for a few seconds as the realization sank in. The fucker had pinned Mary's eyes open, forcing her to watch the abuse in front of a mirror, most likely.

Jessica took another deep breath, then continued, reciting the facts of the autopsy as a true professional.

"TOD is roughly twelve hours before she was found, so she officially died sometime early yesterday morning. She was tortured for hours before that. The victim has scratches and bruising on her arms, which considering the state of the rest of her body, it's hard to tell if they were from an initial struggle, or during her entrapment. She showed signs of blunt force trauma with two separate fractures in her frontal and temporal bones, and mandible. Six teeth missing. Her knees had been shattered, again blunt force trauma. She had twenty-six cigarette burns on her arms, neck, face." Jessica's jaw clenched. "All of this was perimortem. She had rope burns and scratches around her wrists and ankles, so she'd been bound, my guess is the entire time. And the eyes..." Jessica closed her eyes a moment, and Eli tensed waiting for the rest of the sentence. "The eyes were removed perimortem as well. The suspect used a smooth, not serrated, knife, and my guess is a three-and-a-half-inch paring knife. Something like that. The knife would have had to have been small. He was careful, too. There were no punctures to the brain."

"Was any of her hair pulled out?"

"Yes, I checked that almost immediately. Partial hair loss in a five-inch radius, at the crown."

"So, he held her head still while he cut."

She nodded.

"Was there any pattern to the cigarette burns?"

"No. Sporadic."

"What about the tox?"

"Glad you asked." She raised her eyebrows and pulled a piece of paper from the folder.

"Chloral hydrate"

Eli's stomach hit the floor.

"You ever heard of a Mickey? Slip a girl a mickey in her drink? That's it. Although he didn't slip it into her drink. He injected it into her neck." She lifted a close-up photo of Mary's neck. "It's hard to see here, but based on this line of bruising... and you can see the small prick here, with a trace of blood around it."

He squinted and leaned in. One thing was for certain, Jessica had a hell of an eye.

She pointed. "The needle—an inch and a half—went in here, and went in at an angle. He also used more force than necessary, as you can see from the blood and bruising here."

"She struggled initially."

"Exactly. So he got close enough, somehow, then popped her and took her. Very likely no screams, I'd imagine, although that's not my job to determine that."

"Mind if I take this?" He reached for the paper.

"Not at all, but I'm not done. She also had traces of cocaine in her system."

His hand froze on the paper. "Cocaine?"

"Yes. Cocaine. Her nose was covered in it, and I found traces inside her mouth as well. This hit her system after the Mickey." She stared at him a moment. "Again, this isn't my place to assume, but considering how her eyes were pinned open, my guess is that he gave her the drug after she'd fallen unconscious from the beating, to pull her out of it. He'd give it to her to wake her up so he could continue torturing her."

He likes the reaction.

"I don't usually speculate like this, forgive me. It's not my job... this just... feels..."

"Personal."

"Right."

He took the papers from her hands. "Anything else?"

"That's the gist. Details are in those documents. Like I said, I'm going to spend some more time with her tomorrow and I'll let you know if anything else comes up. I'll release her to her family tomorrow morning." She swallowed deeply and shifted her weight. "Let me know what else I can do to help you find this son of a bitch."

He nodded and pushed out the front doors, eager to get the hell out of there. Something about a morgue.

The stifling temperature had dropped with the sun, but was still hovering in the high seventies, and the humidity was still like a wet blanket hanging in the air. He pulled onto Main Street, hit a red light at the town square—the only light in town he'd noticed. He looked around and couldn't help but notice how different Berry Springs was from his neighborhood in the suburbs. It was like a completely different world.

A diner was the hub of the square, with blue-and-white checkered curtains and bright red booths. He counted six cowboy hats inside. Surrounding the diner was Fanny's Farm and Feed, Tad's Tool Shop, which was closing down for the night, and Anita's Flowers.

He watched an elderly man, dressed in a felt cowboy hat and shiny boots open the door for his wife, dressed to the nines for an evening out with her husband.

Small town America, it truly was.

A mixture of jacked-up trucks and Subarus with kayaks on top speckled the square. During his research on the plane ride down, he'd learned that Berry Springs was a huge tourist destination year-round, known for its camping, hiking, fishing, and hunting.

The town had a warm, old-country feel to it that tugged at him.

It reminded him of growing up on his grandfather's ranch in Wyoming.

There was no graffiti, no homeless wanderers. It was a community where the citizens took pride in their town.

A community that would demand answers as soon as they found out one of their own had been beaten to death and left to rot in the woods.

Ten minutes later, Eli walked up a lighted pebble walkway that lead to a quaint, Victorian-style bed-and-breakfast nestled deep in the woods.

Anna Gable's B&B

A bit pricier than he usually liked to spend, the bed-and-breakfast was the only decent lodging with vacancy in the entire town. The festival and heat wave had brought art-lovers and water-sports enthusiasts to the area.

He could hear the hum of a boat on the lake just down the hill, and surprised himself when a moment of jealousy hit him. It had been so long since he'd relaxed on a lake, or the ocean for that matter. Hell, he didn't remember the last time he'd taken a *vacation.* But that was what he'd signed up for. Living his life out of a suitcase was all part of the job.

Serial killers never slept.

So, neither did he.

He walked through the front door.

"Evening." A dark-haired beauty smiled as she cleared dishes from a coffee table, and instead of scanning her head to toe like he usually would, he immediately thought of the other stunner he'd met that evening—Payton Chase.

The smell of fresh paint lingered in the air. The B&B was spotless and obviously recently renovated. Shining hardwood floors, a massive fireplace in the middle of a spacious living area with multiple couches, lounge chairs and one of the biggest flat screens he'd ever seen. A long hallway led down to a kitchen with windows that overlooked an expansive back deck. An antique-looking staircase with carpet runners to the left.

The woman walked up and extended a hand. "I'm Jolene Reeves, owner of the B&B. You must be Mr. Archer?"

"Yes, ma'am."

"Pleasure to meet you. I've got your room all ready. Let me just set these down." She placed the tray on an end table and he caught a glimpse of the massive diamond sparkling on her left hand. Someone emptied their savings account for that rock. Eli understood the significance of engagement rings, a symbol of two people's love for each other, but he never understood the sentiment of spending thousands of dollars on a circle. What was wrong with a good ol' gold band? The image of the sparklers in Payton's ears popped into his mind. She was probably the type to demand a million-dollar ring.

Not for him.

"Need any help with your luggage?"

He glanced down at the small roller he always kept packed. "No, thanks, this is it."

"Okay, right this way." She led him up the staircase. "How was the traffic coming in?"

Traffic? He almost laughed. This place had nothing on DC. "Not bad at all."

"The arts festival is bringing a lot of folks to town."

"That's what I hear."

"You were the last person before I put up the no vacancy sign." They reached the second floor, which was in shambles.

"Remodeling?"

"Yes. Only a few rooms available right now, like I said, you got the last. I purchased the place about a year and a half ago. The basement and first floor have been completely remodeled. I'm working my way up. You're in the top unit, beautiful views. That room is special to me." She smiled and he knew there was much more to that story. He watched the way she held the banister, and how she favored her hips as they made their way up the staircase.

"Congratulations on the engagement," he said. "How far along are you?"

She turned her head, grinning. "You're pretty perceptive for a guy. How long have you been in the FBI?"

His eyebrows tipped up. He'd been careful not to share that information when he'd booked the room.

"What makes you think I'm with the FBI?"

She chuckled. "Honey, I can spot an agent a mile away... and that was before even I got engaged to one."

"What's his name?"

"Ethan Veech. Cyber Crimes. You know him?"

"Actually, yeah, I've heard the name." He searched his memory as they reached the top floor.

She turned and heaved out a breath. *"Phew."* She cocked her head. "You're a profiler aren't you?"

"You should be a detective, Jolene Reeves."

She tipped her head back and laughed. "Anyway, to answer your question, I'm ten weeks and I swear this baby is soaking up every inch of my energy." A smile crossed her tired face. "Worth every second, though."

He watched the joy light her eyes.

A family.

It was a terrifying concept he'd never considered, and one that he'd accepted might never be part of his life.

She opened the door, and he stepped inside. Jolene wasn't kidding about the view. Sweeping windows looked out to a rolling back lawn illuminated by antique lamp posts. Just beyond that, a half moon danced on an ink-black lake. The room had hardwood floors throughout, a small kitchen, and separate bedroom with a four-poster bed.

Not bad at all.

"Can I get you anything?"

"No, thank you. Although I've got half a mind to carry you down the stairs myself."

"I'll make it, thanks. Good to exercise. Ethan will be coming in tomorrow, hopefully, and I'll take a few days to relax. I've left your reservation open, as you requested. Stay as long as you'd like."

"Thanks."

She closed the door and silence engulfed him. He set down his luggage, placed his briefcase on the desk, then walked over to the windows and looked out at the lake. Multiple boats swayed in the water, stars twinkled in the sky above soaring mountains in the distance. A normal person would look at the scenery with appreciation.

Eli Archer looked at it as a roadmap to a homicide.

He turned from the window, his thoughts easily, or perhaps habitually, fading from fantasies of fun to work, and he walked over to the kitchen and yanked open the mini-fridge.

Nice.

Water, soda, juice and a mixture of expensive imports. He grabbed a beer with a wicked-looking wizard on the front—*Brewed in the Ozarks, it said. He hoped that meant it wasn't mixed with a Mickey.* He popped the top and took a swig—not bad.

As he settled into the desk, his mind was already running at warp speed. He grabbed the thick file tagged *Miller, Arnie.* Coffee mug rings and grease stains covered the front. The file had been in many different hands, but none as long as his. He flipped it open. On top lay hours of interview transcripts, which he'd read countless times.

He set them aside.

Next, the investigator's notes and witness interviews— this portion of the file was short. Much too short.

He set them aside.

Finally, he pulled out the section held together with a paper clip titled *Theo LaRouche.* He removed the clip and frowned as he looked at photos of the artist's paintings. He narrowed his eyes as he traced his fingers along the lines of a blurred silhouette of a cloaked man against a stormy land-scape. Beady eyes, a luminescent yellow, peered from under the black hood. It was as if they glowed against the dark, menacing colors. The cape faded into slashes of deep red— angry, violent.

He slowly looked through each image, more of the same —chilling, dark, hostile. Finally, he lifted the last image, its corners crinkled from so many hands examining it.

Sans Couer.

A tingle as fine as demon's fingers tickled up his back as he stared down at the eyeless woman in the painting. Blurred lines outlined a voluptuous young woman in a red gown, with her head dangling from the edge of a muted brown sofa. Her jaw, crookedly slacked open, the tongue limp against the corner of her red lips. Her eyes, vacant, black holes. Soulless.

"*Haunting...*" Payton's words echoed in his head. Yes, haunting.

His finger trailed the words written by him on a yellow post-it on the inside of the folder—

The Couer Killer

That was the name the media had used to sensationalize the psychotic serial killer that was murdering young, innocent women.

The Couer Killer Strikes Again, the headlines read.

He set the painting aside, took a sip of beer to wet the cotton in his mouth, then pulled out the first set of crime scene photos.

Courtney Howard, age 24, 119 lbs., 5'3", auburn hair, blue eyes. Cause of death: Cardiac arrest due to blood loss. Manner of death: Homicide.

He stared down at the black holes where Courtney Howard's eyes had once been. Her face had been beaten so badly they'd had to use her teeth for a positive ID. He pulled out the next group of photos.

Pam Robertson, age 22, 107 lbs., 5'2", red hair, blue eyes. Cause of death: Intracranial Hemorrhage. Manner of death: Homicide.

His throat went dry as he looked at the picture, and the same knot squeezed his stomach. He could still hear her voice, could still see the fear in her eyes when she'd spoken to him the day before she'd been brutally murdered. She'd known. She'd known she was the Couer Killer's next target —a woman's instinct that Eli truly believed was a very real thing. Women were gifted with a certain sixth-sense that men simply were not. Unfortunately, it was only helpful to those who were in tune with themselves enough to listen to it.

His hands trembled as he picked up the interview she'd given hours before she'd been kidnapped.

They'd said it wasn't his fault. Not a single person blamed him for Pam Robertson's death.

But Eli did. Every single night he blamed himself for her death.

He skimmed the interview, although he didn't need to, he could recite it with his eyes closed. Then, he flipped it over and looked at the word that had haunted him every day for the last year.

Shadow.

6

"*P*AYTON ROSE CHASE, I will *not* have this conversation with you again. You *will* be here Saturday night for your father's sixtieth birthday party. End of story."

End of story. One of her stepmother's all-time favorite lines. If Payton had a nickel for every time she'd heard the woman say those words... to her, and her father, for that matter.

Payton gripped the steering wheel as she rounded a tight corner. The narrow mountain roads of Berry Springs were difficult to drive in the dark without listening to one of Charmaine's rants.

"Charmaine, I can't just drop everything—"

"Call me *mother*! Jesus Christ, for the hundredth time! And you sure as hell dropped us, Payton!"

Payton rolled her eyes and inhaled deeply. Charmaine was drunk again, that much was obvious.

"The moment you turned eighteen you turned your back on your father and me. After all we've done for you!"

We've. Payton bit back a laugh.

Charmaine's voice began to pitch. "You don't even call anymore—nothing. It's like you've totally disowned us. After *everything*." She clicked her tongue. "Payton, I have some *very* important people coming to this event..."

And there it was. The real reason her stepmother wanted her at the party. It wasn't because she wanted to see Payton, or because she missed her. Charmaine hadn't given a damn when Payton left for boarding school at the age of twelve—she'd been the one to suggest it, after all—hell, the woman had even called their driver herself. No, her stepmother didn't really want to see her. The forty-five year old stay-at-home-wife just didn't want the cracks in their "perfect family" facade to show. Charmaine wanted Payton at the party for appearance's sake. That was it.

Charmaine continued, "I've got the mayor, three senators, congressmen, and state representatives coming, and some very interested investors. You *will* be there."

Payton's nails dug into the steering wheel. Just the woman's voice was enough to make Payton want to run headfirst into a mountain.

She'd never understood why her father married the woman—or *girl*—back then. Payton had been in preschool when Charmaine and her father had met. The gold digger was only twenty-three years old. They married almost three years to the day after Payton's mother had died of heart disease. Payton didn't remember much of her mother but had heard through the gossips that Charmaine and Anne were as opposite as night and day. Charmaine saw nothing other than the eight figures in Payton's father's bank account, whereas her real mother had only seen love.

That's what the gossips said, anyway.

To this day, Payton held it against her father for marrying such a monster. Not that she could talk to him about it. Arthur Chase owned an international financial consulting firm and was away from home forty-five weeks of the year. He spent his life traveling from country to country, spending months at a time working with a single company. He was brilliant when it came to business and technology. He was resourceful, and a notorious bulldog in the board-room. The man could negotiate his way out of a bank vault... not that he would, he liked money too much. But nothing compared to his tenacity—the man wouldn't back down from anyone, no matter what the cost. He was a workaholic by all counts. Payton had gotten her drive and love of computers from him, and perhaps her strong will, too... okay, fine, her stubbornness. That was just a guess though, because Payton didn't even really know her father.

As Payton had gotten older and learned more about the business, she knew her father could have distributed his workload so he could've stayed home with her more, before she was shipped off to boarding school, of course. But then, she'd realized that he didn't *want* to be home. Arthur didn't want anything to do with anything that reminded him of the loss of his first wife. He didn't want anything to do with the gold digger he'd married out of pure desperation to replace what he'd once had with Payton's real mother.

And that epiphany had only made Payton angrier at her father.

Almost as angry as she was now.

"It's this Saturday, cocktails begin at five, although we have people coming in early so I expect you to be here by noon on Friday. And get a nice dress. A couple. Nice ones. You haven't spent all your damn money, have you, Payton? Is that it? How much do you make anyway at that stupid job of yours... a couple hundred bucks a week?"

Payton's mouth dropped.

As if that weren't enough, the drunk continued, "Bring a date, but if he's some hillbilly redneck, I don't want—"

"That's *enough*, Charmaine." Payton snapped, and that was enough to send Charmaine over the edge—the exact place Payton wanted to drive her car at that moment.

"Don't you *dare* tell me that's enough, you little snot. And hear me... if you don't show up to this party on Saturday night, I'll see to it your father cancels your next trust fund deposit."

Payton's hand trembled with anger. She focused on the dark road ahead and instead of saying one of the thousand vile things rolling around in her head, she did what she knew would get under Charmaine's skin the most. She was calm, and as sweet as sugar. "It was a pleasure speaking with you, Charmaine. Have fun at your party."

Payton clicked off the phone and released a guttural scream as she tossed it on the passenger seat.

She hated that the woman could still get to her, after all these years. Threats were common with her stepmother when she was drunk—which was every night—and the trust fund that Arthur and Anne had set up for her when she was just a baby was a major source of contention between them.

The value was now twenty-three million dollars—enough to make anyone jealous.

Charmaine was as jealous as she was manipulative. And even though Payton knew Charmaine had no influence over Arthur when it came to her, the woman still brought up Payton's trust fund in almost every argument they'd ever had.

Payton took a long, deep breath to steady herself.

She'd planned to grab a salad at Gino's on the way home, but had officially lost her appetite. A crime scene topped off with a phone call from Charmaine would do that to you.

She thought of Eli.

Her embarrassment when he'd knocked the gun from her hands.

The butterflies when he'd pinned her against the tree.

His tall, strong body against hers—that ruggedly handsome face with dark eyes that promised anything but boring.

He'd mentioned a woman's sixth sense, and the moment she'd laid eyes on him—gun aimed and all—she knew in her gut she was safe. She was in no danger—she'd never been so sure of anything in her life.

And after her near-death experience months earlier, she trusted her instinct—and her SIG—now more than anything else.

What were the odds she'd run into a fed while researching Mary's death? Fate? Undoubtedly—the man was a walking bag of secrets that she wanted to get her hands on. It also meant that there was much more to the Mary Freeman homicide than she'd anticipated, and she couldn't help the zing of excitement she felt wondering if this was going to be the story to catapult her into the spotlight.

But, as quickly as she'd noticed the man's sizzling hot sex appeal, she realized that Eli was smart. People smart. No innocent smile or tug at her neckline was going to get her anywhere with this man. Hell, he spent his career reading between the lines.

No—no amount of flirty winks would make Eli Archer allow her to get close to his investigation.

He was a vault.

With twenty deadbolts.

That was okay though, she'd figure out a way to get the information she needed, as she'd done plenty of times before.

Payton always found a way.

She rounded a hairpin corner and flashing lights pulled her attention.

Frank's Bar.

She slowed the car, fighting an internal battle in her head. Did she really want to spend the rest of her evening talking about NAR News gossip—not particularly. Did she want a drink? Like she wanted her next breath. The decision was made when Jax's words echoed in her ear.

"... *you need to make nice with the locals if you're going to get anywhere in your career.*"

She hit the brakes and turned into the small gravel lot. The place was packed, especially for a Tuesday night. Not a single parking spot. She wove around the trucks until sliding into a grassy spot along the woods where a few others had parked. She glanced at the clock—9:04 p.m.

One drink.

After yanking off her ATAC boots and slipping into her black, Louboutin heels, she pulled down the mirror and glanced at her reflection—*holy crap*. Half her makeup had sweated off from her sweltering hike in the woods, leaving only black smudges of mascara below her lash line. Her long, auburn hair had frizzed from the humidity, giving it a finger-in-electrical-socket look—not pretty.

She heaved out a breath, contemplating.

One drink.

After a quick reapply of concealer and lip gloss, she pulled her ball of frizz into a loose bun on the top of her head and snarled as she gazed at her reflection. Oh well, that'll have to do. After smoothing her white, silk blouse and black pencil skirt, she made her way across the parking lot and pushed through the heavy wooden doors.

Along with the sour scent of beer and cedar, loud voices and laughter floated through the room. A few cowboy hats turned toward her, followed by a few whistles and cat calls —maybe she should've kept the boots on. Loud, classic country played from the antique jukebox in the corner that sat underneath a large clock with antlers sticking out of the sides. Hardwood floors ran underneath locally-made wooden tables and chairs. A stone bar lined the left side of the room, with a mirrored wall filled with liquor bottles. A small stage sat in the back. This was her third time to the bar, the first two had been to chase down leads for a few of her stories.

She liked it. It was classic southern honky-tonk.

She skimmed the tables searching for familiar faces, with no luck.

She was just about to leave when—

"Payton! Holy crap, you came!" Pushing her way through the crowd, Gia expertly clutched a martini glass without spilling a drop. Her smile was infectious.

"Wasn't sure if you guys would still be here."

"Are you kidding? This place is hoppin'. We'll be here all night. Jax put our name in for karaoke." She rolled her eyes with a laugh. "Come on, I'll get you a drink," she said as she grabbed Payton's hand guided her to the bar.

"Hey, Billy!" Gia leaned over the bar, her cleavage spilling over her top. Not surprisingly, she snagged the bartender's attention in seconds.

"Hey there, Gia girl." He glanced at Payton and gave her a not-so-subtle once over. The bartender wore a faded red plaid shirt with the sleeves rolled up showcasing an armful of tattoos. His hair was shaggy, giving him the quintessential bad-boy look.

"Have you met Payton Chase?" Gia grabbed Payton and shoved her forward, causing her elbow to swipe an angry-looking trucker's beer on the bar.

"Sorry," she said as she nudged Gia.

The trucker grunted in response, his attention never leaving the baseball game on the television mounted to the wall.

"Don't believe we've met," Billy winked. "You from here?"

"Born and raised."

He frowned—because he should definitely know her, then. She got that a lot.

"Payton here went to boarding school and college on the east coast." Gia winked. "Our little hoity-toity world traveler."

Billy grinned. "That explains it then. Didn't think I'd forget a face like that."

Payton's eyebrow cocked.

"Anyway, what can I get ya, lil' miss?"

"I'll take a vodka cranberry, please."

"Make it a double. She needs to relax." Gia added.

Before Payton could protest, Billy sauntered off to get her drink.

"God, I'm *so glad* you came out!" Gia turned and scanned the crowd as if she was scouting for her next pair of heels. "There's some cute boys here tonight. Lots of out-of-towners in for the festival. You see Clay McDowell? He just moved back from college. Nothing wrong with a younger man, right?"

"Younger man? Please. We're twenty-six, G."

"Don't remind me."

Payton laughed. Gia dreaded every birthday past her twenty-first—being able to officially buy booze was apparently the peak of any woman's life—and Payton had no doubt Gia would be into Botox before too long.

Billy delivered Payton's drink with a wink, and she sipped as she looked over the crowd. Cowboys—a few cute —drunks, more drunks, and some of the tightest pleather skirts she'd ever seen. A motley crew of every southern stereotype imaginable.

Raised voices pulled her attention to the corner of the room where a game of pool was getting out of control.

"Come on, girl, let's get to the table."

"Hey, Payton!" Jax stood from his chair and raised his glass where half the NAR News crew hovered around a large table in the back. Just a few feet away, two blondes sang incoherently on the dance floor—one stumble in their bejeweled cowboy boots and they'd be wearing Jax's pitcher of beer.

She slid into a chair between Gia and the station's tech specialist, Carson Knapp, surprised to see him there. Notoriously quiet, Carson came to work at the same time every day, ate the same thing for lunch every day, left at the same time, and barely spoke to anyone outside of meetings. They'd only exchanged a few words in the entire year she'd worked there. There was a small part of her that felt bad for him, and a small part that also thought he was a bit creepy.

She smiled. "Didn't expect to see you here."

He smiled and for the first time she actually looked at him. Carson was cute, in a boy-next-door way, with a charming smile.

"Right back at ya," he said before taking a sip of his beer. "Who dragged you out?"

"Who do you think?" He nodded toward Jax who was glued to the blondes on the dance floor. "You?"

She nodded toward Gia who was knocking back a shot of whiskey. "Who do you think?"

He laughed. A nice laugh.

She took a sip.

"So, how's your story coming along?"

"Oh, you mean *'Have the Ozarks gone to pot'*?" She rolled her eyes. "Riveting."

He laughed. "So, what are you doing? Just chasing down drug dealers and asking them about their business?" He grinned.

"No, I've actually decided to take a different angle. I'm in the process of interviewing people who recently got their medical license for it. Getting their take and how it's helping them."

"That's totally different than ol' Kip wants, you know."

"I know." She chewed on her bottom lip. "Truth is, he's wanting me to tarnish my hometown, painting it as some shady back-alley place full of addicts. It's not. And marijuana medical licenses are a hot topic right now. I think that's what people really want to hear about."

"Cheers to that," Jax, who was apparently eavesdropping, raised his glass before emptying it and heading back to the bar.

"Ever wish you were as social as that guy?" Carson asked.

She laughed, but hesitated. Did she?

"Well," he tipped up his beer. "Here's to not really wanting to be here, but not having a half-bad time."

"Cheers to that."

With that, she settled in to watch the drunk blondes

serenade Jax in an off-key version of "Friends in Low Places"... Was there any other version, she wondered.

Another highball and four songs later, Payton leaned over to her new friend, Carson.

"I'm going to grab some air on the patio. Save my seat, I don't want to small talk with anyone else."

He laughed and nodded.

Payton pushed away from the table, unnoticed by Jax who was grinding on Miss Boobs-A-Lot, or by Gia who had dragged Clay McDowell onto the dance floor, much to his dismay.

Drink in hand, she weaved through the crowd and stepped onto the back patio. Although every seat was taken, it was calm and quiet, a stark contrast to the bar inside. She walked to the corner and leaned against the railing. A large oak tree strung with lights towered above her, the golden sparkles reflecting in her drink as she mindlessly twirled it in-between her fingers.

Mary Freeman, her stepmother... Eli Archer...

Although the vodka had helped dull the day, her mind was still unsettled.

"Beautiful night, isn't it?"

Startled, she turned.

"Sorry," the man smiled. "Didn't mean to scare you. Name's Ted Davis. They call me Teddy."

She smiled and shook his large, leathery hand. "Payton Chase."

"Nice to meet you."

Ted—or Teddy—wore khaki shorts with a red T-shirt that stretched nicely across his chest and flip-flops on his tanned feet. Based on his bare ring finger, he was single, and based on the striking looks, that was by choice.

He leaned in and she caught a whiff of liquor on his breath.

Great. The only thing Payton hated more than drunks, was dealing with one of them hitting on her. Something about liquor made even the smartest man an incessant idiot on picking up on subtle—or not-so-subtle—body language.

"Gettin' kinda crazy in there isn't it? Your friend's tearing up the dance floor."

"I don't doubt it." She looked away—subtle leave-me-alone cue number one.

"You dance?"

Give me a break. She smiled and kicked out her foot. "Not in these heels." *Or, ever.*

"Too bad." He leaned closer, enough to make her stomach tickle with nerves. That sixth-sense Eli was talking about. She stepped to the side and her hip hit the wooden railing. She was cornered by the drunk—literally.

"Looks like your drink's a little low. Can I get you another?"

"No, thank you." She turned fully away from him now—cue number two.

He slid his hand over hers, getting even closer. "Come on. Just one more. I'd be more than happy to—"

She yanked her hand away. "I said, no thanks, Ted. Now, if you'll excuse me..."

He clamped down on her arm. "Hey, I didn't mean—"

"Payton..."

With eyes cold as ice and a tone Payton hadn't heard since she was a toddler, Eli Archer walked up behind them. "Sorry I'm late."

Ted straightened, bowing up like a Cobra about to strike. *Shit.*

She quickly angled herself between both men, noticing

how tall Eli was. He towered over her and was a good three inches taller than her drunken Casanova. Not even the shadow covering Eli's face could hide the anger vibrating off of him. He looked absolutely terrifying.

"Spec... ah, Eli. Thanks for coming." She turned to Ted. "Pleasure meeting you, Ted Davis."

Cue number three: Get the hell out of here, asshole. She glanced behind him where all conversation had stopped and everyone was staring at them. They were the spectacle of the evening. How embarrassing.

Ted shot her a fiery glance, then one to Eli, before nudging him with his shoulder as he passed. Bad move, apparently.

It happened so fast she still wasn't sure how Eli did it, but like a flash of lightning, Eli had the drunk's arm bent behind his back and his head on the table.

Gasps sounded around them.

Eli leaned down and whispered something into Ted's ear that had his nostrils flaring.

"*Teddy!*" A short brunette came barreling across the patio. "Hey! Let him go!"

Eli released him, standing solid as the Oak beside them as Ted sprung up and stood nose to nose to him.

Payton's heart hammered in her chest.

"Teddy baby, come on, baby, come on." Horrified, the brunette tugged the drunk's arm until finally, he tore his eyes away from Eli, took another look at her, then stumbled across the patio.

Her mouth dropped as she shifted her attention to Eli. "Oh my *God.* That was..."

Cool, calm, and collected, Eli slowly rolled up the shirt-sleeve that had come undone during the scuffle. His hands weren't even shaking... unlike hers. He was still in the same slacks, shoes, and blue button up as when they'd met in the woods, except his hair was a little more mussed, and dark circles shaded his eyes.

"Sorry about that," he said as if he'd simply spilled her drink.

"*You're* sorry? No, *I'm* sorry. You didn't have to..."

"Yes, I did."

"Well. Thank you."

He stared at her for a moment and a flurry of butterflies awoke in her stomach. It was the second time that evening that Eli Archer had given her butterflies. And the second time he'd been protective of her. One thing was for sure, the agent who seemed to get better looking every time she saw him had the Knight in Shining Armor thing down. The women must love him.

Suddenly, behind them—

"Two shots of Patron. On the house." Billy hurriedly crossed the patio and handed them two ice-cold glasses, dressed with salt and a lime. "Sorry about that, Agent Archer." He flickered her a glance. "And, Payton. On the house—doubles. That was Ted Davis, he's harmless. Him and his girlfriend come in here all the time. Get a little sauced up occasionally, but who doesn't?" He grinned. "Anyway, I asked them not to come back tonight. If you need anything else, let me know. Again, sorry."

"Thanks... Mr..." Eli extended his hand, and Payton was taken aback how calm he was after just slamming some dude's face on a table.

"Oh. Billy. I'm the bartender here."

"We haven't met."

"No. Cop buddy in there told me who you were."

Eli nodded. "In that case, I'd like to chat with you later if you have a few minutes."

"Absolutely. Just holler at me when you're ready."

"Will do."

"Well, I guess the word is out," Payton murmured as Billy walked away.

"Was hoping to make my way around the place before it did."

So that was why he was there—to interview the staff of the most popular bar in town.

His gaze pinned her. She swallowed deeply.

"You okay?" He asked.

"Yeah. Just... yeah, yeah, I'm fine."

He set down his shot glass, stuck out his hand and nodded at her purse.

"What?" She lifted it. "You want?" She frowned as she watched him open it up.

"You carry that SIG for protection, right?"

"Right."

"What good's it going to do at the bottom of your bag next time someone harasses you?"

"First, this isn't the Wild West. I'm not going to pop a drunk in a local bar for hitting on me."

The corner of his lip curled up at this.

"Second, a sidearm doesn't exactly go with this outfit, and an ankle holster doesn't go with these heels."

He lingered on her legs a minute in a way that had her hormones waking from hibernation. He handed her the purse. "You know they make bags with side pockets specially for handguns?"

"I'll look into it," she said dismissively, but then frowned intuitively. "You think if Mary Freeman had a gun..."

"I'm not saying that. I'm just saying it's good to be prepared."

"Well, you don't have to worry about that with me." *Not anymore.*

"Good." He scanned the room in the exact way he did the woods when they were on the mountain—suspiciously.

"Are you here alone?" She kicked herself the moment the words came out of her mouth.

A second ticked by as he stared at her. "Yes. You?"

"Yes. I mean, I met some friends inside." She snorted and turned toward the trees that surrounded the bar. "They've taken over the dance floor."

"Not a dancer, huh?"

She laughed. "No."

He cocked his head and rested his elbows on the rail.

"What?"

"Nothing."

She crossed her arms over her chest and cocked her hip onto the rail. "That surprises you?"

"I'd be willing to bet my *Gucci* shirt that you dance."

She grinned. "Ah, so you think because I noticed the brand of your fancy shirt, that, what? I'm a classically trained dancer?"

"That and the two carat earrings you have in your ears, and the two thousand dollar bucket you call a purse."

"Hey, I got this two thousand dollar purse for free."

"Ah... she's a thief."

She laughed. "No. A website called Luxe Trade. Swapped my old one for this beaut."

"You literally trade bags with people?" He said it as if the concept was mind boggling. Had this guy never had a girlfriend in his life?

"Yes, but only authentic bags. You have to show the receipt, serial number. It has to be verified."

"Well, see if any of those pricey bags have pockets for handguns."

She grinned. *"Anyway,* so all that means I dance?"

"Those things lead me to believe you grew up with a silver spoon in your mouth and lived a lifestyle where your parents consider it a civic duty to know how to classically dance. And, you have a staff that called you Miss Chase. But the dead giveaway is the way you angle your feet outward when you stand, and your impeccable posture." His gaze lowered to her legs, bare below the knee, and the look in his eyes sent tingles flying over her skin. "And the long, lean legs." He lingered, again, sending her heart fluttering. "You were a ballet dancer."

"Not bad, Agent Archer. You read the hell out of people, don't you? It's almost like that's your job..." She looked him over. "You're not a traditional agent, are you?"

"What makes you say that?"

"One, you don't have a team with you. So, either the feds don't think Mary Freeman is connected to any other homicides, or you're here to investigate something different. Although you're not. You're obviously here about Mary, just in a different capacity. Two, although you know details of the murder, you're obviously not leading the case. BSPD is. The case wasn't handed to the feds." She narrowed her eyes. "You've been brought in to consult. You're a criminal profiler."

"So you see," he said as he leaned toward her, "I'm afraid I won't be much help in your story, Miss Chase."

"Oh, no, no, no. Not so fast, Archer."

"Archer, huh?"

"That's right." She leaned, shoulder to shoulder, faces inches apart. "You wouldn't be here if you didn't think there was a chance this was connected to another case. So, there's got to be some similarities with other homicides. Am I right? Come on, tell me."

His gaze flickered to her blouse where the top button was dangerously close to popping open. "Is this how you conduct interviews?"

She cocked a brow, straightened and nodded at the table where he'd slammed Ted's face. "Is that how you conduct yours?"

He grinned. A moment of silence slid by as understanding flashed between them. They both were very used to getting what they wanted out of people, and they both had brick walls built around themselves. She wondered if anyone could break through that shell of his, professionally, or emotionally, for that matter.

He wasn't letting her in, that was for sure. So, she'd have to go a different route.

"I drove by Harry's Hardware again. They picked up the car already." She said, redirecting the conversation.

"Not surprising. So, how'd you get the roommate to talk?"

She shrugged.

"You played up the fact you were born and raised here, and could help with the investigation using your journalism background."

"How do you know I was born and raised here?"

"Lucky guess."

"Why do I feel like you get lucky with a lot of guesses? Anyway, yes, and two eyes are better than one, right?"

He glanced down at her shirt again.

"I wanted to get to know Mary from her roommate's perspective, and figured woman to woman, versus cop to woman, might reveal more information. And, the cops had already interviewed Cami, so what the hell."

"Mary was raised here, you were, too, and you're around the same age... and this town is the size of a thimble. How do you not know her personally?"

"Oh..." She took a quick sip. "I left town during seventh grade."

"Where to?"

She looked away. "Boarding school."

He raised his eyebrows. "Where?"

"East coast. And my education away from Berry Springs continued through college." She laughed. "It's funny. I'm from here, but I have felt like an outsider ever since I came back."

"When was that?"

"Less than a year ago."

Something in his eyes flickered.

"I graduated four years ago, accepted the first job I could find there, then saw NAR News had an opening for a journalist so I jumped on it."

"What did you major in?"

"Journalism, minor in Computer Science."

"Interesting combination."

She smiled. "Guess so. I've always been into computers." *Or anything that I could bury my head in to avoid my stepmother.*

"Must've been hard leaving home like that, at such a young age."

She glanced out at the mountains in the distance. He had no idea how hard it was to pack up and leave everything you knew at such a young age. She'd never forgotten the shock, or the feeling of total abandonment when Charmaine told her she was going to boarding school. Truth was, Payton believed that very moment changed her life. Nothing makes you feel more unloved than the person who's supposed to be your parent shutting you out. Nothing makes you more insecure and introverted than starting a new school during the awkward, self-doubting phase of puberty. At a very young age, Payton knew she could only count on herself and she knew that had shaped the woman she was today.

And she sure as hell didn't want to go into all that right then.

"It was hard at times, but I received a good education." She dropped it there and switched the conversation to what she really wanted to be discussing. "Look, Eli, I get that all law enforcement hates the media. I get it. But it doesn't have to be that way. I can be an additional source for you."

"You have an entire department of additional sources."

"Yeah, but you're FBI."

He snorted and looked away.

"I'm going to write this story no matter what, Eli."

"I have no doubt you will, Payton." He looked back at her with an intensity that had her spine straightening. "Just don't be stupid."

She glared back. "I'm not in the habit of making stupid decisions."

"That makes two of us."

They stared at each other for a second, and she knew that was all she was going to get out of him. Eli was a locked box of secrets.

"You gonna drink that shot?" She asked.

His gaze shifted to the sweating glass on the railing.

He picked his up, she picked up hers.

With a twinkle in his narrowed eyes, he said, "To always trusting your instincts."

She tapped his glass.

"To always trusting your instincts."

7

*B*EEP, BEEP.

Eli reached across the desk and turned off his alarm clock.

5:31 a.m.

He glanced out the windows at the darkness still blanketing the mountains. He hadn't even left his desk. He wasn't sure why he even bothered setting his alarm clock every night. Eli habitually woke before five, every single morning. On the nights he slept, anyway.

And last night, was one of those sleepless nights.

It wasn't long before Payton's friends had come looking for her on the patio of Frank's Bar. And it was even a shorter amount of time that her friend Gia began digging into his personal life in a thinly-veiled matchmaking attempt.

He was out the door the moment she'd asked why he'd never been married.

He found himself contemplating that question the short drive back to the B&B. He'd had plenty of girlfriends, had been on plenty of dates... until he joined the Behavioral Analysis Unit. The first case he'd worked on was creating a profile for a serial child molester. He'd crawled into the deepest depths of hell during that six months, and his partner said he'd never climbed back out. Before being accepted into the unit, Eli had worked as a special agent for five years and had seen plenty of shit, but it was nothing compared to analyzing a criminal's head. Eli quickly realized he had something else that no one else did—the freakish ability to envision himself as the suspect, to envision the crime as it took place. For better or worse.

He'd never forget the first time he'd started having visions. He'd closed his eyes and stepped inside the mind of a murdering rapist. He could hear the murder, see it, feel it. By the time his partner had shaken him out of his trance, his heart was pounding so quickly in his chest he thought he was having a heart attack. With each out-of-body experience, he learned to control his physical reaction to the adrenaline coursing through his body.

But even then, he couldn't hide it completely.

"You're getting too close to this Archer." His partner would say. *"You need to take a step back. Get out of his head."*

Get out of his head.

He couldn't.

Eli's ability to *become* his suspect was exactly what made him one of the top criminal profilers at the FBI. It was also what made him detach from every meaningful relationship he'd ever had.

Eli had graduated college with a double major in Criminal Justice and Psychology and had applied to the FBI his first week out of school. In the academy, Eli was known as a fun-loving, good-timing jock who didn't take shit from anyone. He was the tallest and heaviest trainee, with muscles that came from two hours in the gym every morning, seven days a week. He was stronger, faster, and smarter than his trainers. He graduated the top of his class.

The bloom slowly started falling off the rose when he'd lost a buddy in a case that had gone sideways. Mortality hit home, and it sobered him up. Slowly, the long days, death, and the blatant disrespect for human life began to take its toll.

Evil was a very, very real thing.

Then, the rose officially died when he'd joined the BAU. Long days turned into twenty-four-hour days. A constant string of serial killers, pedophiles, rapists consumed every second of his day. Too much evil in the world needed too much of his attention. He kept a permanently packed suitcase next to the front door of his barren, one-bedroom apartment a block from headquarters. He lived, breathed, ate, and drank the job. He didn't sleep.

The job had sucked him in, its ice-cold grasp dragging him further and further into dark depths where the line between fact and make-believe, between good and evil, got blurrier and blurrier. His co-workers, his partner especially, began looking at him differently, began treating him differently. Some days they barely spoke to him. It wasn't until his boss ordered him to see a counselor that he realized how much he'd changed.

"You've become dark, Eli," his boss had said.

Dark.

His boss was right. The happy-go-lucky Eli had been replaced by death. Some days, he wondered if he'd ever see that guy again.

Life sure was easier back then.

Eli set down his tepid coffee and tore his eyes away from the gruesome crime scene photos scattered in front of him. He blew out a breath and leaned back. The air conditioner hummed in the corner, promising another scorcher. He scrubbed his hands over his face.

He needed fresh air... a quick energy refresh.

He pushed out of the chair and threw on his jogging gear. After sliding his phone and shiv into his spandex, he pulled on a pair of shorts, T-shirt, and running shoes and quietly walked downstairs. The smell of fresh coffee woke up his senses.

"Well, good morning." Jolene poked her head out of the kitchen. "Headed for a jog?"

"Morning, and yes. I didn't wake you, did I?"

"No, not at all. This baby did. Pregnancy insomnia, or whatever it's called."

He wished he had something to blame his insomnia on. Oh that's right, he did... dead bodies.

She continued, "Breakfast menu's in your room and there's one on the table in the den. Just let me know what you'd like when you get back and I'll have Greg, the cook, whip it up. Should be here in thirty minutes."

"Thanks, but I'll catch something on the way out. Go rest."

She smiled. "Believe me, I wish I could. You can pick up the jogging trail by the boat docks down the hill. The four-mile will loop around if you follow the green markers. It's a lighted trail, too."

"Green markers. Got it."

She smiled, a hint of pity in her eyes. She knew he hadn't slept. She knew the life of an FBI agent didn't allow for it.

He stepped outside into the humidity, although it was still dark, he swore he could see it swaying like steam around him. He raised his arms over his head and took a deep breath, inhaling the fresh scent of morning mountain air, the scent of the lake in the distance. Bugs chirped around him, birds sang in the trees above.

Berry Springs wasn't half bad. Quaint, charming, except for the most recent homicide. It was a town that embraced nature and wildlife and being outdoors was the only thing that relaxed Eli. Maybe he'd vacation here one day soon... if he took vacations.

He took off in a jog down the hill, toward the wet, moldy scent of lakeshore. In the distance, twinkling lights marked the trailhead. He glanced up at the sky where the stars were just beginning to dim. Thirty minutes to sunrise.

He hit the trails and pushed into a sprint. Pine needles crunched underneath his shoes, sweat began to bead on his forehead, the fresh oxygen awakening his sluggish body from a night hovered over murder books.

One mile down, then two.

The sky was lightening, and he'd already passed two joggers—both male, thankfully. If he had his way, he'd demand no woman be allowed out alone until the suspect was caught. Unfortunately, things didn't work that way. Although the citizens of Berry Springs would be shaken, scared, and even angry that a murderer walked among them, unfortunately, it didn't mean that they would be more cautious or vigilant. No, most people would go about their day as they always did, with the attitude of *"it will never happen to me."*

If he had a nickel for every victim that said, "I never thought this would happen to me."

He thought of Payton going to the crime scene alone the evening before.

Crazy.

He thought of the way her body had felt underneath him against the tree. The spark in her ocean-blue eyes when she'd looked over her shoulder at him. The red of those full lips.

Sexy.

Payton Chase was beautiful, smart, confident, stubborn, and ambitious. Every quality that drew him to a woman. She was also part of the media. Every reason to stay away. It was just a matter of time before she dug up the old articles about the Couer Killer, and connected the dots. If she hadn't already.

He'd just hit his fourth mile when his phone buzzed.

"Archer."

"It's Quinn. Got your email; what time can you meet this morning?"

"As early as you can fit me in."

"Thirty minutes?"

"Sounds good."

"You're at Gable's B&B, right?"

"Right."

"I'll pick you up at the dock on the lake. There's been a development."

8

*E*LI STEPPED ONTO the dock as a boat sliced through the lake. The bright colors of dawn painted the rippling water, dancing under pink clouds moving swiftly overhead.

Jolene had a cup of coffee waiting for him when he'd gotten back from his jog, and he'd had just enough time to grab an ice-cold shower before making his way to the dock. The workday was starting early—just the way he liked it.

"Morning." Quinn skillfully maneuvered the boat to the edge of the dock.

"Morning," Eli said as he stepped into the boat.

"I've got a thermos of coffee in the back."

"Just had a cup, thanks." He met the lieutenant at the head. "What developments?"

"A hunter just called in a skull he found in a creek, just off the lake."

"A human *skull?*"

"Yep." Quinn pulled away from the dock.

"He's sure it's human?"

"He wasn't, but Jessica is. I asked her to come by. Thought you'd want to check it out."

"You thought right."

They started through the lake, into the rising sun. The wind whipped around him as water sprayed up from the sides, cooling Eli's already warmed skin. Damn he needed to get out to the lake more... or, at all.

Quinn continued, "I also thought we'd have our meeting out here, solo, if you don't mind." He cut him a glance. "I'd like to get the full story, your profile, before engaging the team. I'd like to know what we're dealing with before bringing everyone in. First thing I learned when I accepted the job in this town was that gossip and suspicion of outsiders is as common as a concealed carry license. Unfortunately, even at the station. I'll meet with you, get the lay of the land, then pull together a meeting with everyone who needs to be there and lay out the facts. Sound good?"

"Sounds great." He'd had more meetings with small-town law enforcement than he could count and one thing was for certain, he had to work that much harder to convince them he knew what he was talking about. *They* were the experts of *their* town, after all. The fewer people he had to convince, the better. And this way, he'd have the lieutenant on his side going in.

He already liked Lieutenant Quinn Colson.

The boat cut through the water and he raised his voice over the wind. "Did Jessica say how old she thinks the bone is?"

"Nope. It was called in 'bout forty-five minutes ago. I texted Jess immediately. She sent a text just before I picked you up saying she was there, and that it is definitely human. That's all I know."

Eli's mind began to race. "Any recent missing persons?"

Quinn shook his head. "Nope. I'm having Grayson pull a list of all local missing persons over the last ten years, although once we get a better idea of how old the bone is from Jess, we'll narrow it down."

Eli nodded but something in his gut told him they wouldn't need to go back ten years.

Quinn slowed as a dark figure waved from a dock ahead.

"That's Harold. He called it in. We're going to park in his slip and walk up. He owns the rental house my brother's living in. Nice guy. The skull was found just about a quarter-mile from his house."

Quinn pulled into the slip and Harold was already tying the boat by the time they cut the engine. Dressed in pressed, dark-colored Levis, a short-sleeve plaid button-up and straw hat, the man looked to be pushing eighty. Eli guessed he was an early riser, like he was, and liked routine, wearing the same style for decades. Every morning, coffee, paper, shower, and dress for the day, whether he planned to leave the house or not. That was Harold, he'd bet his life.

"Howdy, there." The scent of Old Spice wafted through the air as Harold lifted two mugs. "Made you boys some coffee, and I pulled my side-by-side out for y'all."

Nice guy, indeed.

"Thanks, Harold. We shouldn't be long." Quinn took the mugs and handed one to Eli before starting up the trail that led to Harold's house.

"Y'all let me know if you need anything, ya hear?"

"Yes, sir," Quinn yelled over his back as he jumped over a fallen tree trunk.

Eli hung back to let Harold go ahead.

"No, go on up," the man said. "I'll stay here and make sure no hoodlums or festival hippies mess with the boat."

Eli smiled, nodded. Of course he would.

After a quick hike up the trail, he jumped in the side-by-side next to Quinn and they took off through the woods.

Eli sipped his coffee, paused, twisted his lips and raised his eyebrows. He couldn't fight the grin as he looked at Quinn. "There's Bailey's in this."

Quinn grinned. "Like I said, nice guy."

Eli laughed and took another sip as Quinn did the same. "Alright, should be..."

As they came down a hill, Eli caught a glimpse of Jessica's bright red baseball cap through the trees. Quinn rolled to a stop between two pine trees. They got out, making their way through the thick underbrush.

"Mornin', boys." Jessica looked up and wiped the sweat from her brow with the back of her gloved hand. Eli grabbed a tree branch for stability as he stepped down to the shallow creek that cut through the woods. No shoreline here.

He zeroed in on the skull on the ground.

Jessica's eyes locked on the mug in Quinn's hands. "That Harold's special?"

"Yes ma'am." He handed her the mug, and she chugged for a good two seconds. Eli noticed the bags under her eyes and paleness of her skin. Jessica had gotten as much sleep as he did, and she was more torn up about Mary Freeman than she let on.

She swallowed deeply and licked her lips. "That'll wake you up in the morning, boys. And trust me, you're going to need to be alert for this."

The tone of her voice confirmed what Eli's gut had been telling him on the way over. He kneeled down next to Quinn.

"The jaw is fractured in several places." Jessica looked up, her gaze skirting back and forth between them.

The heavy implication hung in the air for a moment.

She tore her eyes away and back down. "Also several top teeth are missing, but it's impossible to tell if that's from an injury or if they came out as the body deteriorated." She looked at the creek. "The hunter said he literally found it right here. Makes me think it could have been dumped from the lake during the most recent flooding this spring. You'll have to get a team to sift through the creek and search the area for the rest of the body. It'll take days, if not weeks."

"Can you tell how old it is? Time since death?"

"That's a bit more difficult to say. Bones found ten years ago look very similar to bones found five years ago. I can tell you this bone is in decent shape. I'd say within the last few years. I can tell you that the person was older than eighteen because they have their top wisdom teeth. There's no significant bone loss, so I don't think the person is very old at all."

"Can you tell if it's a man or a woman?" He asked.

"My guess is woman. Women tend to have more pointed chins; men more square. Also, can you see the sloping of the jaw here? Women have more of an obtuse angle, men more vertical. The good news here is that they should be able to ID from the teeth."

"Back to the fractures. What can you tell us about that?" Eli asked.

She nodded. "It appears to be perimortem."

"Jess, English." Quinn interrupted.

"Meaning it happened very close to the time of death. There are three categories of trauma in skeletons—antemortem, perimortem, and postmortem. Ante is before death, peri is close to, and post is obviously after." She pointed to the small fracture. "You can tell the stage by the amount of healing around the wound... there doesn't appear to be much here."

Eli watched her closely. Her eyes met his, and then the bomb dropped.

"And… there's a few marks around the orbital bone. I can't tell if it's a knife, but it's definitely something."

Quinn's mouth dropped. "Are you telling me her eyes were cut out?"

"I'm telling you there are small, almost microscopic marks around her eye socket."

Quinn surged to his feet and grabbed his phone.

Wide-eyed, Jessica looked at Eli. "Do you think it's another one? Another woman murdered by Mary's killer?"

Eli looked at the skull as a woman's face began to take shape. "We'll see when they make an ID and go from there."

But Eli didn't need an ID. He already knew her name.

9

"*V*ALERIE WALSH."

Quinn frowned. "Doesn't sound familiar."

"Declared missing up in Hammond county about a year ago..." Eli clamped his mouth shut as a young couple came up behind them.

"What can I get y'all?" A tanned woman with grey dreadlocks running down her back smiled as she wiped her hands on her tie-dyed apron.

"I'll take a double stack, two sausage links, and four slices of bacon. And a water, please. Extra syrup on the side." Quinn—who'd obviously been here before—rattled off without a moment of hesitation.

Eli looked over the hand-written menu tacked up on the small food truck underneath a wooden sign that read *Berry Good Day.*

Considering their proximity to the river, Quinn had suggested they grab breakfast at a "damn good" walk-up food vendor parked outside a popular outfitter that offered kayak, canoe, and fishing adventures. The temperature had already breached eighty, and the heatwave had people of all ages hitting the water. It was just past seven-thirty in the morning, and they'd had to stand in line just to place an order.

Eli looked around as the waitress wrote down Quinn's order. The rising sun glistened off the water. A thickly wooded mountain hugged the far bank of the river, and above them, cliffs that he guessed stretched two-hundred feet. It was a beautiful area with plenty of trees to seek solace from the relentless sun.

He watched a young man and wife slather sunblock on twin two-year-old boys with matching swim trunks and floaties on their arms. A group of teenage girls giggled as the kayak instructor demonstrated safety precautions. A trio of fishermen slowly floated by in their jon boats, waving at the group of elderly women sitting with their feet in the water and with books in their hands.

"And for you, sir?"

He focused again on the menu. "I'll take a fiesta wrap and water, please."

"Good choice." Her smile widened as she looked at Eli. "Name's Shauna. Don't recognize you."

"Just visiting the area."

"Are you now? Well, I'd be happy to offer you a discount for a run on the water. Level's perfect for a smooth canoe ride. I'll even take you myself."

Eli could see the reflection of Quinn's ear-to-ear grin in the window.

Before he could make up an excuse, she winked and handed him two bottles. "Here's your waters. Just think about it. I'll bring the food right out. Sit where y'all'd like."

Quinn was still smirking as they made their way to a secluded table nestled under a rock overhang.

"I think Shauna likes you."

"I think Shauna wants a nice tip."

Quinn laughed as Eli slid into the picnic table and felt a rush of cool air.

"Is there a cave over here?"

"Yep. See over there?" He pointed to a thin crevasse barely visible in the rocks. "Leads to a pretty big cave. You ever been spelunking?"

He laughed a humorless laugh and nodded.

Quinn's eyebrows arched. "Lemme guess... an investigation."

Eli nodded realizing how pathetic his life was. Yep, he'd been spelunking before... following up on a tip that led to the bodies of two missing children.

"Well, you should do it sometime, minus the dead bodies. There's dozens of caves in these mountains." He frowned and Eli knew exactly what the lieutenant was thinking.

"It's not a bad idea..."

Quinn met his gaze. "Don't have the manpower to canvass the caves right now. We'll start with the creek and woods, first. Now, tell me about the other victims. Tell me about Valerie..."

"Let me start with the beginning." He took a quick sip of his water. "A year ago, a young woman, twenty-four, was found in a shallow grave up in Hammond County in Missouri."

"That's just an hour north of here."

"Right. I was called in because her eyes had been removed—"

"Wait, they called in an FBI profiler for one homicide?"

"No, they called me in because it was the second body with missing eyes they'd found in two weeks."

Quinn's brows arched. "Serial killer with a fucked up M.O."

"Exactly, except the eyes would be his signature, not his M.O. His M.O. is what makes him tick, the why's of the crime, which is exactly why I was called. A fucked up M.O, yeah, no doubt about that but that doesn't help us find the guy. So, the first victim, Courtney Howard—her eyes had been removed, she'd been beaten, and her wrists had been sliced."

"Just like Mary."

"Yes."

"Sexual assault?"

"No."

"Just like Mary."

Eli nodded. "Courtney was a twenty-four year old nurse at the assisted living facility in Hammond county. Her fiancé, twenty-nine year old Arnie Miller was a self-employed electrician with three DWIs, one D&D, and one aggravated assault under his belt. Rumor had it he'd roughed up Courtney on multiple occasions, though like most domestic abuse cases, she never called the cops."

Quinn nodded, knowing that situation all too well.

"So, local authorities made him suspect one from minute one, until he provided an alibi for the night of Courtney's murder—his mom. They called me in at this point. Then, the second body was found—beaten, no eyes—and they jumped on him again. The second victim was Pam Robertson." He cleared his throat and took a sip of water. "Pam had reported being followed two days before she was abducted. Said she was doing a late-night grocery run and, quote, someone in a red Ford was watching her from the shadows."

"Please tell me she gave you more than that."

"No, and of course, the corner store where she bought a gallon of milk, cereal, and a box of kitty litter didn't have security cameras in the lot. She also said when she let her cat in later that evening, she felt like she was being watched. This concerned me because she was around the same age, type, and bore a resemblance to Courtney. Fast forward to the next night..."

He paused. He'd just fast forwarded over the biggest mistake of his career. The mistake that kept him up almost every night. The mistake that cost an innocent woman her life.

He continued in his ever cool, even tone as he'd been trained to do. As the brutality of his job had trained him to do—work without emotions.

"Pam Robertson was found almost beaten to death, her eyes had been removed, and she'd been dumped in the woods."

"Jesus... Wait... you said almost."

He shifted in his seat. "That's right. She died four hours after she was found, from her injuries."

Quinn shook his head. "Holy shit."

"Yeah. She was a tough one."

A moment slid by before he continued, "Also, both women had chloral hydrate and cocaine in their systems. We believe the suspect lures them into his vehicle, knocks them out with the chloral, and then uses the cocaine to stimulate them and keep them awake while he tortures them, and now, with Mary I'm wondering if slicing their wrists is the final act. He likes to watch them slowly die."

"So Courtney Howard's wrists were sliced, and our own Mary Freeman's, but not Pam's?"

"Pam technically died of brain hemorrhaging. The ME said she'd been unconscious for some time, which is why I don't think he cut her wrists, which is his ultimate ending. He thought she was already dead, by accident, I believe, so he simply dumped the body."

Quinn shook his head in disgust.

"At this point, needless to say, the story hit national news. They'd dubbed him the Couer Killer. Are you familiar?"

"I wasn't until Grayson mentioned it last night—shocked that the guy knew his paintings. I'm not from here, didn't know about LaRouche. That *Sans Couer* painting is the freakiest damn thing I've seen in my life. You think it's connected? All this to a painting from a dude who died a hundred years ago?"

"Two young women, red hair, missing eyes, close proximity to where the painter was said to have lived... I couldn't ignore the coincidence." He blew out a breath. "I fucking unturned every stone, not that there were that many, and nothing turned up. No connections between the painting, Theo LaRouche, Courtney and Pam. Nothing."

Quinn scratched his chin. "The timing's interesting."

"I agree. I didn't even know there was an art festival this weekend."

"It starts tonight."

"Tonight?"

"Yep. There's a big parade in the next town over, Eureka. Artsy town. The bars that line downtown will have paintings for sale and auctions. It's a big event." He bit his lip. "As I'm saying this, I'm thinking we need to go. Check out the crowd, see if anyone's auctioning a LaRouche knock-off..."

"Or, even take note of the people who are looking at similar art, and make note of the big buyers."

Quinn nodded. "I'll arrange it. So, there's no connection between Pam and Courtney and LaRouche, but what about with Arnie Miller? Did he have a connection with LaRouche, or any interest in creepy-ass paintings?"

"No, nothing. Guy definitely wasn't the artsy type."

"Okay, so how'd they get this guy convicted?"

"They searched Miller's house and found blood in his bathroom, which was then confirmed to be Courtney's. But the nail in his coffin was when they pulled security footage from public areas around Pam's house and saw him on camera—in a red Ford—getting gas five miles from Pam's house the day she was murdered. He was taken into custody and convicted of first-degree murder for both women six months later. That was three months ago."

Quinn took a sip of water while gathering his thoughts. "And now, we find the body of a local Berry Springs woman with no eyes, beaten to death, and the skull of a young woman with tool marks around her eyes...I'm guessing this is where Valerie Walsh comes in."

"Bingo. As I said, Valerie was reported missing around the same time Courtney and Pam were murdered. And, get this, Valerie also resembled the other two women... and so does Mary."

"Is there any connection between the girls other than appearances?"

"Nope, not a single thing. Different schools, didn't even know each other. No family connections, nothing."

"That's interesting. Okay, so Miller kills two, possibly three women a year ago and gets locked up. But now Mary's body turns up like the others..." Quinn studied him for a minute, and Eli let him. He wanted to get Quinn's thoughts and see if they aligned with his.

"The obvious here is that we've got a copycat killer. Cut and dry. But, you don't think it's a copycat killer, do you?"

"No, I don't."

"Then, that means you think Miller is innocent."

"I do."

"Then you think Courtney, Pam, and Valerie's killer is still out there."

"And obviously not done."

They waited a moment for a group of preschoolers to pass by.

Quinn leaned forward on his elbows. "What makes you think Miller is innocent? That's a big fucking deal."

It was a big fucking deal. A deal that could cost people their jobs, hell, possibly his own. "I've thought Miller was innocent from the moment I interviewed him."

"Why?"

"The evidence that led to Miller's conviction was one-hundred percent circumstantial."

"What about Courtney's blood in his house?"

Eli shrugged. "Could've been from any one of their domestic incidents. The girl had a damn bloody lip on her last social media posting. Said she'd fallen in the bathroom—"

"Where the blood was found..."

"Exactly. And hell, he even admitted to roughing her up on multiple occasions. And the mother as an alibi? The woman has dementia and showed signs of abuse as well. He probably threatened her. But what really gets me is that there is even less evidence when it comes to Pam. The only connection Miller has to her is that he was seen getting gas a few miles from her house the day she was killed."

"What did he say he was doing that day?"

"Getting wiring supplies at a shop for his job, two miles from the gas station."

"Was he?"

"Yep. We have him on camera."

Miller's body language on that footage also didn't reflect a man who had just abducted, or was planning to abduct a woman, but that was based on Eli's gut and decades of watching human behavior—not black and white fact.

Eli continued, "Miller claims he went straight home after getting gas, but unfortunately, we couldn't verify that."

"Does anyone else share your opinion?"

"That Miller is innocent?" He laughed. "Hell no, the pressure was so heavy, they wanted a guy in cuffs immediately."

Shauna delivered their food with a wink, then sauntered away with a quick glance over her shoulder.

He thought of Payton.

"There's something else."

Quinn dumped a gallon of syrup on his pancakes and took a bite.

"Pam Robertson woke up for a while in the hospital."

The lieutenant's eyebrows slowly raised as he looked up.

"We attempted to ask her questions, with no response. Not even a kick in blood pressure. She was awake, but wasn't there." A gust of wind blew past him as he looked out at the water, remembering the next moment like the back of his hand. Pam, with bloody, white patches over her non-existent eyes, her face purple and contorted from the swelling and bruising. They couldn't have replicated it in a horror movie. He'd never, ever forget it. "Seconds before she went back under, she whispered something."

Quinn stopped chewing.

"Shadow."

"Shadow?"

Eli nodded and in an attempt to busy his hands, took a bite of his wrap.

"Shadow? What the hell does that mean?"

Eli shook his head and shrugged.

"Who else heard?"

"Only me."

"And you're one-hundred percent that's what she said?"

Yes, he was. "Pretty damn sure."

Quinn frowned, his mind racing now. "You know we have a Shadow Creek... hell, there's even a Shadow Creek Resort."

"All already looked at, extensively. We've ruled out the resort and anyone there; same with the creek, although today's events change that. There is absolutely nothing regarding the word shadow in Arnie Miller's life. We scoured his computer looking for code names, passwords, locations, titles, anything that included the word shadow. Nothing."

Quinn thought for a moment. "But the skull wasn't found at Shadow Creek. That's on the other side of the mountain."

"Could've drifted. Been carried by scavengers."

"So... what? He took the vics there before he killed them, and Pam remembered? She was trying to tell you his location?"

"Possibly. I don't know."

"What about the paintings angle? Are any of LaRouche's paintings named *The Shadow* or something?"

"No. Regardless, it's another clue that links the Couer Killer *here*, to Berry Springs. This town is a common link in all this, LaRouche, Shadow, and now Mary Freeman."

"And it also makes Miller less and less likely."

"Listen, I'm not saying that Miller isn't a piece of shit and doesn't deserve what he got, I'm just saying I don't think he's the Couer Killer."

Quinn blew out a whistle and leaned back. "Holy shit, man."

"My thoughts exactly."

"Shit is going to hit the fan when all this gets out. There will be a retrial... or, hell, they might even just let Miller walk." Quinn leaned forward, eyes narrowed. "Okay, so, if Miller isn't our guy... who is? What's your profile?"

Eli swallowed and wiped his hands with a napkin, thankful to be getting to the nuts and bolts now. "The first thing we look at is to determine if the criminal is organized or disorganized. Organized crimes are almost always premeditated, with little evidence at the scene. Organized criminals know right from wrong, enjoy the hunt—so to speak—and show little to no remorse for their victims. Disorganized, on the other hand, are unplanned, sponta-neous, impulsive crimes that are usually frenzied. With these cases, the suspect usually leaves a pile of evidence at the scene. Disorganized criminals are typically younger—mid-to-upper-twenties—and are usually under the influ-ence of drugs or alcohol and, or, mentally ill. I don't see this with our Couer Killer, in fact, I see the exact opposite. I believe you are looking for an organized criminal, above-average intelligence, with a significant ego that needs to be satisfied. He or she is driven by their need to display control over the victim. That's what makes him tick, and with CK—Couer Killer—this is mostly expressed with the grand finale of slicing the victims' wrists and watching them die. It's the ultimate rush for him—to take the most cherished posses-sion a human can have—their life. This is someone with absolutely no regard for humanity, and has a solid grip on mortality, even his own. I believe he fully understands his actions and believes he will get caught, and fears it."

"Why do you say that?"

"Because he stopped for almost a year, during Miller's trial and after the conviction. Possibly felt like he was given a clean slate. Extensive time between killing sprees is uncommon for serial killers. CK has something to lose, and we need to find out what that is. I believe you're looking for someone who's mid-thirties, has steady employment, a normal life so to speak, and a decent amount of money—"

"Why?"

"Cocaine for one. Why cocaine? There are many different stimulants that he could have used to keep the girls awake, that are a quarter of the cost. I believe he occasionally uses, although not often, and that's his drug of choice. He has a certain comfort level with it, and that's important to him. He strategically tortures his victims—he likes structure, a plan, for things to go his way. Two, the LaRouche connection, assuming there is a connection with CK and the *Sans Couer* painting. Those are considered valuable, expensive paintings."

"Do you think this guy has some of his paintings?"

Eli raised his eyebrows and shrugged. "I'm not going to rule it out, but I do think that our suspect identifies with LaRouche's inner turmoil and creepy-ass paintings. I think CK could battle depression, but he is not mentally ill. He knows exactly what he's doing. I also think he paints, as well... perhaps releases emotions in that way. Or does some sort of art at the very least."

"But LaRouche was said to be crazy... didn't he try to remove his own eyes?"

"That's the rumor."

"But you don't think CK is crazy?"

"You don't have to be mentally ill to be drawn to someone who is. There is a darkness around LaRouche that our guy responds to. No one understood LaRouche, no one understands CK. Tortured minds, kindred spirits type of thing. Cutting out the eyes is his signature. Again, it feeds his ego. He wants to be famous, and I think you'll find he follows the stories on the news. He likes to think he's smarter than us. His MO was the same with both woman, and I believe it was the same with Mary. He picks his victims personally. I have no doubt there is a level of stalking going on beforehand, as Pam said, she felt like she was being watched. He has a type, he picks them out and then lures them into his car, or close enough to him where he sticks them with a needle."

"You used the words 'he or she' earlier."

Eli nodded. "Everything about our suspect screams sexual assault—typical with an organized criminal, someone who gets off on exuding control... but CK doesn't sexually assault the vics. Why? One, there's a chance we're not looking for a man, but a woman. In which case, all the above stands, except of having disdain for human life in general, this woman has disdain for other women. An extremely jealous woman created by someone in her past with—"

"Red hair, pale skin, short stature..."

"Exactly. But, if it's not a woman..." he frowned and inhaled deeply. "This man goes off course from the typical serial killer profile. Like I said, sexual assault happens in almost all man-slash-woman torture cases. So why doesn't he? My guess is that he is either married or in a steady relationship driven by sex. He gets it enough. This man isn't driven by sexual need, he's driven by his need to control someone weaker. He gets off, so to speak, on the woman's pain, not her pleasure."

A moment ticked by. It was a lot of information.

"So," Quinn took a deep breath. "A man or woman,

potentially wealthy, mid-thirties, above-average intelligence, egotistical, and potentially in a relationship. What about the job? Any thoughts on what they actually do for a living?"

"Well, it's hard to ignore the painting angle here. I think CK is possibly involved in the art world somehow, anything creative. Like I said, I think he has some money. Could be inherited or self-made, although I'm leaning toward self-made because of the ego."

"Well, this is a small town. Not a huge pool of people with money."

"I've already pulled the list."

"Okay, has anyone on that list purchased LaRouche's paintings?"

"That's what I'll dive into this morning."

"How do you think he finds his victims?"

"That's a good question, and one that I'm still trying to piece together. I think he stalks them for a while, maybe to the point of obsession. He gets to know their routines, where they live, what they do, then he goes in. This fits Pam's story that someone was following her. Possibly stalks on the internet, too. That's very important to consider. As we've discussed, he has a type. Maybe the women remind him of someone in his past, someone he despises, an ex-girlfriend, an abusive mother, or simply the *Sans Couer* painting. It really might not be much deeper than that. He identifies with the pain in that painting, or with LaRouche when he painted it."

"Or, he could just like pretty girls."

Again, he thought of Payton.

"I don't think so. If the motivation was simply a pretty face, he wouldn't be so exact in his selection."

Quinn paused. "This is all very Vincent Van Gogh. Didn't he cut off his ear or something?"

"Yes. I considered a connection there, too. Van Gogh was born in 1853 in The Netherlands. He started painting in his mid-twenties. It's said he struggled with mental-illness his whole life. He was known for an eccentric argumentative personality and for being very difficult, culminating in the infamous argument with someone where he cut off his ear with a razor blade. It's a definite possibility that LaRouche could have identified with Van Gogh, but in this case, I don't think our suspect does. I think he's inspired by LaRouche's paintings, but like I said, that's it."

"Crazy fucks."

"Again, I don't think our guy is crazy. He knows what he's doing. Hell, he probably gets off on the fact that we think he might be crazy."

Quinn sipped, digesting.

Eli leaned back. "What did you make of the landowner? Gary Powell?"

Quinn exhaled loudly and met his gaze. "Rubs me the wrong way."

"What do you know about him?"

"Lives alone, in an old farmhouse about sixty yards from where Mary was found. Own's all that land. Inherited. Wife left him years ago. Rumor has it he's a drunk."

"Drugs? Past arrests?"

"Two DWIs and according to one of my officers, he was caught with a joint once but they let it go."

Eli shook his head.

"I know. You wouldn't believe—"

"Yes, I would. I worked plenty of cases with small town PDs. Make their own rules."

Quinn eyed him. "I understand it, though. I don't like red tape. I get it."

Eli met his gaze. "I don't either."

They nodded in an unspoken agreement—they'd do whatever they'd need to do to get the Couer Killer off the streets. Even if that meant skirting around red tape. Hell, Eli had built a career off it.

"No cocaine or mickeys found on Gary?"

"No, just a joint, but I'm betting they didn't even search his truck."

"Does he have a connection to Mary?"

"We're looking into that."

"Would be nice to know why the wife left him."

"Meaning, if there was ever a physical confrontation? Not sure. Gossip says it was just because he drank his paychecks. Can't blame a woman for walking away from that Prince Charming."

"I had the pleasure of running into him at the scene, after you left."

"Really?" Quinn leaned forward.

"He didn't like me being on his land although I'm not sure if it had more to do with me being a fed."

"Could be. What's your take on him?"

Eli paused for a moment. "That he's hiding something. Information, or something on that land."

"We'll look into it. Anything else turn up after I left?"

Eli shifted in his seat. "Actually, yes. A woman. You know a Payton Chase?"

Quinn whistled and shook his head while leaning back. "Tell me you're lying. Tell me she did not go out there."

Eli wished he could say he was lying... he also wished he hadn't gotten a little twinge of jealousy at seeing Quinn's reaction to her name. There obviously was a past there. Romantic, maybe?

What the hell did he care?

"I ran into her as I was leaving."

"Was she alone?"

"Just her and a SIG P938."

Quinn's face fell. "Makes sense then."

"What makes sense?"

"Her being out there... the gun."

He leaned forward, and Eli did the same.

"Earlier this year, Payton was investigating a homicide when she was attacked. She was chained to a wall in the guy's house for almost twelve hours."

"Chained to a wall?"

"Yep. She was lucky. He never touched her... I got to her before."

Eli blinked, processing this little—*huge*—piece of information, and suddenly everything began to make sense. The gun, the self-defense moves that had obviously just been learned, the suspicion behind those blue eyes.

Quinn shook his head. "Yeah, our own Payton Chase found the suspect before we did." He shook his head again. "She's a dog with a freakin' bone when she wants something. She's a pistol."

A pistol. Truer words have never been said.

"Y'all need anything else?" Shauna hollered as she wiped down a nearby table.

"No, thanks." Quinn turned back to Eli. "Send me the list you pulled this morning of the wealthiest folks in the area. I'll have the team look at it and see if anyone jumps out. We'll run it through the system, and the DMV, to see if anyone has a red Ford."

"Will do. Let me know what you find in Mary's social media, too. Any new followers over the last few weeks? Messages? Emails?"

Quinn nodded.

"Before Arnie's conviction, we did a deep dive into

anyone in the US who purchased LaRouche's original paintings, but there are several unaccounted for. We knocked off
the verified purchases from the suspect list. During our
search we realized how many copies and knock-offs there
are; posters, prints, hell even Halloween decorations. That
list is ridiculously long, and not all inclusive on top of that.
It would take hundreds of man hours to sift through. I've
already got someone at HQ looking specifically in the area
for any kind of LaRouche or *Sans Couer* purchases, or travels
to see any of his paintings... just anything related to the guy.
Anyone with any kind of connection."

"We need to look at the public computer system, too.
The library. Check the IPs, see if anyone has Googled him."
Quinn paused and ran his fingers through his hair. "Word's
out about Mary. Woke up to my phone ringing. When the
details of how gruesome it was gets out... it's going to be a
witch-hunt. They're going to want someone's head."

"Yes, they are." Eli's eyes leveled on Quinn's. "This time,
though, take your time. This time, though, get the right
guy."

Quinn nodded in understanding. Pressure and panic led
to shoddy police work. The lieutenant stood, Eli remained
seated.

"Quinn." Eli's voice was ice-cold. "Don't forget, our killer
has a type. He won't veer from it. Pay particular attention to
that—you'll stay a step ahead of him. Mid-twenties, red hair,
blue eyes. He's got a type... and he's not done."

As they gazed over the carefree crowd, something deep
in his gut clenched.

He thought of Payton.

10

CHARMAINE GRIMACED AND leaned forward.
Another fucking wrinkle.

She stared back at the reflection in the mirror, her gaze slowly sweeping over the lines of her face. Her fingertip traced the deepening wrinkle next to the corner of her mouth. Nasolabial lines, her doctor had told her. She didn't give a damn what they were called, she just wanted them gone. Which is what she'd told him precisely when she'd marched in there last week to demand more filler.

It's not time for another injection, Mrs. Chase. The lines are barely visible, Mrs. Chase, he'd told her with a touch of annoyance as he loaded her up with samples to tide her over in the meantime.

Stupid, impotent doctor. She paid the guy enough for his services, she should be able to get whatever the hell she wanted, whenever the hell she wanted it.

She exhaled, straightened and cocked her head. Forty-five years old.

Almost fifty!

Her hand trembled as she picked up her two-hundred-dollar bottle of perfume and dabbed it behind her ear. She watched every moment as if she were watching someone else, scrutinizing every dark spot on her skin, every mole, the little flab of skin under her arm.

Forty-five.

Time was an evil bitch. An unrelenting force, pulling her farther and farther away from her youth. Her best years.

She squared her shoulders and smoothed the ivory silk house dress she'd slipped on. It was a gift from her husband, a surprise he'd given her during their last vacation... six years earlier.

Arthur had taken her to Fiji, at her request, and booked the presidential suite—a thatch house on stilts that sprawled over the crystal blue water. They'd spent a week holed up on the island. An entire week of attending every hotel event, every water adventure, every fishing trip, and reading every book on the damn island in an attempt to avoid actually talking to each other. They were years past small talk. Years past being able to drink enough to pretend they were in love.

He'd said the trip was intended to let them get away and reconnect. Truthfully, she'd expected him to tell her he wanted a divorce.

That didn't happen, to her dismay.

Neither did the reconnection, unless you count the ten minutes she'd let him inside her after polishing off a bottle of tequila. He didn't even come. She faked hers. She was good at faking things.

It was almost nineteen years to the day she'd said "I do" to the wealthiest man in town. Arthur had been a true gentleman, wined and dined her, given her gifts, pulled her into his wealthy inner circle. But what she hadn't realized at the time was it was all a facade. All a feeble attempt to replace the wife he'd lost years earlier.

A feeble attempt to find his spoiled, little daughter a new mother.

It was almost immediately after the I-do's that cracks began to show in their marriage. It was as if Arthur had suddenly realized that having another wife was not going to replace the one he really loved.

The one Charmaine would never be. Would never live up to.

And every day—*every single day*—the little brat Payton reminded him that Charmaine was not his true love. Payton looked just like her mother. A timeless beauty that no plastic surgeon could recreate. No amount of Botox, fillers, hair dye, nothing could compare to his precious former wife.

Arthur liked shiny things. Beautiful things. Hell, that was part of the reason she'd married him. But that love of beauty spilled into his work—his assistants, clients, even Payton's babysitter had been beautiful. Each thing, each woman, more beautiful than herself. She couldn't take it. Couldn't take the constant worrying that Arthur was cheating on her. So, she dealt with it, and did what she had to do. First was the babysitter. Charmaine had secretly slashed the eighteen-year old's tire, causing her to drive into a river embankment as she left the house. Charmaine told Arthur half the scotch was gone, so he'd fired her.

They never saw the girl again.

His assistants and clients had been more difficult. Charmaine had driven a few out purely by her incessant, cunning attitude—the way she spoke to them, the side-long glances, each planned and calculated. Each threatening in the most minuscule way, each impossible to ignore.

But that didn't stop her husband. He'd kept hiring young, beautiful women and eventually she'd changed tactics... going after his childhood friend and business partner. If he could have fun at Chase Enterprises, so could she.

The intercom chimed, ripping Charmaine away from her thoughts. Her stomach tickled with nerves.

"Yes?"

"Mr. Raya is here to see you."

She looked in the mirror. "Send him to the library." She glanced at the clock—8:17 a.m. He was early.

She quickly dabbed on sparkly lip gloss, pulled a robe over her gown and padded into the master bedroom. She glanced out the window to the front lawn as she stepped into her slippers. The morning had grown overcast, menacing.

Fitting for the occasion.

Mateo, dressed as impeccably as always in a blue Armani suite, stood with his back to her as she stepped into the library.

"You're early," she said as she closed the double door behind her. The *click* of the lock echoed through the massive room.

He turned.

"My flight leaves in a few hours." Her husband's business partner's gaze was hard, his shoulders tense. He slowly crossed the room. "I don't like that your housekeeper sees me. Why don't you come to the door and let me in for yourself. You know I'm coming, for Christ's sake." His voice was a hard whisper.

"Mona won't say anything. Trust me. I've made sure of that."

Mateo shook his head. "I don't want to know how."

"No, you probably don't." She narrowed his eyes and looked him over. Was he backing out?

"And you're sure Arthur doesn't know?"

Her eyes slitted. "You've known him longer than I have. You tell me. You work next to him every day. Does anything feel off?"

"No."

"Then, no, he doesn't know. When will you be back?"

"Tomorrow. I'm meeting Arthur for a very important business dinner tonight in the city, then he's headed to France for a meeting before the weekend. I'll be back by late afternoon."

"He's definitely going overseas?"

"Right. If anything changes, I'll let you know."

Mateo looked down at her with his dark eyes, as if he was trying to decide something.

It pissed her off.

"Look, if you're having second thoughts..."

"I'm *not* having second thoughts, Char," he hissed.

She cocked an eyebrow and fisted a hand on her hip.

He blew out a breath, took a step back and began pacing.

"I'm putting everything on the line, here. My marriage, my job, everything."

"You won't need a job after this. And you even told me your wife's excited about moving back to Spain. You're going to have more money than you know what to do with. We both will. You've hated working for Arthur for a while now. You said it yourself." Desperation colored her tone. She swallowed it down. Desperation aged you. "Look, technically we can scratch it. I don't want to do this if you're getting cold feet. Like you said; there's too much at stake. But if you're backing out, back out now. They're waiting for the transfer. It's going down this afternoon."

He pinned her as he closed the inches between them. A shiver ran up her spine.

"I'm not backing out, Char. And you want to know why?" He seethed, "You'd take it for yourself. Every penny of it, and you'd hang me for it. You'd pin it on me, because that's who you are. That's how you operate."

Charmaine kept her gaze locked on his even though she wanted to take a step back. Her hands curled to fists.

He was right. She would take all seventeen million dollars they'd spent the last year laundering from Chase Enterprises, run for the border, and set him up for the fall. It would be hard to do, but she'd do it.

Fuck yeah, she'd do it. They were supposed to split the money down the middle, eight-point-five each, but seventeen would be a hell of a lot better.

And he knew it.

What he didn't know was the additional six million she'd been funneling into a secret offshore account for the last five years when she started planning her escape. Arthur had made Charmaine sign an iron-clad prenup that waved her right to most of his assets, no matter how long they were married. She'd get the house, some cars, stocks, if they divorced and that was it. At twenty-three, she'd been stupid enough to sign. Dear little beautiful Payton, on the other hand, was on the receiving end of a twenty-three-million-dollar trust fund, receiving deposits every year until she turned thirty-five, then she got the whole shebang.

Lucky bitch.

The additional six million would be a hell of a cushion if her little deal with Mateo fell through. And the money would be *hers*. All hers. And she deserved every penny of it for living in a loveless marriage for decades.

She stared back at him and felt her pulse begin to race.

"I want to know right now, Raya, are you in or are you out? The bank is expecting our deposit. Everything's in place."

He glowered down at her and her mind spun with ideas on how to make him take the fall.

His phone rang. Two rings passed as he stared at her like a boxer in a ring. Finally, he reached into his pocket, turned his back to her and answered.

She grit her veneers as she listened to one side of the conversation.

"Yes... seven-thirty is fine. Yes, six. Thanks." A low chuckle. "I'll make note of that, thanks."

Her eyes narrowed as she watched the smug smile cross his face. He glanced at her from the corner of his eye.

"Yes, this number is fine. See you then." He hung up and turned toward her.

"Who was that?" She asked, although they both knew it was none of her business.

"Tori, from work. Confirming our client dinner tonight."

Her jaw twitched. She'd met Tori—another young, sexy number. "You said, *see you then?*"

"Yeah, in New York. She'll be with us."

Jealously twisted in her stomach. Was Tori banging her husband? Mateo, even? Emotions began to swirl inside her. "Mateo, are you in, or are you fucking out? Right now. Tell me right fucking—"

His hand grabbed the back of her head and yanked her to him. Eyes narrowed with venom, he stared at her a moment before his lips crushed down on hers, his tongue forcefully shoving into her mouth. She kissed back, hard, matching his intensity. She ripped off his belt and undid his designer slacks as he tugged off her robe.

Her hand swept down his boxers onto his erection. Goosebumps flew over her flesh and she felt the familiar rush between her legs, a rush only Mateo Raya could give her—had given her a dozen times since they devised their plan months earlier. The sex had been an unexpected bonus.

She folded him out of his pants and stroked. Long, hard, deep strokes until he gripped her by the waist and heaved her onto the desk that sat in the corner of the library. One sweep of her hand sent Arthur's new laptop clattering to the floor, along with a Tiffany lamp and stack of folders. She'd blame housekeeping.

Mateo's breath was heavy, frenzied, as he yanked up her gown and nudged her legs apart. His hold on her hair so tight, her scalp tingled as he drove into her with a force that had her toes curling and a *yelp* catching in her throat.

He yanked back her head, burying his face in her neck as he bored into her. She felt the sheen of sweat from his forehead on her cheek, listened to the wheezing inhale as he pounded her so hard her teeth chattered.

A familiar tingling swept across her delicate skin. She squeezed her eyes shut, willing the sensation to go away. Instead, she yanked her head out of his fist, ripping out some of her hair in the process, met his eyes and spat every vile, twisted, perverted thing she could into his ear. Sweat trickled down his cheek. His chest heaved, his body tensed. He was close.

Now, it was time to close the deal.

She grabbed his face, pressing her freshly applied acrylic nails into his cheeks.

"Are you in or out, Mateo?" She hissed as he fucked her.

His wild gaze locked on hers, barely able to focus through the sensation overtaking his body.

"Fucking in, you fucking bitch."

A grin spread across her face as he exploded inside her.

Putty in her fucking hands.

Putty. In her hands.

Panting, he pulled away, his tanned skin flushed red. He narrowed his eyes and looked at her open legs, lingering for a moment.

No, she didn't come.

Her gaze bored into him. *No, you can't make me come. You're not good enough.*

It was something she could hold over his head.

Control.

It was all about control. And no one knew control better than Charmaine.

He lifted an eyebrow, as if he didn't care.

He cared. And it ate him up that he couldn't please her the way she did him, and that was the entire point. Power. *She* had it.

He zipped up his pants and turned away from her.

"You've got the papers drafted up?" He asked, his voice low and gravelly as he buckled his belt.

"Leaving them for him on Sunday, after I leave."

"Divorce papers... a hell of a birthday gift." Mateo headed out the door. Without looking back he said, "You are one cold woman, Charmaine."

He had no idea.

11

*E*LI ROLLED TO a stop underneath a lush maple tree next to the B&B. He grabbed his cell phone, briefcase, and tepid ice-tea before pushing out of the car. The sound of boat engines mingled with distant laughter as he walked down the pebble path that led to the front porch. It was just past five in the afternoon, and he was exhausted already. He'd spent half the day fighting the growing crowd of festival-goers and visiting local art shops. There was no way in hell the timing of the festival and Mary's murder were a coincidence, and his gut told him that the Couer Killer would take part in the festivities. Eli posed as a well-meaning tourist looking for a birthday present for his fake wife, who was spending the day at the spa.

"What kind of art are you interested in?"

"My wife likes post-impressionism paintings, I think it's called. Anything like that?"

"I think you'll find most shops here carry more modern paintings, but I have a catalog you can look through..."

"What about Theo LaRouche, do you carry anything from him?"

"No, I wish..."

The answer was the same in every shop.

The hours spent meandering through a sea of tourists had gotten him nothing but sweat-soaked boxers. Not a single lead. After that, he'd spent the afternoon visiting the surrounding pharmacies, inquiring about chloral hydrate prescriptions, then he'd visited the seediest bars in the area, asking about Mickeys. He figured a Mickey was less readily available and requested than cocaine, so maybe it would open up a lead.

So far, nothing. Nada. Zip.

A bead of sweat rolled down his back as he stepped through the front door of Gable's B&B. Thick clouds had moved in during the afternoon, but the humidity was still stifling.

Suffocating.

The rush of cool air sent goosebumps over his body. He took a deep breath and spied Jolene checking in a young couple who looked like they'd already been out on the lake.

He didn't blame them.

He started up the staircase—

"Hey, Agent Archer," Jolene called out.

The couple jogged past him up the staircase—God he remembered the days when he'd had that much energy. He turned as Jolene motioned him into the hall. "Have a minute?"

No. "Sure."

He followed her into the kitchen where the bottom half of a man's body stuck out from under the sink.

"Hey, Ethan, this is Special Agent Archer with the FBI."

A grunt, squeak of a pipe, then the man scooted out of the sink. He wiped his hands on his pants. "Ethan Veech, Cyber Crimes. It's nice to meet you." He quickly stood, and they shook hands. "Your reputation precedes you. It's an honor, really."

Jolene smirked at her fiancé.

Ethan laughed, "Hey, I'm not too proud to say it. Archer's one of the best profilers at the FBI. Been around a while. Right?"

"Longer than I care to admit, and you're one to talk. I heard of the work you did on the Castner case. Tracked a group of home-grown terrorists through their internet footprint. Impressive." After Jolene had mentioned the agent's name earlier, Eli had looked the guy up and instantly remembered hearing about his computer sleuthing skills. Ethan Veech was quickly working his way up to being one of the top agents in his division.

"Everything's traceable these days," Ethan said. "Just have to know where to look. Unlike your job... hard to predict a serial killer's next move. *That* takes some instinct."

Jolene rolled her eyes. "You guys want to hug and get it over with or can we move on?"

Eli grinned. Jolene had spunk.

She turned to Ethan. "*Anyway,* although he didn't tell me," Jolene flashed a grin at Eli, "I think Agent Archer is here about the body that was found off Summit Mountain."

Ethan's eyebrows tipped up. "Yeah?"

He nodded. It was pointless to pretend anymore. The entire town was talking about it. And, Ethan was one of his own. "It's potentially connected to an old case I worked. I'm working to determine that." Eli cast a glance at Jolene's belly. "I'd ask if that was why you were here, too, but I'm guessing you have more pressing matters to attend to."

An ear-to-ear smile stretched across the agent's face. "Due late winter."

Jolene exhaled loudly. "Thank God I won't be in my

third trimester in this heat. Seriously, this heatwave is unreal." She placed her hand on her stomach and glanced out the window where the clouds blanketed the setting sun. "Supposed to get some rain tonight. Summer thunderstorm. Hope it cools it down."

"Cool down or not, you need to be off your feet, Jo." Ethan frowned. "You do too much around here."

She heaved herself up on the kitchen counter and smiled. "Not while you're here. I'm just going to watch you work." She smiled and scanned him from head to toe. "And enjoy this beautiful view while I have it."

Ethan put his hand on her belly and kissed her cheek.

Eli smiled. Ethan was younger than him, with a cocky vibe that usually rubbed Eli the wrong way, but the way the kid's face lit talking about his future child made Eli wonder how long he'd been with the FBI. Ethan still had that spark, the *I'm-going-to-save-the-world* attitude that had left Eli years ago.

It would come. *The darkness would come,* he thought. With each dead body, the light would dim little by little. Shadows would creep in.

But then, as he watched the way Ethan smiled at his pregnant fiancé, Eli wondered if the kid had enough light around him to chase out the darkness. Enough love and distraction at the end of the day to refocus, unwind, relax.

Love—light—that he didn't have in his own life.

"I'm here to give her some relief and work on the place before heading back."

"He travels back and forth between Virginia and here. Splits his time about sixty-forty. Although I'm pushing for fifty-fifty, especially when this baby comes."

Ethan smiled, again, before refocusing on Eli. He frowned. "What can you tell me about the case?"

"I'll get some coffee on," Jolene said.

Twenty minutes and one iced coffee later, Eli had downloaded Ethan on the Couer Killer case—he'd already known a few details—and they'd exchanged information with Ethan offering to assist in any way he could while he was in town.

Eli left Ethan in the kitchen hovered over a detailed to-do list Jolene had drawn up for him—trim the shrubs, paint the porch swing to match the new pillows she'd picked out, replace some shingles on the roof...

As Eli made his way up the staircase, he thought of his own to-do list and how different it was. Watching the interaction between Jolene and Ethan had stirred something in him. Maybe it was because Ethan was an FBI agent who'd somehow managed to make a relationship work.

Why couldn't he?

So, was it him? Maybe it wasn't the job. Maybe it was him.

He frowned.

Insecurity was an emotion Eli didn't allow. Insecurity led to shoddy, irrational decisions. Bad decisions. Eli rarely doubted himself so what the hell was his problem now?

Feeling out-of-sorts, he stepped into his room and cranked the AC. He grabbed a bottle of water from the mini fridge and sat down where papers and gruesome photos scattered the desk. He pulled out an image of Valerie Walsh, envisioning the skull pulled from the creek. Did it belong to the attractive red head staring back at him in the photo? He studied it, as he had done a million times before. Bright, round eyes, a perfect smile, wide with excitement for the future she'd never have. Silky, wavy hair that hung just below her shoulders. He set the picture to the side, and looked from picture to picture—Courtney Howard, Pam Robertson, Mary Freeman, Valerie Walsh.

Auburn hair. Blue eyes. Short. Mid-twenties.

Payton Chase.

A chill snaked up his spine. She'd fit right into this line up... it was something he'd thought the moment he'd met her in the woods, and something he was trying his best not to get too worked up about. He couldn't go around telling everyone with auburn hair and blue eyes to stay inside and lock their doors. He just needed to find the bastard.

In deep thought, he signed into his computer and after six different log-ins into secured databases, he typed *Chase, Payton* in the search field.

Before Eli realized it, an hour had gone by and he'd learned more than anticipated about the wealthy, small-town journalist.

As he'd expected, Payton was born and raised with a silver spoon in her mouth, on the outskirts of Berry Springs. Her father, Arthur Chase, came from a long line of venture capitalists who'd left a hefty inheritance to their only son. Arthur started his own business and over the decades became wealthy in his own right.

Unfortunately, Chase's bank account couldn't save Payton's mother from passing away much too young. Eli found the marriage record of Charmaine Bisset and Arthur Chase along with some very risqué pictures from Charmaine's social media account—pre-marriage, of course. Charmaine was the type of woman to break necks when she walked into the room—tall, svelte, platinum blonde hair against faux-tanned skin. He knew that type of woman very well—pre-BAU, of course.

She was the *exact opposite* of Payton.

He'd found Payton's social media account and confirmed

her attendance at a very prestigious and expensive boarding school in Maryland—all girls. She went on to college to graduate with honors. She'd danced ballet the first few years and was featured in several articles. The woman was an overachiever who'd obviously worked her ass off. Grades like that didn't come easily at schools like that. He found himself clicking through each picture, reading her posts, checking out her friends. He lingered on each photo, searching the lines of her face, her body, the smile, those eyes. He was drawn in. Mesmerized. She pulled at him like a magnet. His mind wandered in ways he'd never imaged—imagining her belly like Jolene's, with his baby inside. When he'd started going through her pictures for the third time, he'd made himself stop.

Frustrated—at himself, the case, and the fact that Payton had captivated an hour of his life—he pushed out of the chair and mindlessly walked around his room, stretching his back. He paused at the sweeping windows and looked at the lake shimmering below.

The sun was resting on the mountain, dusk creeping up. Beams of light shot down from the thick cloud cover, dotting the mountainside in the distance. Boats swayed in the black water, families scurried about the shoreline, packing up to head home for the evening. The young couple he'd seen in the lobby dragged their kayaks out of the water.

Not a single person acting as if they were concerned there was a killer lurking in the mountains.

He scanned each face, each body, watching the way they moved, assessing their body language. Could CK be there? Scoping out the scene?

Was the next victim mingling among the others, having no clue that her life was about to be brutally cut short?

He zeroed in on a young man, tall, fit, walking along the

shoreline. He was alone. Eli glanced around the room, searching for a pair of binoculars. No luck.

He leaned closer to the window, making note of the color of the man's shirt, shorts, color of his hair, the darkening on his left arm indicating a tattoo, the width of his stride, his gait...

The man was alone, on the beach. No cooler, no friends, no smile. It didn't fit.

Eli grabbed his room key from the desk, then turned back to the window for one more glance just as a young girl, followed by a wobbling toddler and pregnant wife jumped into the man's arms.

He froze, watching the loving interaction of the family, then heaved out a sigh. Not his killer. The toddler took off along the rocky beach but before he could reach the water, the man picked him up and twirled him in the air. The toddler flung out his arms, pretending to be an airplane.

He shook his head. Definitely not CK.

What the *hell* was wrong with him? He was on-edge, off his game, and apparently not thinking straight.

Eli stepped away from the window and decided he needed a quick break to clear his head. After an ice-cold shower, he slid into a T-shirt, faded pair of Levi's and grabbed a beer from the mini-fridge. He settled in behind his desk and dove into Berry Springs's richest. There can't be that many, right?

The sun dipped below the mountains as Eli went down the list, one by one, researching each family. Some wealthy by inheritance, some wealthy by pure luck, most wealthy by farming or raising chickens and livestock. None providing any red flags to make him think they were associated with Mary Freeman's murder.

Minutes ticked into an hour and he reached up and

turned on the lamp. He drank the last drop of his beer and leaned back, staring at his computer.

Payton.

He leaned forward again and skimmed the list, landing on Arthur Chase, with Chase Enterprises. He pulled up the estimate of their estate on the outskirts of town—three-point-two million dollars. Their land was estimated to be worth about a million, their home, over two, which was equivalent to at least a ten-million-dollar house where he was from. He looked at an aerial view and found himself surprised that it appeared to be a showy, grander-looking home with all the bells and whistles. Nothing like the other farm houses of Berry Springs's richest that he'd looked at. He zoomed out, noting another expansive home just past the Chase's property-line.

A quick search told him the house belonged to Mateo Raya—Arthur Chase's business partner, apparently.

He clicked through a few screens and stopped on a family portrait he'd pulled during his deep dive—turned into obsession—of Payton's social media. There was only one family photo... only *one.* He studied Arthur. Thinning, gray hair, deep-set wrinkles and bags under eyes that matched the lifeless smile on his face. His arm protectively squeezed a much younger Payton next to him, who wore a flowing white dress, and the same forced smile. Then his gaze settled on Charmaine, standing on the other side of Arthur, with her head cocked to the side and a smile that looked like it was made for magazines. She was dressed in a skin-tight dress and even in the photo, her jewelry twinkled. Her skin was flawless, unlike her husband's, her dress and handbag reflected an extravagant lifestyle, unlike the wrinkled shirt and slacks that Arthur wore.

He glanced back at the sprawling estate and realized that it didn't reflect Arthur, it reflected Charmaine.

He brought up his email and clicked through until he found the list of people and companies who had purchased LaRouche paintings over the last five years. He skimmed the name—no Chase.

Humph.

He exited out of his email and clicked on the folder named *Robertson, Pam,* and scanned through the long list of documents, not sure what he was looking for until he came to a spreadsheet entitled: *Sotheby's.*

He clicked it open and scanned the names who'd attended a rare post-impressionism painting auction at the famous New York auction house over the last ten years.

Chase, Arthur

Chase, Charmaine

His eyebrows lifted. Payton's parents had attended a rare painting auction exactly two years ago. He narrowed his eyes, staring at the family picture, again.

Humph.

He picked up his phone, and five minutes later was sitting in the kitchen next to cyber crimes expert, Ethan Veech. Jolene delivered two Jack and Cokes to the table. He was really beginning to like this woman.

"Okay, Arthur Chase, and... spell the first name again..."

Eli spelled *Charmaine* as Ethan clicked on his keyboard. "And you think they have a connection to the girl that was found yesterday?"

"Mary Freeman, and no, not necessarily, but I believe our suspect lives in the area, possibly in Berry Springs—"

"Weren't the other CK vics killed in Missouri?"

"Yes, but that's less than an hour north of here. Not uncommon for serial killers to hunt within a sixty-mile radius of where they live. Like I said, I think this guy has something to lose. Victims in his hometown would be too risky."

"Then you don't think he killed Mary."

"I didn't say that. According to everyone in the country, the Couer Killer was found, convicted, and locked up months ago. CK doesn't feel the need to be as careful anymore, because someone else was convicted."

Ethan nodded. "Good point. Sorry for interrupting, okay you were saying..."

"I was saying I don't necessarily think there's a connection, but the Chases have money, live in the area, and have an interest in high value paintings."

Ethan's fingertips danced over the keyboard. "It'll take me a bit to dig into Arthur's company, but I should be able to give you a top-line opinion in a sec..."

As Ethan clicked through several programs, Eli brought up a spreadsheet on his computer. "I have the list of people who've purchased LaRouche paintings in the last five years. Any way you can drill deeper into it? Or perhaps expand it?"

"Send it to me." A few seconds passed as Ethan studied the screen. "Okay, so everything with Chase Enterprises looks legit. His business finances and home finances. Damn, his daughter is getting a nice chunk of change."

Eli wanted to ask how much, but stopped himself. He'd already dived into Payton's personal life enough for one evening... and stared at her pictures enough for a lifetime.

"Hang on..." Ethan frowned and leaned forward, his fingers typing at a dizzying speed. Eli glanced up at Jolene. She smiled and shook her head—*I don't know how he does it.*

"Charmaine opened an offshore account six years ago."

This had Jolene frowning and stepping forward. "Which one?"

"Aebi Bank, Switzerland."

She cocked a brow. "I've used that bank..."

Both Ethan and Eli looked up at her.

"Don't ask," she said to Eli.

Ethan looked at Eli. "Right. Don't ask."

"Alright, then." There was much more to Jolene than met the eye, and if he had to guess it was something to do with something illegal in her past... but, he wasn't going to ask.

She continued, "Aebi is a fantastic bank for hiding assets. Offshore accounts have less regulation and transparency, but Aebi in particular is notorious in the black market for catering to hidden assets."

And, there it was—Jolene's past... but, he wasn't going to ask.

Ethan nodded. "Charmaine opened the account under a different name, but used her social security number. Not the smartest tool in the shed. Her husband isn't on the account, and it appears..." more clicking... "that she deposits increments around the end of the month, every month dating back six years."

Jolene laughed. "She's taking money from her husband."

"Can you confirm that?" Eli asked Ethan.

"*Hmm*....so, she's wiring money to the offshore account from two separate accounts. One is coming directly from an account under Chase Enterprises, and one is coming from a local bank."

"Wait, directly from Chase Enterprises?"

"According to this, yeah. But those deposits aren't coming from her—she has no legal rights to his company. Someone else deposits the money."

Jolene frowned. "That doesn't make sense."

Eli leaned back. "Unless she's working with someone

inside the company. Is there any way we can see who makes those deposits?"

"Only if they transferred from a personal account... and, bingo. Yep, what an idiot. It's a man named Mateo Raya."

Eli's eyebrows popped up. "He owns a house right next to the Chases."

"Maybe they're all a little closer than it appears."

"So, what about the other account? You said there's two."

"The other account is linked to someone named Dustin Bisset."

"Who the hell is Dustin Bisset?"

"Well, according to this birth certificate... it's Charmaine's son."

12

*P*AYTON NUDGED THE tiny pink umbrella to the side of her cup and sipped her radioactive-looking drink. Sugar and... pure grain alcohol.

Nice.

But what did she expect at a festival?

She watched a tattooed, glittery woman belly-dance in the middle of a sea of people, most of whom didn't even notice her—surprising considering the woman was wearing only a bralette as a top, and had balloons for boobs. Then again, the dancer was dressed not unlike half the women and teenagers, meandering through the closed-off streets, listening to the bands, browsing the art tents, tasting the exotic food from the street vendors. The woman, Payton guessed was mid-fifties, swayed effortlessly to the jazz music blaring from the street band, the streetlights sparkling off the beads and charms that decorated her generous hips. So confident, so carefree. She moved effortlessly to the music, as if she were a part of it. As if the music was moving her. The Summit Mountain Arts Festival always drew in some very interesting crowds. It was one of the few times you'd see less cowboy hats than baseball caps. The opening-night of the festival was the biggest event, and tonight was no different, even with storms lurking in the area. Thick cloud cover greedily absorbed the waning light of dusk, and the scent of impending rain perfumed the summer breeze. The electricity was thick in the air. Energy, moving all around her, just like the carefree belly dancer.

Payton's gaze shifted to a small group coming down a narrow staircase, each had extravagant masks over their eyes. Sparkling glitter, feathers, beads, very Mardi Gras. She'd never seen so many masks at the festival before, then again, she hadn't been in over a decade.

"Helllllo? Payton?"

Payton tore her gaze away from bustling crowd and turned to Jax. "I'm sorry... what?"

Sitting across the table from her, Gia released an annoyed exhale.

They'd snagged the last table at a small, charming Mexican restaurant downtown. Colorful tiles accented the large rock building, with flickering lampposts lighting the sidewalk. The restaurant had two patios, one in front along the street, and a bar with every brand of tequila imaginable lined the back patio which was much more secluded and private than the front. They'd chosen the front to watch the parade. The building backed up to a rock cliff on the mountain that flanked downtown. Very unique, very popular. Only open during the summer months, the restaurant was a favorite spot for both locals and tourists. Tourists loved the view and proximity to shopping, and locals loved it not only because of the romantic atmosphere but because it was one of the only restaurants in the area that didn't have pool tables, dart boards, jukeboxes, or spit cups. It was where everyone in Berry Springs took their dates... just like tonight.

"I said, are you gonna eat that?" Jax nodded to the table.

"Oh." She looked at the soggy nachos on her plate. "No, you go ahead. Knock yourself out."

"Payton," Gia's voice sounded eerily like Payton's step-mother's, and also not unlike her stepmother, Gia was sporting a very decent buzz. "I think I need to go to the bathroom."

Payton wrinkled her nose and glanced over her shoulder at the line of porta potties against the trees. There was a constant line for the bathroom inside the restaurant, so everyone was avoiding those.

"Knock yourself out."

Gia thrust a nod toward the trees. "Bathroom."

Payton rolled her eyes and slid out of the chair. She followed Gia through the crowd, ignoring a few whistles.

They reached the porta potties and Gia spun around, the fringe on her skirt flapping with the attitude in her hips. *"Girl."* She fisted a hand on her hip. "What is wrong with you tonight?"

Payton sighed and glanced at the table in the distance. "I'm sorry... I just don't enjoy being set up."

"It's not a set up. Well, I mean... I guess it kind of turned out like that, but I didn't mean it to, I promise." Gia pulled a makeup compact out of her faux alligator-skin purse and checked her lipstick. "I invited you as a cushion for my first time hanging out with Clay, and then Jax invited himself along." She sighed and turned toward her. "He likes you, girl. It's *sooooo* obvious."

It *was* obvious. Payton had gotten the vibe Jax was inter-ested in her since he'd offered to show her around the office on her first day at NAR News. He'd subtly flirt with her and she'd constantly catch him watching her from across the room. She should be flattered; Jax was attractive, smart, fit, and had a job—all good qualities in a man—but she wasn't. If she had to be honest, she really didn't even like him that much.

Just then, a group of bikers pushed their way past them, causing Payton to stumble and Gia to giggle. She caught herself on a parking meter and as she looked up to scowl at the leather-clad men, her eyes locked on a figure frozen in the hustling crowd, staring straight at her. Her stomach dropped—an instant response. The skin, pale as milk... the eyes... she froze. A *Sans Couer* mask? She narrowed her eyes, pushed past the bikers—who were now flirting with Gia— and just as she stepped onto the sidewalk, another group, this time a bachelorette party blocked her. Dammit! She shuffled around, only to realize the figure was gone. Was she imagining things? Paranoia perhaps?

"Payton," Gia grabbed her arm. "You should have saved me... although one was kind of cute. God, my dad would have a heart attack."

Payton took one last look into the crowd then turned back. She was being paranoid. Crazy. "Sorry. Thought I saw someone I knew."

"Anyway, we were talking about Jax..."

Payton blew out a breath of frustration. "I'm just not into him... like that, anyway." She took a deep breath, pushed the fake masked man out of her head, yanked out her lip gloss from her purse and dabbed some on. She was hot and looked like crap, she assumed. Gia, Clay, and Jax had picked her up from her house, but only minutes after she'd walked in, leaving her no time to change. She was still wearing her professional black slacks, sleeveless blouse, and heels that she'd worn to work. Definitely not something she would've chosen for an arts festival, or a first-date, for that matter... even if she'd wanted it to be.

"I get it, Pay, I do, but I just wish you'd give him a chance... hell, give *anyone* a chance."

She slid the gloss back into her purse. "I'm not going to stay here, in Berry Springs, forever you know. I'm not staying at NAR News for my entire career. I'll move ten times before I land my dream job. It's how it goes."

"But that doesn't mean you can't still have fun, Payton. It doesn't mean you can't kiss a boy, or," Gia wagged her fingers in air, *"gasp,* have sex with one." She laughed and drew her for a hug. "Let's get back to the table before some young college girls swoop up our men."

"God forbid."

They walked back into the restaurant where Clay and Jax were in the middle of a heated debate about which team was better, the 1927 Yankees or the 1998 Yankees. Both had played college ball, and both had an ego to match.

"More baseball?" Gia groaned as she sat down.

"Oh, you want more? Okay, 'cause I can go all night." Clay winked and slid his arm around Gia.

"I doubt that." Jax grinned, then turned to Payton. "You okay?"

"Yeah. Sorry, just didn't get much sleep last night." She took a deep sip of her neon-blue drink.

"I told you, you shouldn't have gone out to that crime scene."

Gia's eyes widened. "To Mary Freeman's? You went out there? To the woods?"

"It was on my way home." Another sip. *Geez,* why did Jax have to bring that up *now*? When she'd agreed to go to the festival she'd promised herself two things: that she wouldn't talk about work, and that she would pretend that the only reason she agreed to go wasn't to scope out the crowd and look for anyone in eyeless masks, or anyone looking at LaRouche paintings.

"Oh, *yeah,* like everyone just stops by to check out a murder scene on their way home." Jax looked at Gia. "Payton's trying to nail the story before Lanie does. Which would be quite the feat."

Gia's face dropped. "You need to be careful with that. You know what happened…"

"Last time?" She felt her defenses creep up, along with a slight buzz from the tequila shot earlier. "Yes, I'm very aware what happened last time I went hunting a killer, and it won't happen again."

Jax grinned at Gia. "Did she show you her gun?"

Payton elbowed him. She didn't want anyone to know she'd gotten her conceal carry license, but when Jax had gone snooping for a pack of gum in her purse, he'd found it.

Gia's mouth gaped. "You got a *gun?*"

"Oh, come on, every around here carries guns." She tried to make light of it, but the truth was, having it in her purse made her uncomfortable.

Gia turned to her date. "Do *you* carry?"

Clay shook his head. "Nope. Dad does though." He grinned and flexed. "I've got my own guns."

Gia laughed and flicked her hair—her trademark flirt. Payton grinned—the guy was toast.

Gia shrugged. "Hell, maybe I need to get one." She grinned as Clay flexed his bicep again. "Not one of *those*, a real gun." She shook her head. "I still can't believe it happened. Poor, poor girl."

Jax took a swig of his beer, then leaned in. "Have you guys heard the details yet?"

Eager to hear the gruesome details, Gia and Clay simultaneously leaned forward.

"No." Gia said in a loud whisper. "What happened?"

Jax's face hardened as he looked from Gia to Clay, then to Payton. In a hushed voice, he said, "I hear she was beaten to death. Knees shattered, jaw broken, completely unrecognizable. *Bad.*"

Gia gasped, and Payton found herself scanning the crowd again as a chill snaked up her spine.

"Heard she was tortured for hours before she finally died."

A rumble of thunder sounded in the distance, but no one's eyes left Jax.

He continued, "Get this... I heard the guy burned her, too. While she was still alive."

Gia visibly shuddered across the table, and Clay protectively wrapped his arm around her. "Sick fuck," he said.

Jax nodded, his eyes darkening. "I'm not done."

Payton's stomach dipped. She didn't want to hear it again.

"Her eyes were cut out."

"*What?*" Gia squeaked, as the fork she was holding clattered onto the ground, followed by a crack of thunder.

A few heads turned in their direction.

"*Shhh!*" Jax rolled his eyes.

"Are you freaking *kidding* me?"

"That's what I heard."

Payton narrowed her eyes. "Where did you hear all this?" She'd heard it from her contact, Ellen from BSPD dispatch, but she didn't think anyone else knew the gruesome details.

"Like you, I will not reveal my sources."

Payton's eyes narrowed. "Only one other person saw her

body besides the cops and they're keeping the information locked tighter than a vault."

"Who else saw her?" Clay asked.

"The guy who called her in. The owner of the land, where she was found." She turned back to Jax. "You talked to Gary Powell."

Jax innocently shrugged.

"How do you know him? I hear that guy's a hermit."

"You *heard* that, or is it because you went by his house earlier today, and he didn't answer the door?"

Payton's eyebrows tipped up. "Do you have a tracker on my car or something?"

He winked. "Nothing gets by me, sweetheart."

Gia's face had paled. "Do they have any suspects?"

Payton thought of Eli... for the hundredth time that day.

"Don't think so." Jax said. "They brought in a fed to help out."

Clay picked up his beer. "Let's hope they find the guy soon. Anyone who could do something like that..." His voice trailed off as a flash of lightning cut through the sky. A few *yelps* sounded from the crowd, but the music, dancing, and drinking kept going.

Silence fell over the table. Payton's gaze slid behind Clay to the table of college-aged girls giggling and having a good time behind them. Girls' night out.

She got a sick feeling hoping they all made it home.

Rain began to dot their table.

"Well, guys, between this conversation and the weather, I'm about ready to head home and securely lock all my doors and windows." Gia glanced over the shoulder. "Where the heck is our waiter? I haven't seen him in like fifteen minutes."

"I'll find him," Payton said a bit too eagerly. She, too, was ready to get home, not only to end this awkward kind-of-double-date, but to spend some time digging into Gary Powell more. There was something there. She was missing something. Why had the guy talked to Jax, but not answered the door when she'd dropped by? She got up from the table and spied their waiter stepping through the doors that led to the back patio. People were already beginning to make their way out of the sprinkles of rain. A massive oak tree decorated with lanterns sprouted out of the patio floor, streaks of water shimmered against the rock cliff that walled the back. The thatch-roof covered bar with dangling decorative lights swayed in the rainy breeze. It was like she'd escaped to a secret oasis.

A gust of wind blew past her as she stepped outside. The storm blowing in had already cooled the temperatures a good ten degrees. It was much quieter, with fewer drunks. She paused and took a deep breath, inhaling the fresh scent of rain and appreciating a break from the noise out front.

When she opened her eyes, she saw him.

13

*E*LI ARCHER SAT at the end of the bar with his hands wrapped around an ice-cold beer. He was in a deep conversation with the bartender who was ignoring the angry glances from the few people wanting one more drink before the rain hit.

As if sensing her, Eli slowly glanced over his shoulder, the swaying lights on the thatch roof above the bar casting a dim glow over his face. The moment their eyes met, goosebumps prickled her skin.

He watched her as she moved through the crowd.

"Hey." She squeezed past a busty blonde who was no doubt planning to make a move on the handsome agent.

He stood, his hand sweeping over her back, the touch sending tingles across her skin. "Here, sit."

"Oh, no, thanks. I'm actually about to head out. Didn't expect to see you here."

"Couldn't resist the art."

She grinned. "No offense, but I don't take you as an artsy kind of guy."

He cocked a brow. "Why's that?"

She glanced at the bartender who was hypnotized by the hot blonde's belly shirt. "For one, artsy guys wouldn't come to an art festival only to interview local bartenders about a recent homicide."

"You got me there."

"Have you gathered any useful information?"

"Some." His gaze slipped past her. "Hot date?"

She laughed, then wondered why he'd asked. Their waiter breezed by and she asked him to bring the check to the table as soon as he could. Eli watched her every move, like a hawk.

When the waiter disappeared, she stared back at him for a moment. The sprinkle of rain had stopped, but based on the thunder in the distance, more was on its way. A drop dripped from the awning down her face.

He swiped it away.

She looked him over—he was dressed casually, in a simple grey T-shirt that hung taut over his wide shoulders and muscular chest, faded jeans and flip-flops. It was a stark contrast to when she'd first met him, and a glimpse of someone who was exponentially more relaxed than the one she'd met. But it was intentional. The relaxed, casual veneer had been planned, calculated.

Everything about this man was calculated, everything about him was for the job.

"Can I get you a drink?" The bartender asked over his shoulder while skillfully filling two pints.

"Vodka cranberry," Eli answered for her.

She didn't need another, but she didn't argue. She wanted to know if anything unusual had turned up during the day regarding the investigation, but also... the little butterflies flittering around in her stomach told her she was excited to see him.

Someone bumped her shoulder, and she stumbled. Eli grabbed her arm and quickly stepped behind her, steadying her. "Thanks," she said as he guided her onto the stool and positioned himself between her and the dissipating crowd.

"Enjoy." The bartender placed her drink on the napkin. She sipped, eyeing Eli over the rim, into those dark brown eyes that were watching her again.

"Do you come here a lot?" He asked, then glanced in the direction of their table. Had he seen her with Jax? Did he think it was a date? Of course he did... and why did she care so much?

She shook her head. "No. My friend, Gia, dragged me out tonight."

He looked up at the twinkling tree. "Worse places to be dragged."

"True. Have you walked through the festival?"

He nodded, sipped his beer. "Not one for crowds, although I did see a nipple."

She laughed. "Cheers to that, then."

He smirked.

"Have you eaten?" She asked.

"No."

"You should. Food's delicious here. Get the tacos."

"Tacos, huh?" He sipped. "You didn't eat your nachos."

She narrowed her eyes with a slight grin. "You were watching me."

He sipped again. He had been watching her. For how long, she wondered.

"Well, under the circumstances, Agent Archer, you're lucky that doesn't get you a call to dispatch."

"Creepy man watching a woman in a bar?"

"Exactly."

He stared at her for a minute. "Let me get you dinner. A real dinner that you'll actually eat."

More butterflies. "Ah... well, I came here with—"

"There you are." Gia sauntered through the crowed, laser-locked on Eli.

Payton stood. Shit. "Sorry, Gia. This is Special Agent Eli Archer..."

"*Special agent,* huh?" Gia wobbled on her heels as she stuck out her hand with a flirty smile. In the five minutes since Payton had left the table, Gia had gotten drunk. Very drunk.

"Nice to meet you." They shook hands, Gia didn't let go. He flickered a desperate glance to her.

"Okaaay, let's go," Payton said with a laugh as she physically separated Gia's hand from Eli's.

"Oh. *no. You* stay." She said to Payton, then winked at Eli, then back to Payton. "I'll see you tomorrow." Gia leaned in to her ear. "Remember what I said in the bathroom?" Payton cast an amused glance at Eli—Gia's whisper was loud enough for the entire bar to hear. "You need to have some fun, Pay. You know, some steaming, *hot*—"

"Alrighty." Payton yanked her head away. "You need to get to bed, Gia. Alone, preferably."

Gia snorted, wobbled again. "By my choice. I'm not too sure about Clay."

Payton shifted her gaze to their table, where Jax was standing with his arms crossed over his chest, and a pissed off look on his face.

This was insanely awkward.

"Do you have a ride?" Eli asked Gia.

"Yeah. Clay didn't even drink. He's pulling the car around." She looked at Payton. "Call your driver, make him come pick you up. Drink, eat, *have fun.*" Another wink, then she sauntered back into the restaurant and grabbed her purse from the table where Jax was no longer scowling. Good, maybe he was already in the car.

Payton shook her head. She was going to catch shit tomorrow, no doubt about it.

"Driver, huh?"

She was hoping Eli hadn't heard that. She'd wanted to kick Gia the moment the words came out of her buzzed mouth. "Not mine. My stepmother has one."

He nodded to the stool for her to sit, again. "Must be nice."

She shrugged as she sat, and wrapped her hands around her sweating cocktail. She'd rather have a pap smear than talk about her family.

"You two aren't close."

She snorted. "What makes you say that?"

"You called her step*mother*. Most people would say 'step-mom' or drop the 'step' all together."

She took a quick sip avoiding eye contact. "It's complicated."

"Most 'steps' are."

She thought of she and Charmaine's argument earlier and blew out a breath. "No, we're not close, and yeah, my stepmother has a twenty-four hour on-call driver." She looked at him and rolled her eyes. "She also has a twenty-four hour on-call bartender, if you catch my drift." Truth was, Payton wasn't sure if she'd ever been around Charmaine when she wasn't drinking. Even in the morning.

She continued, feeling a surprising release just talking about it. Or, maybe it was the vodka. "They—my dad and her—have a house by the lake just outside of town. My dad hired the driver after she totaled car number three."

"Yikes."

"Yeah."

"Why doesn't he drive her around?"

"He's never home. Has a place in New York where he stays ninety percent of the time." She laughed. "He gave her this old truck he keeps to drive around the property once, telling her if she was going to keep wrecking his cars, he wasn't going to allow her to drive a nice one. The woman walked out and we didn't see her for a week." Payton grinned. "Best week of my life."

"What kind of truck was it?"

"An old, red Ford."

Eli stared at her for a moment, then took a swig of his beer.

She grabbed a menu from behind the counter, relaxing into the buzz grabbing hold. "You know, I might just get an order of tacos, and you're going to get an order, too." She glanced at him. "Not negotiable."

He grinned and held up his empty bottle to the bartender. "Alright, then."

After rattling off their order and ordering another round of drinks, she turned to Eli. "Did anything come up with Mary's car?"

"Not as of this afternoon."

"No prints, nothing?"

He shook his head.

"He must lure them into his car somehow. Maybe asks to use their phone, pretends his vehicle is broken down." A shudder swept over her as she heard Jax's voice in her head describing the body. "Did you see her?" Her voice lowered. "Mary's body?"

She watched his jaw twitch—an un-hideable reaction to his emotion, even for the stoic agent. Yes, he saw Mary, and yes, it must have been horrific.

"It was the same way with Pam Robertson, wasn't it?"

His neck snapped toward her, surprised.

Nerve, hit.

"How do you know about that?"

"Maybe when you start taking me seriously as a journalist, I'll tell you."

He stared at her.

"This is what journalists do, Eli. We investigate crimes." Truth was, she'd spent the entire afternoon researching similar cases, and it wasn't long before she was knee-deep in Pam Roberston and Courtney Howard's homicides. The information she'd pulled was only bits and pieces, but what she was able to gather was that Eli had been called in to profile the Couer Killer and had taken it upon himself to watch over a suspected target—Pam—who claimed she'd felt like she was being 'stalked.' At two in the morning, according to his statement, he'd felt confident that Pam was in for the night and decided to do a drive-by of another suspected target's house, the girl's friend. Except Pam wasn't in for the night—she'd gone out the back exit of her apartment building to walk her neighbor's dog that she was watching while the couple was on vacation. She never made it back to her apartment.

Pam was found beaten near death with her eyes removed. According to the death certificate, she'd died the day she was found. Eli was by her side.

He narrowed his eyes, assessing her, obviously not liking the topic or the fact that she was meddling.

He looked away and took a deep sip of his beer.

"It wasn't your fault, you know."

He stared at his beer, twisting the bottle in his hands.

"You had no idea she was going to sneak out the back door."

He finally looked at her, anger flashing across his face. "I should've. I should've taken laps around the house. I should have never left."

Payton saw the pain in his eyes as he spoke. She now understood Eli's commitment to the case. Eli blamed himself for Pam's death, and now, with Mary's murder, it was apparent that the wrong guy was put behind bars, and the real killer was still out there. Eli had been handed a second chance to help catch the guy.

During her research, Payton was given a glimpse into the terrifying world Eli lived day to day, and suddenly the dark, brooding eyes made sense. She'd also learned Eli had no kids and had never been married... which perhaps was more surprising than him dropping the ball on a surveillance mission. Eli was tall, with a body like a tank and a kind of rough-around-the-edges sexy that brought women to their knees. Case in point: Gia. But the thing that made Payton look twice were his eyes, dark, almost black as coal with a depth that seemed to stare into your soul. After researching him, she knew those eyes had seen more than enough evil for two lifetimes, and held more secrets than that.

And as he stared back at her now, she wanted to peel back the layers—the many, many layers—that made up Eli Archer. Remove those bricks one by one until the real Eli bared his soul to her.

She had a feeling the real Eli was much different than the man sitting next to her.

That maybe he'd forgotten who that man was.

The rain had started up again, except this time no one moved. The crowd had left. Paid their bills and headed home for the evening. Payton and Eli had the bar to themselves.

He flagged down the waiter, and with an edge to his voice said, "Can I get a shot of Patron? Double."

He didn't want to talk about Pam, or his "mistake." Message received.

He swallowed the shot—no salt, no lime, no wince— then sat it on the table and switched conversations. "So, how long has your father been in New York?"

"You mean how long has he had the apartment?"

"No, this visit."

She thought for a moment. When was the last time she'd spoken with him? Days? No, weeks.

"At least two weeks. He'd been in Australia for months before that."

"Bet that's tough on a marriage."

"Maybe. If they loved each other."

He looked at her. "They don't?"

She smiled, looked down. "No. No they don't."

"You don't like her."

She laughed out loud. "The feeling is mutual, trust me."

"I doubt that."

"Then tell that to the back of her hand when I was in sixth grade." She clamped her mouth shut. Why the *hell* did she just tell him that?

"She *hit* you?"

"No. No, no, no, I mean, yes. Technically. Look, it was only once, and I didn't..." She was taken aback by the tense lines of his face, by the fire in his eyes. "I shouldn't have said anything."

"Did you tell your dad?"

"Hell no. I... didn't want to bring attention to it. I didn't want to have to suffer through another argument between them... I know it sounds silly, but I was embarrassed. Like, in a weird way, I allowed it to happen. It was my fault, or something. Makes no sense, I know."

"It's not silly, Payton. It's very common. More than half of all abuse incidents go unreported."

"Abuse?" She laughed. "*No,* I wouldn't categorize—"

"If she slapped you, that's abuse." His tone was ice cold, and she wondered how many child abuse cases he'd worked in his career. "Did it ever happen again?" He asked.

"No. Never." She cut him a glance with a slight smirk. "I told her if she ever did it again, I'd shatter every piece of her precious China sets."

"China sets? You're ruthless."

"Charmaine collects all kinds of pointless things. Rare jewelry, purses, sculptures, art... I think she even has some old Russian dolls worth six figures. But her China? She displays it in a massive glass case and freaks out if there's one speck of dirt on it. They're her pride and joy when people come over." She snorted. "What a life. Anyway, we pretty much stopped speaking after that incident... and the streak continues."

"Your dad didn't notice?"

"Notice what?"

"The decline in you and your stepmom's relationship."

"I don't think you realize how much my dad is away. If not on a job, he's holed up in his New York apartment."

"You should've told your dad."

She shrugged—she knew that, and kicked herself many times for not doing it. But she was young and emotional and learning good decisions from bad. Maybe if she had told her father, he would have left Charmaine, and maybe, just maybe, their relationship would be more than a hug on the holidays.

"Was that the only abuse in your house?"

"My dad wouldn't hurt anyone."

He stared back at her and she laughed. "You mean did Charmaine ever hurt my dad? I strongly doubt that. He might turn a cheek to her drinking, attitude, and God-knows-what-else, but he wouldn't turn a cheek to her fist. Trust me there. Also, he's her damn meal ticket. Woman has never worked a single freaking day of her life."

"You said God-knows-what-else. What do you mean? Is she into drugs?"

"No, I don't think that's something Dad would tolerate."

"You were talking about affairs, then."

"Wouldn't put it past her. Either of them." She shifted in her seat, incredibly uncomfortable now. She was embarrassed by her family. They had all the money in the world, but that didn't help. She'd do anything to have different roots.

"Then why are they still together?" Eli asked.

"If I had a nickel for every time I'd wondered that." She sipped her drink. "I'd have one-trillion nickels."

"That's a lot of coins."

She grunted.

"Not that you'd need them, though." She looked over at the small smirk on his face. "Can I ask you something?"

She cocked a brow. "I think you've asked your fair share of questions this evening, Agent Archer."

"Why do you work?"

"Oh, you mean because I'm so rich? I should just spend the day sipping Champagne out of a golden flute while slathering thousand-dollar anti-aging lotion all over my body?"

His eyes twinkled. "That I'd like to see."

"Then go glance in the windows of my father's house. I'm sure that exact thing is happening right now."

He wrinkled his nose.

"Hey, Charmaine's very pretty, you know. Just ask her." She glanced down at her body. "We couldn't look more different."

He leaned in. "Not all men like bleached-blondes with fake breasts, Payton."

She looked into his eyes and... more butterflies. Her cheeks began to flush and she looked down. "Anyway, you asked why I work." She raised her chin and looked him square in the eye. "Because I love it. I like to work."

"The independence."

"Exactly." She narrowed her eyes. "Quit trying to figure me out, Agent Archer."

"Right back at ya, Payton."

She smiled. "It's what I do." She thoughtfully stirred her drink. "I've always wanted to be an investigative journalist. I remember when my mom was still alive, my dad would come home and tell us all these stories about third-world countries, and show us pictures and tell us how different things were. He wanted us to know we were lucky to live in America. He'd tell us about the crime and injustice, and I remember being so abnormally interested for my age." She looked at him and grinned as her gaze swept over his body —the body protected by a thick brick wall. "I love solving mysteries."

His eyes narrowed with an intensity that had her heart skipping a beat. Inches from her face now, he whispered, "This is one mystery that would take some time, Miss Chase."

She leaned closer, almost touching his lips. "I've got all the time in the world, Agent Archer," she whispered.

Her pulse picked up. She licked her lips.

He pulled away.

She took a quick breath—not realizing she'd been holding it—and turned away.

At that moment three things became evident: There was something mutual sizzling between her and Eli. Whether it was lust or something more, she didn't know. Two, maybe information about the Mary Freeman case wouldn't be so hard to pull from that brick wall sitting next to her.

Three—the vodka had officially hit home.

"Well, I should..."

He sat unmoving, his gaze locked on hers so penetrating a lump formed in her throat.

"... head on out."

"Call that driver of yours."

She snorted. "I wouldn't give Charmaine the satisfaction."

"You could call your brother."

She frowned. "My brother?"

14

THE PASSENGER SIDE door slammed as Eli started the engine. He felt Payton's glare on him like the devil's fork, scorching him from the seat as she dropped her eight-hundred-dollar purse on the floorboard.

"*Talk.*"

He flicked on his high beams as they pulled onto the dark mountain road, buying a moment while he contemplated how to respond. How the hell was he supposed to know she didn't know she had a stepbrother? That she didn't know Charmaine had a child?

One thing he was one hundred percent certain of now was that the Chase family was loaded with secrets... secrets that raised more than one red flag with his current case. Arthur Chase's old, red Ford, a conniving stepmother with a temper and penchant for fine art, the close proximity to the victims, the money, and now, a mysterious stepson who had apparently been cast aside at birth. All signs were pointing Eli to dig deeper into the Chase family, and now, he had the daughter—the sizzling hot, stubborn, drop-dead gorgeous daughter—in his damn passenger seat... the absolute *last* place she should be. Hell, he needed to be formally interviewing her, not giving her a damn ride home—not putting him next to her when all he could think about was getting her out of that silky shirt that ran like liquid gold over her breasts.

"I said, *talk*," she repeated.

He stopped at a four-way and glanced at the clock—8:30 p.m.—before asking, "Which way?"

She heaved out an impatient breath. "Right, and then take a left at the next road. I live about five minutes from here. Now, talk, Archer."

"Okay... Charmaine got pregnant when she was sixteen, had a boy, and gave him up for adoption when he was six months old."

"How the hell do you know this?"

He cut her a glance.

"Oh, that's right, the FBI can dig into anyone's personal life." She rolled her eyes.

"Well, that's the pot calling the kettle black."

She glanced out the side window, avoiding his gaze.

That's right, I wasn't the only one digging into someone else's personal life. He didn't like that she knew anything about his personal life, and especially about the details surrounding Pam Robertson... although she didn't know them all. She didn't know that each victim had red hair, blue eyes, and were spitting images of her. She didn't know that with every moment he spent with her, he became more and more desperate to find the son of a bitch... to keep *her* safe—the woman that seemed to completely captivate him. The moment he found out about Dustin, a new possible scenario had started to link together... the son of Charmaine, jealous of the stepdaughter who lived a lavish lifestyle after his mother had given him away as thoughtlessly as a stick of gum. Dustin probably despised Payton, and everyone that looked like her. Jealousy and money. Two very common motivations for murder.

"Who was the dad?"

"According to the birth certificate, some guy named Corbin."

"What was the boy's name?"

"Dustin Bisset."

"She kept her last name for her child?"

"Apparently."

She stared out the window for a moment. It was a shock —would've been a shock to anyone. He decided to leave the money laundering out of the story for now, at least until he figured out how—or if—it connected. Payton was having a hard enough time digesting her long lost stepbrother.

"Charmaine is forty-five now... so he'd be close to thirty years old."

Eli nodded—he'd already done the math. The age fit the Couer Killer profile.

"Where is he?"

"I don't know. I was honestly hoping you could tell me that, before I realized you didn't know about it."

"What about the dad? Where is he?"

Just give him an hour, he thought. "Not sure, either." He glanced over at her. The glow of the radio illuminated the lines of her face. The anger was fading, confusion setting in.

"I wonder... *God,* there's *no way* my dad knows. He would've told me. Somehow it would've come up through the years. And furthermore, my dad would have tried to get Charmaine to reconnect with him."

"Would he, Payton? You told me yourself that you and he don't have a solid relationship. Why would he care to foster a relationship with his wife's son?"

She paused for a moment. "The guy my dad was before my mom died would've wanted to reconnect a family... but, you're right, I guess. Maybe he didn't care." She shook her head in disbelief.

"Left here?"

"Yes. I'm the last driveway on the left."

He turned onto a freshly paved road, shiny from the rain. Dense woods lined both sides. They were mid-way up the mountain, he guessed. "So Charmaine never said anything about him at all? Maybe you've forgotten?"

"You really think I would forget that I had a stepbrother, Archer?"

There was a bite to her tone when she said his last name, and he imagined her addressing him like that while she slapped him around in bed.

She suddenly laughed a humorless laugh, shaking him from his sexual fantasy. "I've always wished I had a sibling," she said. "I just *cannot* believe this. You've got to track him down."

That, and figure out how long your dad has driven an old, red Ford, and if he was in town for any of the murders, and check if Charmaine has purchased any of LaRouche's art, and if anything in the Chase household connects to the word shadow...

"Eli." She interrupted the long list of immediate to-dos running through his head, the list that he needed to keep from her. "Why were you digging into my family?"

"Why were you digging into me?" He glanced at her as she opened her mouth, but then she closed it and looked away.

He knew why—it was the same reason he'd gone through every *single* picture in her social media account. Multiple times.

She crossed her arms over her chest—defiant. "I'll find Dustin if you won't help me."

He had no doubt she would. Dammit, she was stubborn.

He turned left at the end of the road, next to a shiny mailbox with begonias spilling over the base. The driveway took a turn and opened up to a large, manicured lawn speckled with soaring oak and maple trees. In the center, a white plantation-style house with a wraparound porch that was illuminated under dim, golden lights. Meticulously manicured shrubs lined the house with a colorful array of flowers blooming along the walkway that led from the circle drive to the front steps.

He rolled to a stop, wondering if she lived alone.

She grabbed her purse and stared at him with a look he couldn't quite read—an unfamiliar occurrence for him.

"Want to come in?" She asked.

Yes. "No..." He paused. "I mean, I've got a lot to do, Payton."

"Murder never sleeps."

"No, no it doesn't."

She gazed through the windshield as if wanting to say something. Sprinkles of rain fell from the tree towering above and dotted the windshield.

"You can't just drop this bomb on me... and..." she shook her head again but this time he swore he saw the glisten of tears in her eyes.

She was *crying?!*

Christ. Cold-blooded killers, rapists, drug-addicts, he knew how to handle them all. A crying woman, not so much.

"Whatever." She pushed out the door. "Thanks for the ride." And slammed it.

Shit.

Go, Eli. Go home.

He watched her stomp up the walkway, her long hair blowing in the breeze, her steps a little unsteady on those spike heels.

Those sexy, sexy, heels.

Go. Home. Eli. It's not your job to protect her. Go home.

With a groan, he shoved the car into park and got out. As she inserted the key into the front door, she looked over her shoulder with a look that suggested she'd known he'd cave. And instead of waiting for him, she pushed through the door and left it open as she disappeared into the house.

Why did he feel like she somehow had gotten control of the situation now?

Wow, this woman knew how to manipulate. He'd be impressed if it weren't for the fact *he* was the one being manipulated.

He stepped inside a modern, open floor-plan house with sweeping windows that overlooked the woods. Subtle white, gray, earthy wood tones; clean and minimalistic—exactly the opposite of what he imagined her eccentric stepmom lived in. There was no clutter, just the bare necessities arranged in a sleek way that resembled a showhouse. It was undoubtedly a very expensive home with top-of-the-line appliances and all the bells and whistles, but the extravagant taste was hidden expertly well. As if she were embarrassed.

A light clicked on the in the kitchen.

"Do you always leave your front porch lights on?" He crossed the room as she pulled two beers from the fridge.

"Only when there's a murderer on the loose."

Or after you were brutally attacked and tied up in a basement for twelve hours.

She popped the top and handed him a pricey import.

"Where are you staying?" She asked abruptly.

"A B&B by the lake."

She nodded, eyeing him. Approval or disapproval? Thinly veiled invite to stay at her house? The thought excited him, so he forced it away.

"You've got a nice place here. You live alone?"

She nodded.

"A lot to maintain."

She shrugged. "Keeps me busy on the weekends, when I'm not working of course."

"You take care of it?" He couldn't hide his surprise.

The corner of her lip curled up. "Expecting maids and a butler?"

"More or less."

"No. I take care of it myself." She said with a mix of pride and anger.

"In spite of Charmaine's lifestyle."

She sipped her beer, avoiding eye contact.

"You can't let her control your life. Even if you don't realize it."

She paused, then looked at him with slitted eyes. "I want to know why you're digging into my family. And don't give me some bullshit answer, Eli. I want to know the truth."

He watched her closely, the attitude thick in an attempt to mask the emotions she was feeling inside. He assumed she did that a lot.

She continued, "You've got a lot on the line with this case. When Arnie Miller's lawyer talks to the media—and you know he will—the pressure to find the real Couer Killer is going to be turned up a million degrees. All eyes will be on you to predict his next move. You can't afford to spend your time snooping around people you don't believe are connected."

The rain picked up outside, a light buzz on the roof.

"Your family clicks off several check points on my profile. Along with several other Berry Springs citizens."

"What points, exactly?"

"I believe the suspect has money, has something to lose. There seems to be a connection with Berry Springs and the other two victims, so I believe he lives here, has a house here, or visits frequently. I believe the suspect has a strong interest in art, LaRouche in particular, who also happens to have lived here."

"Kind of vague."

Yeah, considering he wasn't telling her everything.

"What age does your profile say the suspect is?"

"My guess is thirties."

She blinked. "That would be the age of my stepbrother."

He raised his eyebrows.

"You think it's him?"

Eli sipped again and watched her wheels turn. "Payton, let me ask you something."

"Yes?"

"Does the word *shadow* mean anything to you?"

"Shadow?"

He nodded.

"Other than the obvious, no. Why?"

Just then, a chorus of distant barks broke the silence.

He straightened, his instincts kicking to alert. "You have dogs?"

She set down her drink, with a look that shared the same instant concern. "No. My neighbor does. Their property runs just beyond those trees."

He frowned and looked out the window into the darkness. "Hit the lights," he said as his hand slid to the gun on his belt, hidden under his shirt.

When the kitchen went dark he stepped next to the window and peered outside.

Seconds of silence ticked by as he focused on the line of woods that hugged her house. Suddenly, a flash of movement just beyond the tree line.

He drew his weapon. "Get back from the window." He crouched down. "And stay here."

"Did you see someone?" She whispered from the shadows.

Someone, something—he wasn't sure—but it was his gut telling him danger was close by.

"Were you expecting anyone tonight?" He whispered.

"No. And especially not coming up from the woods."

"Seeing anyone?" He turned fully to her, the outside porch light spilling onto her face.

She pinned him with her gaze. "... No."

A moment passed between them as they stared back at each other.

"Okay, you stay *here*, Payton, you understand?"

"It's my house, Eli."

He clenched his jaw. Every second they spent arguing was an opportunity for whoever the hell was lurking around her house to get away. "I don't care if it's your house. I'm a federal agent and I'm telling you to stand down." Anger began to pump through his veins. *Damn* this woman's independence. *"Stay."*

He stood, steering clear of the windows, and as he stepped out of the kitchen, he heard a shuffle behind him. He spun around, nose to nose with Nancy Drew.

"Get back in the kitchen."

"No!" She hissed. "Why? I have every right—"

"Because all the fucking victims look like you, Payton!" He yelled.

Her eyes popped in shock and she took a step back.

He ground his teeth and growled in frustration. "You resemble every single victim. You must've not noticed during your deep dive into my personal life." He said in a loud whisper. "The killer has a type... and you're it."

Her mouth slowly dropped.

He grabbed her shoulders half wanting to slap sense into her, and half wanting to kiss the shit out of her. "Now you understand, right?"

He saw fear as she nodded.

He exhaled. "Okay, get back into the kitchen and wait for me there. Do not come out unless I tell you to."

Damn this woman.

He waited until she faded into the shadows before turning and jogging through the house.

Considering the porch lights would announce him coming out the back door, he slipped out the front door, assuming the creeper was still coming up from the back.

Eli squatted, did a quick sweep of his surroundings, then darted into the woods.

He stopped.

The rain wet his shoulders as he slid behind a tree, taking a moment to get his bearings. The raindrops hampered his ability to hear footsteps, a twig breaking, or any other tell-tale sign that someone was close.

He'd have to move, relying only on sight, which was shit.

He gripped his Glock and slipped through the woods; silent, skillfully, as he'd been trained to do.

He kept his eye on the edge where the lights of the porch provided an outline of the trees... and someone slowly moving from tree to tree.

A blaze of fury heated him from the inside out. Someone

was watching—*stalking*—Payton. What if he hadn't been here tonight?

He slid his finger over the trigger, gritted his teeth and moved forward, quickly, as the figure slipped from tree to tree. He traced the outline, the height, weight of the person. The movement.

Could this be the Couer Killer? His pulse picked up at the thought and a fresh rush of urgency shot through him. This could all be over tonight.

He slowed as he crept closer, breathing slowly in and out of his nose, his senses hyper alert to everything around him —the rain sliding down his face, the pitter-patter of the drops on the leaves above, the breeze sweeping over his damp clothes.

The figure stopped, his gaze fixed directly on the kitchen windows.

How long had he been watching?

Then, the dark silhouette burst from the trees into the backyard and Eli lunged forward, sprinting through the woods at full speed. A branch sliced his cheek.

He didn't notice.

"Stop! FBI!"

The figure stumbled giving Eli a chance to leap onto his back.

They tumbled to the ground, and in under two-seconds, Eli had the man flipped onto his stomach with his hands bent behind his back.

The man spat, cussed, and as he turned his face, Eli recognized the profile immediately.

Gary Powell.

15

"*E*LI!"

Payton, who had apparently been watching from the window, barreled down the lawn. The night was pitch-black, her silhouette outlined by the porch lights in the background.

His grip tightened on the body beneath him, and Gary flinched, spitting another curse.

"Here." Winded, and wide-eyed, she held up a pair of handcuffs. "Use these."

He tipped a brow.

A grin cracked the shock on her face and she innocently shrugged.

Cuffs. Why the hell did this woman have cuffs? And more importantly, who had used them on her? He pushed the jealousy out of his head. *Not now, Eli.*

"Get my phone out of my pocket and call Lieutenant Quinn Colson, tell him I've got Gary Powell trespassing on your land."

"*Gary Powell?*"

"Make the call," he said sharply.

She took one more look at Gary, then at him with a questioning look in her eyes.

Could it be him?

Eli nodded to his pocket—*make the call.*

She pulled his cell, and he waited until she stepped away.

"You want to tell me why you're stalking Payton Chase?"

Gary spat and laughed. "I ain't stalkin' nobody." The smell of liquor was hot on his breath.

"Then what the fuck were you doing creeping around in her woods after dark?"

"I ain't got to defend myself to *anyone,*" the man hissed.

"Right now, Mr. Powell, you've got to defend lurking around a woman's house two day's after another woman was found beaten to death on your land."

"They're on their way." Payton walked up and glowered down at Gary, then said, "Decided you finally wanted to chat, Gary?" Her eyebrow cocked with attitude.

Eli's gazed snapped to her. She'd tried to interview him? About Mary? He wished he could say he was surprised.

"I don't talk to the press," Gary hissed.

"You might just have to now."

Sirens pierced the silence as red and blue lights bounced off the trees. A second later, flashlights flickered as Lieutenant Colson and Officer Grayson came jogging down the dark hill.

Eli pulled Gary to his feet, and as Grayson guided the drunk to the car, Eli updated Quinn, and confirmed that Payton had gone to Gary's house yesterday in an attempt to interview him regarding the body found on his land. She apparently was met with silence, which made the fact that he was caught on her land even more interesting.

There was absolutely no doubt in Eli's mind that something was going on with the landowner—whether that included removing eyeballs and beating women to death was to-be-determined.

After asking Eli to sit in on the interview later to get his thoughts, Quinn and Grayson left as quickly as they'd come.

"You're reckless, Payton," he said to her as the patrol car disappeared into the night. He kept his gaze straight ahead as they started walking up the lawn.

"Hey. I wanted to interview the guy, that's it. And, I didn't realize... how the hell was I supposed to know I looked like all the other victims, Eli? Maybe if you would've told me—"

"I thought our little self-defense lesson in the woods would be enough to scare you to your senses."

"This is my *job*, Eli. I was doing my job by visiting Gary for an interview..." Her tone and quick delivery told him he wasn't the only one pissed off at that moment. "Maybe if you'd done *your job* by telling me... Shit, maybe if you'd told the other girls... " Her voice trailed off as she stepped onto the porch.

The insinuation felt like a blade piercing his chest. She was stubborn, manipulative, and knew how to hurt. He breezed right past her and kept walking.

"Eli." She turned and blew out a breath. "I'm sorry. *Dammit.* I didn't mean it, I'm just... and... and I get that you can't tell me stuff like that... Eli?"

He inhaled deeply through his nose feeling like he was about to internally combust.

"*Eli.*"

His name came off her tongue like a crack of a whip.

He stopped at his car and could feel her stare boring into his back. The only thing more maddening than this woman's gall, was the fact that he'd stopped. That he wasn't halfway down the driveway by now. That he'd actually considered turning around.

That he was goddamn glad she'd called after him.

Shit, Eli.

"Eli." Her voice was softer now. "I'm sorry."

Common sense was telling him to get in the fucking car, but he didn't move. What the *fuck* was wrong with him?

He heard soft footsteps behind him.

"Eli."

He turned and her eyes rounded. "Holy *shit.*"

He frowned.

"Your face. *Geez,* Eli." She grabbed his arm and stepped closer. "I didn't notice down there because it was so dark. You've got a hell of a scratch on your face. It might need stitches."

It was the first time the pain registered, followed by the wetness on his cheek, and he remembered something snagging him while he ran through the woods. Tree branch one, Eli zero.

Her hand swept down his arm to his hand, leaving a trail of goosebumps on his skin. "Let me..." she said softly as she tugged at him. "Come inside for just a minute."

He stared back at her. Her eyebrows furrowed in concern and guilt for saying what she did. She bit her bottom lip, begging, and squeezed his hand. "Please, Eli, come in."

As if being pulled like a magnet, his foot moved forward, then the next, then the next.

Payton Chase was absolutely, one-hundred percent, fucking irresistible.

He followed her inside, like a dog on a damn leash. She led him through the house and he thought of the handcuffs and searched for any signs of a man—or men, for that matter.

They stepped into her bedroom where a subtle come-hither scent lingered in the air. Something light and fresh, clean, with a touch of flowers. It smelled like *her.*

A massive four-poster bed against a wall of windows was the focal point of the room, and like the rest of the house, it was modern, clean, and minimalistic with only a reading nook next to a lounge chair, and big-screen TV that almost gave him an erection.

Next, he was led into a bathroom—fit for a queen.

Fit for Payton.

White marble, two-person shower, another sitting area, and an entire wall that looked like some sort of female command center with shelves of cosmetics, a makeup desk with lighted mirrors, and a red velvet chair that looked like the only thing missing was the crown dangling from the armrest. It was the only outwardly extravagant area of her house... until he glanced in her closet.

A sweep of insecurity sent a shock through his system.

He'd never be able to provide that for her. Who the hell owned that many pairs of shoes?!

She finally let go of his hand, then dropped to her knees next to the cabinet.

Cotton balls, peroxide, butterfly stitches, none of which was included in his insta-fantasy the moment her face was inches from his groin. She stood, grabbed a washcloth and ran it under warm water.

Her eyes met his.

His heart gave a kick.

She dabbed the washcloth against his face, slowly, gently, womanly. His heart started to pound, so hard that he feared she could hear it against the silence of the room.

His gaze drifted down to the soft breath escaping the thin line between her full lips. The rise and fall of her chest.

She ran the washcloth under the sink, the water washing away pink from his blood.

She dabbed again, then locked onto his gaze.

A moment ticked by, although it felt like an eternity.

"I'm sorry," she whispered.

Me, too, he thought, *for all the things I didn't tell you... for all the things I haven't.* Dammit, he couldn't get involved with this girl. Not right now.

Before he could pull away, she pulled up on her tip-toes and kissed him, a soft sweep across the lips before she settled in.

His heart tripped in his chest.

Her tongue met his and every thought racing through his mind melted. He gave in—to *her*—taking her with a need, an urgency he'd never felt before. He swept his hand to the back of her head and fisted her soft, auburn hair.

A soft groan escaped her lips, and he grabbed tighter, tilting her head back so he could have his way with her. The groan set him over the edge, the blood funneling between his legs, his mind single-focused now. The focus of a wild animal about to devour its prey.

He wrapped his arms around her waist and lifted her onto the counter. Something tipped, then shattered on the marble floor.

She didn't care. If anything, based on the tightening grip of her hands on his back, it turned her on.

She wrapped those long legs around his waist. He pressed his erection into her, and just knowing what was behind the thin black fabric of her panties sent another round of tingles over his skin.

He yanked her silk blouse out of her pants and slid his hand onto her breast.

Lace. Of course Payton Chase wore lingerie that was completely irresistible to every man on the planet.

She fumbled with his belt and licked her way to his ear. Warm, wet tongue, a nip, and then, "Eli..."

His phone rang.

Shit.

She froze, then pulled away.

Dammit!

He pulled back and looked at her. Her cheeks were flushed, her lips wet and swollen, her eyes round with surprise.

Yeah, he felt it too.

The phone stopped screaming—they both glanced at it from the corner of their eye—then rang again immediately.

"You need to get that," she whispered, her breath heavy.

"I know." But he didn't move as he stared back at her. "I know," he repeated, then clenched his jaw and peeled himself away.

Inwardly, he was spitting every cuss word in the world as he answered the phone.

And his heart dropped to his feet.

16

*E*LI TOSSED HIS phone on the passenger seat and turned on his high beams as he bumped down the narrow dirt road, deep in the woods. He glanced up at the sky, hoping to see a few stars that would promise a clear sky to come—no luck. The cloud cover was still thick with the threat of more rain.

Hopefully that wouldn't hamper all the favors he'd just called in. His first call was to Ethan Veech to update him on the evening's event—minus the kiss with his new obsession —and get him to locate Dustin Bisset, STAT. Next, he'd called his partner, updating him, and requesting more manpower be sent to Berry Springs.

The heat just got turned up.

Up ahead, his lights bounced off red taillights of a patrol car and a blacked-out pickup. Flashlights bounced off the trees in the distance and just as he turned off the ignition, the bright glow of Klieg lights popped through the trees, illuminating the crime scene.

A ball formed in his gut.

Another one.

The moment he'd heard the tone in Grayson's voice when he'd answered the phone, he knew. And he did everything in his damn power to conceal his reaction from Payton, who was undoubtedly eavesdropping from the bathroom. But true to Payton Chase form, she was a master of reading people. Seeing through people.

Just like him.

She knew. Her eyes said it all as she nodded when he'd told her *"Something's come up."*

The only benefit was that there was no time to feel the weight of awkwardness from their surprise make-out session.

He grabbed the key from the ignition as the realization hit him like a ton of bricks.

If she wouldn't have pulled away from him, he wouldn't have answered that phone. Hell, if she hadn't pulled away from him, he wasn't sure if he'd have noticed a bomb exploding in the next room.

If she wouldn't have pulled away, he would've carried her to bed and would be buried deep inside her this very second.

It would have been the first time, in his entire career, that he would have put a woman before the job.

The thought sent a shiver of emotions up his spine.

What the fuck was going on with him?

Feeling completely off his game, he grit his teeth, grabbed his bag, slid his phone into his pocket and got out. The rain had cooled things down, but it was still steamy... kind of like the kiss he'd just had.

He pushed Payton Chase away. He needed to focus. Now was not the time to be lusting after a journalist—of all damn professions—whose family was number one on his suspect list.

Again, what the *hell* was he doing?

Lights at his back stretched his silhouette across the muddy ground. He turned, shaded his eyes.

A black Tahoe skidded to a stop in the mud.

Wearing a shockingly tight black dress and heels, Jessica Heathrow jumped out. Although he'd only met Jessica twice, he got the vibe she wasn't a "little black dress" kind of gal. And heels? No way.

He wondered if she'd lost some sort of bet.

"Don't look at me like that," she said as she slammed the door and clicked on her flashlight, bag in hand.

"Well, good evening to you, too."

She snorted. "Good evening, my ass." She stomped past him, wobbling on her tiptoes through the soggy ground. Her face squeezed with anger. "I was on the first goddamn date in six damn months," she mumbled.

He fell into step with her as they descended into the woods. He inched closer, hyper aware of each wobble. He didn't know a lot about women, except for one thing—heels and mud don't mix.

She continued, ranting into the wind at no one in partic-ular, it seemed. "I've turned this guy down three times. *Three* times over the last year. Why? Because I'm a freaking worka-holic, that's why. But you know why else? I've become a cynic. A terrible Debbie Downer cynic." The buzz of bugs around them increased as they walked deeper in the woods, and Eli wondered if they were trying to drown out her rant. She spoke louder. "Nothing works out the way people intend it to. Nothing is perfect. Death is real, evil is real. I deal with the finality of death every day, and the devastation it leaves in its wake. It's my job. So why would a relationship work out? Why would love work out when there's so much evil in the world?"

He kept his gaze ahead as her words hit home, perhaps now more than ever.

"And when I saw Mary's body. Saw what someone had done her." She finally looked at him. "Eli, it really got to me. And, oddly enough, had the opposite effect on me. It made me realize that because there is so much evil in the world, because life is so short, why the fuck not give things a chance? It's not like I'm going to be around forever. Why not try to allow myself at least the opportunity to try, to let someone love me?"

A knot grabbed his throat.

"So, I get the first night off in freaking *weeks* and I decide to grab my balls—so to speak—and I called ol' Judson back and told him I'd go on a date with him. He's asked me out a hundred times. I dressed up real nice, *as you can see*, and he took me to the Evening Shade Inn. And, Eli? I'll be damned if I wasn't having a nice time." She laughed a humorless laugh. "Then, in an ironic twist of fate, my phone rings just as dinner arrives. It's Colson, calling me up to tell me another girl has been found." She looked down and shook her head. "Judson's still there. On our date without me." A moment passed and Eli could hear faint voices through the trees.

She looked at him. "*Another one,* Eli."

There was a touch of accusation in the frustration of her tone and it crawled under his skin like ants. Mostly because she was right. It was past time he caught this son of a bitch. The right guy, this time.

Jessica continued, "Heard they brought in ol' drunk Powell. You think it's him?"

God, I hope so.

A fly zipped past him, then another, then another, their little black bodies darting around against the background of harsh fluorescent light. The flies always came first.

"We'll find out soon enough."

Officer Grayson and a younger officer he hadn't met turned as they stepped out of the brush. The young officer's face was pale, eyes round. Grayson's face, on the other hand, was stone-cold—a look of experience with death.

"Oh my *God*," Jessica said breathlessly as she looked down at the ground.

Eli's gut twisted as he stared at the woman sprawled out in the muddy grass.

It wasn't the size of her grotesquely swollen, beaten face, and her lips, split and protruding from the skull. It wasn't the flattened nose against shattered bone, it wasn't the red, oozing dots all over her skin from cigarette burns, or the gaping, puffed up slices of flesh on her wrists. It wasn't the way the bottom half of her legs seemed dislocated from her kneecap in a way that made her look like a puppet on a string.

It wasn't even the holes in her head where her eyes had been removed.

It was the long, dark auburn hair, the height, the weight, hell, even the pricy clothes.

It was as if he was staring down at Payton Chase.

The hair on the back of his neck stood on its end.

Jessica covered her mouth with her hand and shook her head.

A long moment of silence settled around everyone as they gaped down at the Devil's work.

Finally, Jessica took a deep breath, squared her shoulders and instantly became the professional, emotionless, infamous medical examiner he'd initially met. She squatted down and pulled gloves and booties from her bag. The mood instantly switched from shock-and-awe, to let's-get-to-work.

"Special Agent Archer," Officer Grayson said, "This is Officer Hayes."

Eli nodded at the officer, but the kid was studying Jessica with a cocked head as he scratched the top of his head.

Jessica's gaze snapped up. "It's a dress, Hayes. Go fuck yourself."

Hayes frowned, clearly confused. Eli looked at Grayson, who had the same perplexed expression as he looked down at the usually masculine medical examiner.

She heaved out a breath as she snapped on blue latex gloves. "What? Surprised I'm not covered in scales?"

"I just..." Hayes stuttered, "Uh, I've never seen you dressed... were you at a funeral?"

Eli bit his cheek.

"I was on a fucking date, alright? With a *man,* to answer your next question. Lay the fuck off me."

Hayes tore his eyes away and held up his hands to surrender. "Sorry."

"Who found her?" Eli asked, returning to the subject at hand.

"Some teenagers," Grayson said, looked back at the body. "Out smoking pot. Started wandering, walked right up on her."

"Whose land is this?" He swatted a fly and kneeled down next to Jessica.

"Not Gary Powell's if that's what you're asking. Land belongs to the city."

"How far is it from where Mary's body was found?"

"'Bout a hundred yards."

"Our suspect's getting cocky." And things were about to escalate.

Grayson nodded. "Cocky's good."

That was true, but not always. More often than not, cockiness led to mistakes, which left a trail of breadcrumbs to the suspect, but *only* if they caught the mistakes.

"It's the exact same scenario." Jessica said as she examined the body. "Exact. Torture, including the eyes, was done perimortem." Her gaze trailed down to the wrists. "Then he sliced her wrists. Exactly like Mary."

"TOD?"

"I'd say around twelve hours ago."

Grayson looked at Eli. "So right after Mary was found. He murdered these girls back to back."

The knot in Eli's stomach tightened.

Yes, things were escalating.

17

*P*AYTON PARKED BEHIND a white van, the last in a long line of party supplies and catering vehicles that crowded the driveway. She glanced at the clock —10:04 p.m.—then back to the house, all lit up.

Of course Charmaine was awake. Like a vampire, that woman never slept.

She grabbed her purse and pushed out of the car, her stomach knotting with her nerves as she looked up at the white columns of the colonial-style brick mansion she'd grown up in.

The mansion she hadn't stepped foot inside of since last Christmas.

A shadow moved quickly past the front windows, then back, then disappeared again.

As she walked up the steps, the front door opened.

Charmaine narrowed her blood-shot eyes and looked Payton over.

Payton met the icy welcome with a look of her own.

"What're you doing here?"

Payton pushed passed her. "Oh, you know, just stopped by for a chat."

Charmaine hesitated, leaving the door open.

Payton stepped deeper into the foyer. She wasn't going anywhere. Technically, this was her house just as much as Charmaine's, although she'd rather sleep in the morgue instead of staying a night under the expensive roof.

She looked around—new paint on the walls, new furniture, new carpeting on the double staircase. Charmaine had been busy since the holidays.

"Payton, dear. Let me get your purse."

Payton turned to see Mona, the housekeeper, shuffling across the marble floor avoiding eye contact with Charmaine. Payton had always had a great relationship with Mona, and the two had even shared a few cracks about Charmaine in the past, but that mischievous twinkle was long gone from Mona's eyes now. Payton also noticed that the housekeeper was wearing an official uniform instead of her usual long shirt and sweater—no doubt a new demand from her boss. A fresh wave of anger flushed through her system as she glanced at Charmaine.

What a delusional, out-of-touch witch.

"Can I get you a drink?" Mona asked Payton.

"Get me some more wine," Charmaine interrupted.

"How *dare* you talk to her like that," Payton snapped.

Both Mona and Charmaine froze, their eyes wide with shock. Mona quickly turned and disappeared down the hall while Payton watched the color of her stepmother's face turn from a paleness created by thousand-dollar skin brighteners, to red with fury.

The woman was physically trembling with anger.

It reminded Payton of the day Charmaine had slapped her across the face, and her body tensed in response to the horrible memory. But she stood strong, staring back at the monster in front of her.

"Don't you *ever* speak to me like that again, Payton." Spittle fell from Charmaine's lips as she took an unsteady step forward.

She was drunk.

Shocker.

Payton held her ground. "Mona has been with us since I was a little girl. She deserves *respect*."

Charmaine threw her head back and cackled. "What the hell do you know about respect, Payton?"

"I know enough to know not to treat anyone else like trash, like you just did with Mona."

"You little, spoiled brat." She seethed, inching closer and closer. "You completely abandoned us—"

"Abandoned us? *You?*" This time she stepped forward. "You sent me off to boarding school two-thousand miles away when I was in seventh grade. *Twelve* years old! Do you have any idea what that felt like?"

"It was your father's decision."

"Bullshit! You convinced him to do it. I heard the entire argument from the bathroom door. I was *devastated,* Charmaine." Her fists clenched at her side. "I was so young, so vulnerable, and you cast me aside like an obnoxious puppy. Something you're apparently very used to."

Charmaine didn't catch the quip about abandoning her own son. "Well, forgive me if I don't feel sorry for you while you're wallowing in your twenty-million-dollar inheritance, *Payton,*" she said instead.

"That's what this is all about isn't it? It's all about money with you. Always has been. You married my dad for his money, you hate me because I get a chunk of it. You're the spoiled brat, Charmaine. And my dad will come to his senses one day. One day he'll see you for what you really are and throw you out on your overly-Botoxed face."

"Bitch!" She threw her wineglass on the floor. "I'm going to tell your father, you little *bitch.*" Tears of rage welled in her drunk eyes. "I'm going to tell him what a little monster you are." She dipped down and started gathering the shards of glass.

Mona stood in the doorway, her mouth gaping open.

Payton glowered down at Charmaine. "Go ahead, and hey, while you're at it, why don't you tell him about your son?"

The shock froze Charmaine's face, verifying what Payton already assumed—her dad had no idea about his long-lost stepson.

The drunk slowly rose, her mouth gaping.

Payton watched her body begin to tremble, wild madness contorting her face.

Then, everything happened so fast.

A *whoosh* of air as Charmaine swung a shard of glass at Payton's face—

Payton lunged backward—

"*Pop, pop!*" Glass exploded around them.

Payton watched Charmaine's eyes bulge, then roll back in her head as her body crumbled to the ground.

"*Charmaine!*"

Payton fell to her knees and took her stepmother's head in her hand. Blood pooled on the white marble floor below her limp body.

"*Mona!* Call 911!"

As Mona's pitched voice faded behind her, Payton shifted her gaze to the shattered front windows.

Mona rushed over. "Oh, my *God!* Oh, my..." she sobbed

and fell to the ground. "The cops are on their way. Oh, my God!"

Payton scrambled to her feet. "Stay here with Charmaine."

Mona nodded as Payton grabbed her SIG from her purse, then burst out the front door. Under the haze of the lampposts, she saw a figure sprinting down the driveway.

Adrenaline shot through her as she sprinted down the driveway, her eyes locked on the dark silhouette just ahead. The figure turned into the woods but Payton stayed on the driveway to cut him off on the road.

He had to go somewhere right?

The growl of an engine had her stopping at the edge of the dirt road just as a four-wheeler skidded out of the tree line right next to her.

She recognized him instantly. Her mouth dropped—it was Mateo Raya, her father's best friend and business partner.

Their eyes met for a brief second before he spun onto the dirt, kicking rocks into her face.

Sirens wailed, lights flashed through the darkness as a patrol car sped down the road, facing the four-wheeler head on. Lights silhouetted Mateo, and the gun on his hip. He slammed the brakes, did a one-eighty and disappeared into the woods. The patrol car skidded to a stop, and Officer Grayson burst out of the driver's door, gun drawn—directly at her.

"Owen, no!" Eli jumped out of the passenger door. "That's Payton." His eyes flashed to her. "Put down your goddamn gun, Payton!"

She dropped the gun she'd didn't realize was still in her hand. "It's him," she screamed and pointed. "On the four-wheeler!"

Grayson took off into the woods as Eli sprinted to her.

More sirens, more lights, more shouting from the road.

"Are you okay?" He grabbed her face in her hands as she stared at him blankly, trying to form a sentence.

Gunshots in the distance.

"Get down!"

He pushed her to the ground and threw his body over hers. The ground was hot, sweltering. Rocks pressed into her back as her chest heaved against her wildly beating heart. A bead of sweat ran down her face.

Then, an eerie silence settled around them.

Eli lifted his head. His breath was heavy but steady. In a calm, strong voice he said, "Are you okay?"

She squirmed underneath him. "Yes, yes, but Charmaine isn't."

He lifted off her, but kept his hand gripped on her arm as she sprang up. The ambulance maneuvered between the cars and zoomed up the driveway as Officer Grayson emerged from the woods, guiding a cuffed and bleeding Mateo Raya.

Payton lunged forward, but Eli grabbed her shoulders and yanked her back.

"No." He said firmly, positioning himself between her and Mateo.

"Bastard!" She screamed as tears swam in her eyes.

She struggled against him, but he held firm. "This man was my father's best friend, Eli," she seethed. "He was the best man at their wedding for Christ's sake!"

"Nothing will be gained from you attacking him, Payton.

You'll spend a night in jail and possibly lose your job." His gaze landed on a scrape on her neck, anger instantly shooting through him. "Where did you get that? Did he do that to you?"

She reached up and touched her face, then closed her eyes, struggling to remember through the chaos going on around them. "Glass, maybe. He shot Charmaine through the window. Glass was everywhere."

Jesus Christ, Payton could've been shot. Had Mateo intended to shoot Payton, too, but missed? Eli ground his teeth and forced himself to stay put instead of dragging the son of a bitch behind them out of the patrol car.

"Are you hurt anywhere else?"

"No, I'm fine."

Just then, Officer Hayes jogged up. "Eli, Grayson wants to talk to you."

He tore his eyes away from Payton. "Is he okay? Grayson?"

Hayes snorted. "Bullets are no match for that guy." His gaze shifted to Payton. "You okay?"

"Yes, I need to..." Her voice trailed off as she looked at the house in the distance. "Charmaine."

Eli quickly turned to Hayes. "Interview Payton. She needs to give a statement while its fresh in her head."

Keep her here so she doesn't go up to the house, he meant—Hayes nodded in understanding.

"I'll be right back." He grabbed Payton's hand. "I'll be right back, okay? You need to tell Hayes everything that happened."

She nodded, and he took one more look at her face before turning and jogging down the road.

Grayson slammed the car door in Mateo's face and turned to him. The officer was covered in mud, and oddly enough, looked as comfortable as could be. "You think he's our guy?"

Eli glanced in the window where Mateo sank against the backseat with a scowl on his face.

"Could be." He quickly downloaded Grayson on what he and Ethan had uncovered during their deep dive into the Chases' bank accounts—about Charmaine and Mateo working together to transfer Arthur's money into offshore accounts.

"Okay, so how the hell does that connect to the eyeless bodies dropping around town?"

Truth was, Eli didn't know.

"We need to check Mateo's alibis for the night Mary was murdered, and for last night, too, assuming that's when our Jane Doe was murdered. Is Jessica still there?"

"Yes, and Colson is there now, too."

"Good. And check to see if he has an alibi for the dates of Courtney Howard, Pam Robertson, and the day Valerie Walsh went missing. Did Jessica get an ID on the skull, yet?"

"Not yet, and this new body will set her back. Might be time to get some more boots on the ground here."

"Already working on that."

Four victims tortured to death, one missing girl, and one unidentified skull.

He looked back at Payton—and one who looks like all the rest.

"We're stretched thin," Grayson said, "especially with this new arrest."

"Have you interviewed Gary Powell yet?"

"No. Got the call about Jane Doe while he was still being booked in. Detective Walker's getting ready to talk to him, but when we got this call I asked him to hold off for a bit. He's just waiting for my okay."

"Tell him to wait. I want to be there. Gary knows something. He's hiding something. That guy is connected to all this, and I want to find out how."

"Wonder if he knows Mateo. Maybe they're in this together. Maybe it's the Couer *Killers*." Grayson's gaze flickered over Eli's shoulder to Payton. He lowered his voice and said, "Ever notice how much that girl looks like the rest of the victims?"

He looked over his shoulder again, and this time, Payton's eyes met his. His gut twisted.

"Someone needs to keep an eye on her." Grayson said. "She could be next."

Eli tore his eyes away.

Yes, she could be next. Every inch of his body told him so.

18

*E*LI STOOD BEHIND the two-way mirror watching Gary pick at his nails on the table. The chaos in the station turned into a distant buzz in his ears as he analyzed the body language, the expression on the man's face. The drunkenness had faded along with the attitude when they'd left Gary in the tank for hours while dealing with the circus at Payton's parents' house.

Mateo Raya was still in the process of being booked. They'd interview him next.

And down the hall, Payton Chase sat in Police Chief David McCord's office, available to answer any more questions the police might have about the shooting, at his suggestion. After they'd visited the hospital where Charmaine had been rushed to surgery, Eli asked Payton to come with him to the station. It was a thinly veiled attempt to keep her in his sights until he could confirm if either Gary or Mateo were the real Couer Killer.

And time was ticking.

He stepped inside the tiny, white room.

Detective Dean Walker gave him a nod then turned back

to Gary. He'd already begun the interview, taking the time to establish a casual rhythm in an attempt to gain trust and learn the guy's ticks and body language. They were just getting to the good stuff.

Gary's eyes flared as he looked at Eli.

"Gary, I believe you know Special Agent Archer."

"Know him from tacklin' and cuffing me," he sneered.

"He'll just be observing if that's alright with you."

Gary shifted in his seat and grunted. "Like I have a choice."

"The sooner we get some questions answered, the sooner you get out of here, surely you don't mind that. It's late, we're all tired."

A subtle shake of his head.

"Good. As I was saying, you can imagine you gave Miss Chase quite the scare when she saw you on her land, after dark. What were you doing?"

"I'd lost my dog."

"Bullshit." Eli stepped forward.

Dean shot him a look, then refocused on Gary. "You and I both know that's as true as if I told you your ex-wife was a good cook."

The corner of Gary's lip curled up, and it was then that Eli realized Detective Dean Walker was a hell of an interviewer. Dean was born and raised in Berry Springs, and was obviously using that to connect to Gary and calm his defenses. He stepped back to the corner.

"Why do you think I gained so much weight after the divorce?" Gary said with a devilish grin.

With a matching smile, Dean turned toward Eli, "The former Mrs. Powell was an avid cooker, although she'd experiment with recipes. She'd bring all sorts of... odd dishes to the farmer's market, or drop off hordes of food here at the station as a 'thank you for your service'." He glanced back at Gary. "Our police dog, Keyo, was always very grateful."

Gary chuckled.

Dean leaned forward on his forearms. "Gary, tell me what you were doing spying on Payton."

"I wasn't spying..." He blew out a whiskey breath and leaned back. "She came to my house the day before, and I know she works at NAR News. Damn media," he seethed, veering off topic. "That's the problem with the world, if you ask me. They need to stay out of everyone's business. Anyway, I figured it was about the body, or somethin' about some story she was writing so I didn't answer."

"So, you didn't answer because you didn't want to be quoted in the paper. That doesn't explain why you went sneaking around her house later, Gary."

The man looked down at his hands.

"Gary, you've got two DWIs on record. You get charged for trespassing, the judge is going to throw the book at you. Why don't you tell me what you were doing tonight, Gary? Maybe we can work something out."

A minute of silence dragged out.

Finally, Gary rolled his eyes, defeated. "Alright. I didn't answer the damn door for Payton yesterday because I was afraid she'd uncovered my little side job."

"What side job?"

A minute ticked by, then Gary shook his head, and confessed. "I've got some pot plants on my land. Do a little peddling on the side. Not many, and only pot, I promise." He shrugged. "I've always liked to garden and when the wife left me... I spent all my time outside, planting everything you could imagine. Well, one day, after a bottle of Jack I decided to try my hand at a marijuana bush and I'll be damned if that thing didn't thrive. So, I started selling a bit here and there, and that's that. A little extra income and something to do. I don't smoke, don't like it, but it's something to do that gives me some extra money."

"What makes you think Payton would be inquiring about that, instead of the body found on your land?"

"Because she's doing some story about pot in the Ozarks."

"And how did you know that?"

"A friend told me."

"A friend, who?"

Gary glanced at Eli, then back at Dean, then shifted uncomfortably in his seat. "Kid named Jax. Works with Payton."

"Jax buys pot from you."

Gary nonchalantly shrugged, not wanting to rat out a customer. "Anyway, so I guess you could say between that and Mary, I got a little spooked. Got drunk and thought it'd be a good idea to go ask her what she knew and tell her to stay out of my business. Never did like journalists. I took off walking, 'cause I didn't want to get another DWI, and that's the story."

Dean crossed his arms over his chest. "Sounds like you don't make the best decisions when you're drunk, Gary."

Eli stepped forward, placed his palms on the table and narrowed his eyes. "That's not all though, Gary. You're not telling us everything."

Gary looked down, shifted again.

Dean glanced at Eli with tipped eyebrows.

"What aren't you telling us about Mary?" Eli asked.

"Nothing, man, I don't know anything about her."

Eli felt the heat rise up his neck as he stared at the drunk.

"You know if you're withholding anything from us, you're an accessory to murder," Dean said, his voice low, menacing.

Eli leaned in. "And combine that with your DWIs you'll be locked in a cage, and the only thing you'll be growing is a hard on for your new cellmate. Gets real fucking lonely in jail, Gary."

Gary's eyes rounded as he looked up. "Fine. *Jesus.* I... I saw someone on my land the night before I found her."

"Who?"

"I swear I don't know. But I thought it was maybe one of my customers, so I didn't say anything. Didn't want to bring any attention to it. I don't like people in my business, including you. I like to be left the hell alone."

"What time was this?"

"Around two-thirty in the morning. I saw the headlights in the woods and grabbed my binoculars."

"What kind of vehicle was it?"

"A truck."

"What kind? Chevy? Ford?"

"Don't know."

"Color?"

"Don't know... but this stuck out to me..."

"What?"

"It was towing a trailer."

Eli was in the hall and on the phone with Ethan before the interview was even over.

"Dude do you know how many people own camper trailers in Berry Springs? Or, the surrounding counties, for that matter? Did he give you a description? A color at least?"

"He said it was small; smaller than the length of the truck, and light colored."

"So a pop-up trailer, maybe? Door, window, place to sleep, and that's about it."

"Exactly. Or, possibly a fifth-wheel trailer, but check the pop-ups first."

"Either way, definitely enough room to torture someone to death."

"And easy to hide, easy to clean up."

It all started to make sense... The Couer Killer abducted the girls and held them captive in a camper. No house to track or leave evidence, no risk of being seen or heard. He'd have his way with them and then drive straight to the drop point. Only one place for trace evidence. It was smart.

"And this guy didn't see any markings on the camper, or anything on it to help narrow this down?"

"No. It was nighttime, and he was looking through binoculars."

"Well, shit."

"Once you get the names, run it through CODIS first, then compare them with anyone who's purchased LaRouche paintings."

"Will do."

"Have you nailed down Dustin Bisset's location?"

"Not yet. Will let you know as soon as I do."

"Thanks, Ethan. How's Jolene?"

"Almost as ready to nail this son of a bitch as I am."

He thought of Payton.

"Let me know when you get anything."

"Will do, man."

Click.

19

*P*AYTON CLICKED OFF the phone and looked at the clock—1:14 a.m. She walked to the edge of the patio and took a deep breath in an attempt to ease her racing pulse. Although her body felt like it had been run over by a Mack truck, her head was still going a million miles a minute, especially after the phone call she'd just had with her father that went something like—

"Hey Dad, uh, long time no talk, so, Charmaine tried to attack me with a piece of broken glass, but then got shot, and oh, she's stealing from you and having an affair with your best friend."

She looked out to the dark mountains, listened to the sound of the woods at night, the light breeze of the wind. She could not believe the evening she'd just had, and it wasn't even close to over.

She turned, looked through the windows of her patio and saw his silhouette on the phone in the kitchen. Her heart gave a little kick. Eli had never left her side.

The tiniest smile crossed her lips. She slid her phone

into her pocket and stepped inside. She could barely hear Eli's hushed voice as she walked into the living room, giving him some space in the kitchen. Whoever he was talking to, it wasn't good. She watched him for a moment, in the same T-shirt and jeans he'd been wearing at the festival earlier, although now they were covered in dirt and grass stains from attacking Gary, and damp with sweat from hours in the interview room. Her gaze drifted to the way the shirt clung to his chest, and watched the way his muscles flexed as he paced back and forth. His tanned bicep flexed as he ran his fingers through his mussed hair, and at that moment, he looked more like a soldier than a famous FBI agent.

Strong, confident, with the hint of pent-up anger that was about to burst at the seams.

His eyes met hers—locked—and he paused, then said something into the phone and hung up. He set the phone on the counter and crossed the living room. He looked good in her house.

It fit. *He* fit.

"Did you talk to your dad?" He frowned, sweeping a finger down her arm.

She nodded and sighed, suddenly feeling the heaviness of exhaustion from the evening. "He's on the next flight out, from France." She sank onto the couch. "Should be here tomorrow morning sometime."

"How'd he take everything?" Eli sat on the edge of the seat next to her.

She snorted. "Honestly? Honestly, I think he's more upset about Mateo than anything else. More than Charmaine, more than the money." She shook her head and stared blankly at the wall, the image of Charmaine lying in the hospital bed moments before they'd taken her back for surgery flashed through her head. For a fleeting moment, Charmaine's eyes opened and focused on Payton, then quickly drifted closed again. Mona had showed up, worried sick about her boss. And although it was beyond Payton's understanding, she seemed to genuinely care for Charmaine's well-being. After Mona promised she'd call after Charmaine was awake, Payton left with Eli, at his request, to the station where he would begin to unravel the mess of the evening. He'd told her that she was needed for more interviews, but the look in his eyes gave him away. He didn't want her to be alone, and that thought warmed her from the inside out. It wasn't just because she didn't want to be alone, either, it was because he, Eli Archer, wanted to be the one with her. To take care of her. To make sure nothing happened to her. Eli Archer, the insanely hot special agent who'd kissed her like their next breath depended on it.

His phone beeped from the counter although he didn't budge.

She looked over her shoulder at the kitchen, then back at him. "You can get that."

"I will," he said, his eyes never leaving hers.

"Were you on the phone with the hospital?"

He nodded.

"How is she?"

"She's stable; she'll be okay. The bullet passed through her just below the ribcage. Missed major organs. She'll spend a few nights in the hospital then be released."

Payton inhaled and nodded. On the way to her house, Eli had told Payton about the money Charmaine was swindling from her father, and about the affair with Mateo. Payton wasn't surprised at all at Charmaine's deceitful behavior, but was with Mateo's. It was a blow to the family. Although the case would take months to iron out, the motivation seemed clear—Mateo decided seventeen million dollars was a hell of a lot better than eight-point-five.

Mateo had turned the tables on the greedy, cold-hearted Charmaine, and she'd fallen for it.

It was greed over human life.

Damn money.

"Is Mateo talking?"

"Not really. He lawyered up real quick. He'll be charged with attempted murder, among other things."

"I heard the talk around the station. Seems everyone thinks he's our Couer Killer."

"Yes, that is the talk."

She cocked her head. "But you don't think so."

He glanced down, his mind racing. Then, pushed off the couch and began pacing.

"Doesn't fit," he said as he ran his fingers through his hair.

"What doesn't fit?"

"The gun. Shooting. CK gets off on the kidnap and the torture. A gun would be too quick for him. It doesn't fit my profile. Mateo doesn't fit my profile."

"What about Gary, then?"

"Gary's a drunk who meant no harm. He's got a few pot plants and thought that's why you'd come to his house. After a handle of Jack, he made the stupid decision to confront you about it. That was it. He's a drunk idiot, but not our killer."

She paused, then said, "I know you think Mateo doesn't fit the bill, but a killer's a killer, and there was an obvious reason to kill Charmaine—money. And you said it yourself, there're red flags with my family. There's connections."

"Yes, but your family is in a long list that I'm still sifting through."

"What about Dustin? Have you tracked him yet?"

"Not yet."

She stood. "Dustin's got to be it, then. He's the connection."

He looked back at her and held her gaze for a moment, the intensity tensing her.

"What?"

"Dustin isn't the only one I'm worried about." He stopped pacing. "The connection is *you,* Payton."

A chill slowly skirted up her spine. "Because I look like the others."

"Yes."

She leaned forward on her elbows. "When were you going to tell me about the body found tonight?"

He closed his eyes and muttered, *"Goddammit."*

"I heard at the station, and got more than a few stares. Everyone thinks I'm next, don't they?"

He turned his back to her and walked to the window. A minute of silence stretched between them.

She stood, slowly crossed the room and wrapped her arms around him from behind. His body was as tense as a rock. She pressed her cheek to his back.

"I'm not good at this, Payton." His voice was low and deep.

She felt the rise and fall of his chest.

"I'm not either," she whispered.

He turned, with a look that sent her stomach tickling. There was so much behind those dark, sad eyes. So much she wanted to learn, to understand, to ease the pain buried deep below the chocolate irises. He was an ocean of secrets, a broken man. But not all hope was lost. She wanted to remind him of the man she saw glimpses of—during the twinkle in his eyes as he looked at her, the curve of his lip when she smarted off, the smiles that escaped him for the split seconds he let his guard down.

The way he was looking at her now.

She reached up and ran a finger down his tight, stubbled jaw.

"Let's crash and burn together then," she whispered.

As soon as the words left her lips, he took her head in her hands and kissed her.

She tasted warm and sweet, with a hint of surrender that ignited a white-hot, uncontrollable burn of need inside him. A need to be on top of her, be inside her, be *hers.*

When he fumbled with the teeny-tiny buttons of her shirt for a nanosecond too long, he gripped the silk and ripped it open, the buttons clattering to the floor. Her kiss deepened, intensified, reflecting the hunger that was coursing through his body like a shot of speed.

She yanked off his belt while he undid her black lace bra, the thin fabric sweeping down her body before hitting the floor.

Jesus. Christ.

Her breasts were round, firm, with tiny pink nipples peaked just for him. His cock hardened to cement.

She was every one of his fantasies.

His heart galloped in his chest at breakneck speed as he gripped her waist and lifted her off the floor.

"Bedroom?" His voice was low, husky, needy.

She wrapped her arms around his neck and legs around his waist. "Yes, *now,*" she said between frenzied kisses on his neck.

Holy fuck, he'd never wanted a woman so bad in his life.

He carried her through the house, concentrating on putting one foot in front of the other. Not that it would matter if he fell, he'd spring right back up with the erection he was sporting.

He stepped into the bedroom, the moonlight spilling in from the sweeping windows. He slid her onto the bed, her deep auburn hair spilling over the white comforter. God, she was beautiful, and he hadn't even seen the whole thing, yet. He leaned into her breasts, kissing, licking while she kicked off her heels and he slid down her pants.

Her bare skin was so soft, so sweet. Like silk.

He straightened and looked her over, naked except for the black, lace panties to match the bra. His finger trailed the printed flowers barely hiding the dark shading of her hair, before slowly sliding them down her legs.

He got onto his knees.

She smelled like vanilla.

His hands stroked her knees, her thighs, the back of her legs as he kissed his way to her inner thigh, closer, closer, until she spread her knees and opened herself up fully to him.

Oh, my God.

He slid his hand up her stomach as he licked her inner lips, teasing her before finally sliding over her folds. She gripped his hands that were gripping her breasts, her chest rising and falling heavily. He pressed into her, licking slowly, settling into a rhythm before sliding his tongue over her tiny, swollen bud.

A soft groan escaped her lips as he slowly circled, again and again, before inserting a finger... and then two.

"Oh, God, Eli..."

Her voice, the low timbre, the rush of wetness had him throbbing, losing all sense of control. He licked faster, savoring the flavor of her, and moved his fingers with her quickening breaths.

"Eli... *Eli.*" She grabbed his head. "Get up here."

At that moment, she could have told him to kill someone and he would have. He slid out of his boxers and stood over her, looking down at her body on the bed, legs spread, lips swollen, eyes ablaze with lust.

"I want to look at you," he said, stepping between her legs.

"Wait." She lifted up on her elbows and slowly got onto her hands and knees. "I want to return the favor."

He inhaled deeply as she took him with her hand, squeezing, slowly stroking, then took him with her mouth.

He'd officially entered heaven.

His eyes drifted closed as her lips slid back and forth over him, his mind slowly evaporating, his body melting into the sensation that was sending goosebumps over his body. He looked down at her, slowly moving back and forth, and only wanted one thing—to bury himself inside her. As if reading his thoughts, she looked up at him, then slid onto her back, and spread her legs.

Jesus.

His gaze swept over her body, his heart like a drum as he gripped her thighs and slowly pushed into her. She closed her eyes and groaned, her hand finding her breast as she closed around him.

The heat, the wetness.

Payton Chase.

He moved in and out, his fingers sliding over her clit with each thrust, matching the rhythm.

"Eli..." She squirmed beneath him, the expression on her face telling him she was close.

So was he.

He rubbed her faster, spearing into her, sweat beading on his forehead as his body began to tense from head to toe.

Just as he was about to lose his mind, she thrust her hips forward and screamed his name as she came over him. His orgasm was a blur of shattering euphoria as he poured himself into her.

He gazed down at the puffy eyes looking at him, at the tiniest smile on her beautiful, angelic face.

And he knew, he was in love.

The moonlight streamed in through the windows, outlining the curves of Payton's body as she lay asleep, her pale, silky skin naked on top of the comforter.

He stroked the top of her head and watched the slow rise and fall of her breath for what seemed like forever, memorizing every inch of her body.

It was like he was hypnotized.

Entranced.

And he realized he'd been that way since the moment he'd laid eyes on her in the woods. He'd never felt so captivated and consumed by a woman in his life.

He'd never felt this way before about anyone.

His finger traced the small cut on her throat imagining what he would do if someone hurt her.

Cigarette burns on flesh flashed through his head. A lump caught in his throat and his face hardened.

Four women were already dead, and every inch of his gut was screaming that Payton was next on the list.

His body tensed, the shadow of darkness beginning to creep back in, greedily taking away the moments of happiness, peace, light, from him, as it always did.

He grabbed a throw blanket from the bottom of the bed and lightly draped it over her.

After one last look, he silently pushed out of bed and padded into the living room.

3:47 a.m.

Naked, he walked to the window and stared out into the darkness.

It was coming.

20

"*I*'LL BE THERE in ten minutes." Eli clicked off the phone and stepped back into the hospital room. Payton looked up from the e-reader in her hand.

He nodded to the hall, and she followed him out.

"Why do they keep hospitals so damn cold," she asked while wrapping her arms around herself.

"To make the transition to the morgue easier."

She grinned.

He flagged down a nurse. "Can you bring some more blankets into this room, please?"

"Of course." The nurse flashed a flirty smile, which did not go unnoticed by Payton, before walking away.

"Has Charmaine woken up yet?"

"No. She's been asleep since we got here. Not that she's going to be happy to see me or anything."

"What time will your dad be here?"

Payton glanced at her watch. "A few hours."

"Okay." He shifted his weight. "I've got to get to a task force meeting at the station that starts at nine."

"Anything new?"

"They ID'd the skull found in the woods. It's Valerie's, and the markings around her eyes appear to be from a blade."

Her mouth dropped. "Oh, my God, Eli. So that's—"

"Five, including the body found yesterday."

"ID on her, yet?"

He shook his head.

"Anything else?" She squeezed herself tighter and shuddered, and Eli knew it had nothing to do with the chill in the hospital.

"Mary's car's been processed—no prints or anything, so that's a dead end."

"What about her cell phone?"

"Just got the dump this morning. Got two guys scouring it now. But I don't think our guy communicates with them before the abduction. He stalks them, that's it."

"What's going on with Mateo?"

"Lawyer's not letting him talk. We're pushing for warrants."

"What about Gary?"

"He's home and probably six into a twelve pack by now."

"My stepbrother?"

"Haven't located him yet." His narrowed gaze flickered to the nurses behind the counter, then to the exits. Always looking, always suspicious. He didn't like leaving her, even at a public place with security, cameras, and medical professionals. Hell, in his neurotic mind, a jail cell wouldn't even be secure enough.

"Stop. Eli, I'm fine. I'm in a hospital, around a hundred people. And my dad will be here soon. I'm safe. *Go.* Go to your meeting. You've got to nail this bastard, Eli."

He hated to admit it, but she was right. He couldn't nail the bastard sitting in a waiting room.

"What time will your meeting be over?" She asked.

He didn't bother explaining to her that regardless of the meeting ending, he'd still be buried in work. He hadn't slept a wink last night—that made two in a row—not even after hours of exploring every line, curve, and crevice of the woman he was now certain could rip his heart out of his chest. The thought both excited him and scared the shit out of him. Instead of falling asleep beside the sleeping beauty, he'd spent the rest of the night, or early morning rather, going over files he had stored in his phone. He'd officially given up on sleep until they caught the Couer Killer.

She frowned at the expression on his face, and he snapped to casual. He didn't want her to worry about him. "I'll come by and pick you up for lunch, okay?"

She smiled, nodded.

He searched her face, her lips, trying to ignore the twist in his gut for leaving her. Maybe they could have the meeting at the hospital...

His phone rang.

"Go, Eli. I've got my evil stepmother and steamy romantic suspense book to get back to." She winked.

"Okay." He nodded but paused. "I'll be back," he said as he squeezed her hand, before turning and jogging down the hall.

~

Eli turned at the *tap, tap, tap* on the conference room door.

Right on time. Not that he expected less.

"Guys, this is Ethan Veech, FBI Cyber Crimes."

Carrying a briefcase and stack of folders, Ethan stepped into the crowded conference room perfumed with stale coffee, Old Spice, musty breath from a night filled with too much booze and too little sleep, and the sour scent of man-sweat that accompanied urgency and desperation. They'd closed the door for privacy, which only added to the humidity that had snaked its way in from outside. It was supposed to be another scorcher, which was nothing compared to the heat the BSPD was feeling.

Ethan pulled his laptop from his bag, unfazed by the eyes boring into him. Although he was young, he carried himself with the confidence of a seasoned agent.

Eli respected that.

"Ethan, I believe you've met most everyone in the room before, but if not, Police Chief David McCord, Lieutenant Quinn Colson, Detective Dean Walker, Officer Jasper Hayes, Officer Travis Willard, and the newest member of the force, Officer Owen Grayson."

Nods of acknowledgment around the room as Ethan pushed aside papers and gruesome crime scene photos that scattered the conference table.

Eli walked to the front of the room. "I've asked Ethan to help us track down the Couer Killer, and he's here to provide a few updates. To re-cap, we have five victims that we know of associated, or loosely associated with CK. Courtney Howard, Pam Robertson, and missing person Valerie Walsh from last year, and now, Mary Freeman and our unidentified Jane Doe."

"Right." Ethan logged into his laptop. "We'll start from the beginning—as you all know, last year Courtney Howard and Pam Robertson were both killed—drugged, abducted, beaten, and had both eyes removed. Before Pam was abducted, she reported being followed by someone in a, quote, old, red Ford. She was abducted the next day, found hours later and moments before she died, she whispered the word *Shadow*. Arnie Miller was tried and convicted of both murders, although we're operating now on the assumption Miller was falsely convicted." He clicked a few more keys. "You all are aware of Eli's profile, so I won't go into that. I researched a list Eli was provided from HQ regarding anyone who's purchased LaRouche paintings in the last five years—that was a dead end." He looked up. "But I'd like to dig into the list of the wealthiest folks in the area as well..."

Quinn leaned forward. "I took that list and ran it through the system to see if anyone had a record—no hits. Then, I had Jonas run it through the DMV database, and no one has, quote, an old, red Ford registered to their names. I also took a second look at the employees at Shadow Creek Resort, as well as residents who live close to or along Shadow Creek—nothing worth noting."

"Do we have an ID on Jane Doe, yet?"

Quinn shook his head. "There's no recent missing persons reported in the area."

"Could be someone vacationing from out of town, or maybe friends and family haven't even noticed she's gone, yet," Hayes said.

It always surprised Eli how long it took for some families to realize their loved one was missing... and that was even if they ever did. He turned to Ethan. "Let's get back to your update."

"Eli asked me to look into a Mr. Arthur Chase and Charmaine Chase due to their similarities with the Couer Killer profile, and the fact they'd recently visited a high-profile art auction in New York, plus, he recently uncovered that Arthur owns a red Ford."

Colson frowned at Ethan. "Where did you get that information?"

"His daughter, Payton. The truck isn't registered, which

is why it didn't come up in your searches. He uses it to haul stuff around his land."

The Chief sat up.

Ethan continued, "I did a deep dive into the Chases' finances where I discovered Charmaine had been swindling money from her husband over the last few years. Upon further digging, I realized she had been working with Arthur's business partner, Mateo Raya. And we all know how that deal has turned out."

"The DA's already left me two voicemails," McCord shook his head. "Wants to know if we think Mateo's the real Couer Killer."

"Well, let's not be too quick to name him a suspect yet." Eli nodded to Ethan to continue.

"As I was saying, in my deep dive into the Chases, I discovered that Charmaine Bisset had a baby at age sixteen, a boy, Dustin Bisset, whom she put up for adoption when he was six months old."

Eyebrows shot up around the room.

Eli cut in, "It's important to note here that Charmaine kept her son a secret from Arthur Chase and her stepdaughter, Payton."

"How old is this kid now?"

"Thirty years old."

"That fits the age of your profile," McCord said. "Are Charmaine and him in contact at all?"

"Not that we can tell, although that will be one of the first questions we ask Charmaine today during her interview."

"Where's he now?"

Ethan nodded, clicked a few keys. "There are several Dustin Bissets in the US, but one stood out." Ethan pulled up a mug shot of a droopy-eyed kid with a mop of dread-locks, a bloody lip, and tattoos coloring his neck.

Everyone in the room leaned forward.

"This is Dustin Bisset, at age twenty-three, booked for pubic intox, drunk and disorderly, assault, and resisting arrest."

"Nice." Grayson narrowed his eyes, giving Ethan his undivided attention.

"Right. So this guy seems to be quite a drifter. Hippie-type. Grew up in Oklahoma, left town at eighteen. I tracked down an old high school buddy who clammed up at the word FBI, but did tell me that Dustin was a loner, no girl-friends, partied hard—those were his words exactly—and after high school, Dustin got a job with a construction company, and they lost touch. Or so he says. This is where the kid falls off the grid for a while. Maybe sleeping on friends' couches, earning cash wages. Picks up again with this beauty." He nodded to the mug shot on the computer. "Bar fight. His last known location was Tulsa, Oklahoma, where he rented an apartment for six months, two months ago."

"Tulsa... not too far from here."

Eli nodded. Yeah, this guy looked good on paper.

"I've got a call into the landlord. Haven't heard back."

"What about a vehicle?"

"None registered to his name."

"Probably didn't register it."

"Or, stolen."

"Cell phone?"

"Nothing under his name."

"Dude, there's no way a guy his age doesn't have a cell phone."

"Agreed. Could be a burner."

Quinn looked at him with a cocked eyebrow—yeah, this guy was looking real good.

"Marriage certificate?" Eli asked.

"Nope." Ethan shifted back to his computer. "He got a job at a fast-food joint about forty-five minutes west of here. Spoke with the assistant manager on duty and asked him to send me Dustin's work schedule for the last few weeks, to confirm if he was or wasn't working on the days of Mary's and Jane Doe's murders. I also asked him what kind of vehicle he drives..." his voice trailed off as he glanced at his beeping phone.

"Well?" The Chief asked impatiently.

Ethan shifted his attention back to the table. "Guy said I needed to speak with the actual manager on both points. Was sketched out as fuck, if you ask me. According to assistant manager Dewey Doss, the manager should be in around noon."

Everyone looked at the clock—that was less than an hour.

"Is he supposed to work today?"

"Ol' Dewey said he didn't know." Ethan rolled his eyes.

"Okay, so we'll know if Dustin Bisset has an alibi, or not, within in the hour. If he doesn't, we hunt him down."

Nods around the room.

"What about the camper Gary said he saw on his land?" McCord asked.

Ethan pulled a piece a paper from his bag and slid it across the table to the chief. "There's the list of everyone who owns a camper, and or, a trailer in Berry Springs and the surrounding counties." The chief glanced at the long list and Ethan smiled. "Guess southerners like the outdoors."

"What's highlighted?"

"Folks with some sort of record. I think there's a few

DWIs, one domestic. I'd start checking with those first, of course."

Quinn snagged the paper. "I'm on it."

Eli glanced at the list. "That's great, but remember, a lot of people *rent* camper trailers. We need to find those companies and pull their records, too."

Quinn nodded to Hayes. "Get on it."

"Yes, sir."

The Chief frowned. "So, Gary Powell is a drunk who was worried that Payton Chase had uncovered his little pot operation, that's it with him. What about Mateo? Does no one consider him a viable suspect? His damn lawyer isn't letting him talk, so we haven't even been able to confirm his alibis, or lack thereof." He looked at Eli. "Why aren't we focusing more on him?"

Eli took a second to respond. This was one of the most frustrating aspects of working with local law enforcement. It was their names on the line—their job to protect the citizens of their small town. Sure, they'd be quick to blame the feds when a suspect wasn't apprehended, but at the end of the day, if the citizens of Berry Springs didn't feel safe, they looked to the local police department—and to the chief specifically. Mateo Raya shot a woman in cold blood last night. The same day they'd found another mutilated body, a mysterious skull, and two days after finding Mary. Coincidence? The Chief didn't want to think so. He wanted Eli to tie Mateo up in a nice bow, so that this nightmare would be over and everyone could move on with their lives. Afterall, there couldn't be more than one killer roaming Berry Springs, right?

All eyes were on him. He started, slowly and carefully, "The motivation for Mateo to kill Charmaine is clear—"

"Seventeen-million percent clear." Grayson said.

Eli flickered a glance to Grayson, thankful for his support. The comment let the chief know he was on his side on this.

"Exactly," Eli nodded. "That's a lot of money. And money is one of the top motivators in all homicides. I know you've seen that during your tenure here."

McCord cleared his throat. "Yes, I have, but that doesn't mean that Raya didn't kill the other girls."

"The motivation, the MO, is completely different. And the lack of signature that CK likes so much. I'm not saying it's *not* him, I'm just saying it doesn't add up with the other homicides, which are almost identical. All of CK's victims are young, red-haired, blue-eyed women, too. Charmaine is none of those."

The room stilled as everyone watched McCord chew it over. Finally he sat back, resigned.

Grayson looked at Eli. "Speaking of identical..."

Eli's eyes met the military man's eyes, with immediate understanding, and he felt his shoulders instantly tense.

"What else do we have on Payton Chase?" Grayson asked, then addressed the group. "All the victims look remarkably like Payton Chase."

Hayes leaned forward. "Damn, dude, you're right." The young officer pushed out of the chair and eyed the crime scene photos. "I didn't even notice but now that you said something..."

"Who do we have on her?" Grayson asked.

Eli glanced at the clock. "Me."

21

PAYTON'S E-READER CLATTERED to the floor, and she awoke with a start. She immediately looked at Charmaine, who hadn't stirred. Phew. She sat up, feeling dizzy with exhaustion, and glanced at the clock ticking loudly on the stark, white walls.

10:11 a.m.

Geez. She must've fallen asleep while reading—apparently the love scenes in her book paled in comparison to her night with Eli. It wasn't even midday, and she was struggling to keep her eyes open—not that she was complaining. She'd replay last night every night of her life if he'd let her. Screw sleep.

She thought of Eli being in a high-pressure, high-stakes meeting and hoped he was holding up better than she was, although she didn't get the vibe he was someone who slept much, anyway.

Hard to believe after the energy he'd had last night.

Three times.

Three. Times.

The first was magical, soul-stirring, best sex she'd ever had.

The second was hot, steamy, greedy, ravenous.

The third was something out of a restricted movie she'd stumbled upon late one night.

She'd fallen asleep in a euphoric, coma-like state sometime after three in the morning, only to wake up to the smell of coffee brewing at six. She'd never forget walking out of the bedroom and seeing Eli standing in her kitchen, buck naked, filling two cups of coffee.

It jarred her—in a kind of nerve-wracking, exciting way that made her stomach flip-flop. She could get used to that.

She could get used to him.

She'd watched him for a moment, mixing cream and sugar and imagined him fitting in her life.

Exciting. Terrifying.

His face was paler than she was used to seeing, his eyes puffy and shaded with exhaustion, and she'd realized he'd spent what precious time they'd had to sleep working.

But when he turned and saw her, a smile crossed his lips. A smile she'd never seen before.

Soft.

Sweet.

Surrender.

They'd sipped their coffee together at the table, and oddly enough, talked about normal things—both needing a break from death, if only for a short time.

An hour later, they'd dropped by Eli's room at the B&B to grab a change of clothes then made their way to the hospital. Eli's phone rang the entire way, setting the stage for another chaotic day.

A machine beeped in the corner of the hospital room.

Again, Charmaine didn't stir. Payton checked her phone—no messages. She peeled herself off the plastic board they called a couch and smoothed her wrinkled shirt. She'd thrown on what had been on the top of the clean laundry pile in her room—an old, faded concert T, shorts and sandals. After watching Charmaine's breathing for a moment, she silently padded to the bathroom and flicked the lights.

Holy shit.

She blinked—because there was no way the reflection in the mirror was correct—and opened her eyes again.

She looked like *roadkill.* Her auburn hair was knotted in a messy, crooked bun on the top of her head, looking anything but bedhead sexy. Her skin gaunt and gray against the bright red scrape down her neck. Her eyes were blood-shot and puffy.

Then, she felt a soreness below, a feeling she wasn't used to. A smile found her lips.

Eli.

She stared at her reflection as flashes of the night before came back, one by one all tangled in her bedsheets. Her body responded in a way that told her she was ready for round four.

She shook the thoughts from her head.

Coffee.

She needed coffee.

After grabbing her cell phone and purse, she stepped into the blinding white hallway, and right into a nurse she didn't recognize.

"Oh. Sorry."

"Oh, no, I'm sorry." The nurse looked at the door number, then back at Payton. "Are you Mrs. Chase's daughter?"

Stepdaughter. "Yes."

"Great. I was just coming by to check her vitals. How are you holding up?"

Like a piece of string cheese. "Fine. Any idea when she'll be able to go home?"

"Usually within forty-eight hours, but that's up to the doc. I'd say no later than the day after tomorrow if all's well."

And then all hell would break loose in the Chase family. God, she was dreading the downfall from this. Not only the betrayal, the hurt and pain her father would go through, but then the divorce discussions, and the relentless town gossip that would ensue for days following—weeks, even. It was going to be a nightmare.

Her stomach sank just thinking about it.

"My dad should be here within a few hours. I'm going to head down and grab some coffee."

"Sounds good. We'll keep a good eye on her. I'll be in and out for about ten minutes. Breakfast is served until ten-thirty; if you hurry, you can catch it. Take your time, dear."

"Thanks."

She chose the staircase to get fresh blood pumping through her veins, then stepped onto the basement level where the cafeteria was. A middle-aged nurse sat in the corner reading a book with a muscled-up shirtless man on the cover.

She thought of Eli—that guy had nothing on him—and immediately did an inward eye-roll at herself. Sheesh, one night of earth-shattering sex and she couldn't get the man, or sex for that matter, off her mind.

After filling a Styrofoam cup with coffee, she grabbed a cup of strawberries and checked out. As she contemplated a place to sit, a shiver caught her—if the hospital was Antarctica, the basement was an ice-box. She glanced out the windows at the overcast morning, the plants swaying back and forth in the breeze.

Fresh, warm air. That's exactly what she needed.

She grabbed a napkin, found an *EXIT* sign and made her way down the hall. The summer air felt like heaven as she stepped outside. Delivery trucks were parked to the right of her, dumpsters to the left. A large, brick utility shed with massive air conditioners and other equipment were just past that. She looked around and spied a picnic table nestled along the tree line across the lot. Payton took a deep breath as she weaved through the trucks, the fresh, mountain air like a shot of espresso.

She set her phone and purse on the aged, splintered picnic table and slid in. Her view of the hospital was blocked by the trucks, but that was okay. She needed a break from the place, if only a mental escape. A breeze swept past her and the AC units kicked in, drowning out the sound of anything else, the loud hum was soothing, almost. Zoning out, she sipped her coffee and watched a burly man carry boxes down a sloped entrance into the hospital. His muscular body reminded her of Eli and she wondered again how he was doing. Maybe a quick call just to check in. He probably wanted to make sure she was okay, too, right? Before she could talk herself out of it, she picked up her phone and dialed his number. When there was no answer, she hung up and blew out a breath.

"Hey, there."

She jumped at the voice behind her, the phone tumbling out of her hands. She quickly looked over her shoulder.

"Whoops, sorry, didn't mean to startle you." The man smiled widely and leaned on the rake he was holding. He was wearing a navy maintenance uniform, complete with dirt-stained knees.

"That's alright," she said, looking him over. She recognized him, there was no question about that. But from where? "I'm sorry, have we met?"

A gust of wind blew her napkin from the table. As the man shifted forward to catch it, a sharp prick of a needle pierced her neck.

22

*E*LI GLANCED AT his cell phone one more time as he walked across the hospital parking lot.

Why wasn't Payton answering his calls or texts?

He'd texted her from the station telling her he was on his way.

No response.

So, he'd called.

No answer.

Maybe she'd fallen asleep, or perhaps was in a deep conversation with her father. They sure as hell had a lot of ground to cover. He ignored the faint warning bell in his gut, telling himself he was simply sleep-deprived and over-reacting.

She was asleep; that was all. She was safe.

He strode through the main entrance and down the hall, ignoring the glances from the nurses. The door to Charmaine's room was ajar, a dim light shining from the corner. He nudged it open an inch and tapped on the thick wood.

A second passed.

He knocked again, the warning in his stomach beginning to swirl like an impending storm.

Slowly, he pushed the door open and stepped inside. An e-book sat on the cushion of the couch, a crumpled blanket next to it. Charmaine slept soundly in her bed. A twinge of panic had his pulse picking up as he checked the bathroom —no Payton.

"Sir?" A voice whispered behind him

He spun around, startling the nurse with his expression.

"Can I help you with something?"

"Payton Chase, Charmaine's stepdaughter. Do you know where she is?" He tried to rein in the slight tone of panic in his voice.

"Yes, she went to the cafeteria to get some coffee. Is... is everything okay?"

Coffee. Of course.

He started out of the room, but paused. "If we miss each other... if you see her before I do, tell her Eli's here and to wait for me right here. To not leave this room."

"Will do."

He followed the signs that led to the basement cafeteria, each step a little faster than the last.

He was losing his mind. Of course she was okay. And just a few more steps would confirm that. He rounded the corner into the cafeteria... No Payton.

"Excuse me..."

The cashier looked up from the bottle of water she was swiping over the scanner. "Yes?"

"Did a woman, mid-twenties, auburn hair, pretty, come down her recently?"

The cashier bit her lip, thinking. "Yes... yes. She got some coffee."

"How long ago was this?"

"Oh, gosh, an hour maybe."

His stomach dropped.

An hour.

"Do you know where she went?"

"Hmm, I don't think she sat down with it..."

His gaze shifted to the windows. "Thank you."

He stepped out of the cafeteria, paused and looked up and down the hall. Where would she have gone?

He focused on the EXIT sign.

"Why do they keep hospitals so damn cold..." Payton's voice echoed in his head

He jogged down the hall, pushed out the metal door and stepped into the sweltering heat. A warm, humid breeze swept past him as he scanned the area.

"Sir?" He jogged up to a delivery man stepping into his truck.

"Yeah?"

"Did you see a girl out here? Twenties, red hair?"

"Think so, maybe, 'bout an hour ago."

"Was she alone?"

"Not sure. Sorry."

Son of a bitch.

His heart raced as he jogged up the concrete ramp and looked around. He pulled his phone from his pocket and dialed her number...

Ring... ring.

His gaze snapped to the jingling sound of a cell phone underneath a picnic table in the distance.

Shit.

He sprinted across the lot, kneeled down and grabbed the hot-pink cell phone from the dead grass.

Payton.

~

Eli.

She could see him, feel his body against hers.

Memories of the night before flashed through her mind like an erotic movie on repeat. The heat in his eyes as he looked down at her, the power of his thrust, the tautness of skin around a body that rivaled the lead actor in any R-rated movie.

Warmth spread over her, intensifying the floating sensation she was already feeling.

She wiggled her fingers and reached out to touch him...

Her arm didn't move. A dull pain squeezed the tiny muscles in her wrists.

She opened her eyes, blinked.

A wave of nausea swept over her. No euphoric floating sensation... no, it was a lightheadedness that made her want to vomit. Sweat rolled down her face, the salty liquid spreading over her lips.

She was sick.

She was sick?

She blinked again.

Where the hell was she? She tried to pull memories, but everything was blank. Confusion had her squinting, searching for anything to tell her what the hell was going on.

Gray surrounded her. Silver floor, silver walls. She was in a small space, her nose less than six inches from a wall.

She tried to reach forward again but was restricted. Then, her eyes shot open as panic shot through her system like shards of ice.

She was on her side. She was *tied-up.*

She tried to move her legs—also bound.

Her heart went from zero to sixty in a split-second, pounding in her ears like a drum before the sacrifice.

Stop, Payton. Think.

She closed her eyes in an attempt to get ahold of the hysteria threatening a panic attack.

Think, Payton.

She'd been here before, taken and tied up by a monster. She'd made it through it. She could do it again.

Eli.

Oh, God, Eli. Where was he?

Her mind tried to piece together the last moments before her world started spinning. She remembered needing fresh air... she remembered the hum of the air conditioners in the distance... someone coming up to her... then, the sting on her throat.

Her eyes rounded in horror.

The Couer Killer had her.

Eli! Her body wanted to scream for him. She had to tell him, somehow.

She had to get the fuck out of there. She had to survive.

Holding her breath, she listened. The faint sound of birds chirped outside, but it was silent in... where the hell was she?

Was she alone?

She inhaled the stagnant smell of cigarette smoke and chemicals, slowly turned her head and looked upward to a shiny, silver ceiling. A silver ceiling? Was she in a mobile home? To her left was a bench-like seat, covered in plastic. To her right—chains. Four rusted chains with cuffs on the end, where another bench had once been.

Oh, my God.

Multiple, rusted bolts pushed up from the gray tiled floor. A crusty, deep-red color stained the corners.

Blood.

She lifted her head—*holy shit,* she was in a camper. A small counter with a sink and cabinets sat under a small window covered with a ratted, brown curtain. A thin stream of light shone through the slit. It was still daytime. But, what day?

Ahead, an elevated bed—no sheets, no pillow or blanket —with drawers underneath. To the left, a thin door.

And a video camera secured on a tripod sat in the corner.

Oh, my God. The sick fuck was going to video her torture.

She sat still for a moment confirming she was alone in the small space. This was her chance.

She gritted her teeth and bucked, bile rising to her throat. The bind cut into her skin, the warmth of blood ran over her skin, and for a moment, she thought... maybe she could slit her own wrists before the son of a bitch had the chance.

No, Payton, don't think like that.

She bucked onto her back and groaned as she pulled herself up using what core strength she had. The head rush made her vision spin.

Her gaze snapped to movement outside. She froze as the silver handle turned.

The door opened and a masked, dark silhouette outlined by bright sunlight stepped inside. Behind him, woods. She was in the middle of the woods, just like Mary Freeman had been.

The door closed and her captor came into view.

23

*P*AYTON RELEASED A guttural howl through her gag as the tip of the cigarette sizzled in the thin skin below her ear. He'd started on her arms and had moved up to the base of her neck.

Adrenaline flooded her veins like an earthquake, trembling underneath skin that felt like acid had dripped all over.

She'd stopped counting at ten burns.

She stopped caring about the nasty scars she'd have dotting all over her body sometime after that.

She'd never felt a pain so unbearable. Not even when he'd taken the baseball bat to her face, knocking out two teeth, after she'd fought him as he chained her. She'd been swallowing blood ever since.

The cigarette smoke in the camper was so thick it made her want to vomit. In fact, she thought she had vomited.

He didn't care. He'd slowly inhaled at least half a pack while he'd burned holes into her skin.

Her wrists were chained to the wall, open slightly as if she were begging for something. Her ankles, chained to the floor. He'd leaned a mirror up in front of them, so she could see what he was doing to her. So she could watch him torture her. See the blood. She'd stopped looking after the blood dripped from her chin.

He flicked the cigarette aside, then turned back to her, his face hidden behind a mask with black holes for eyes. The *Sans Coeur* Halloween mask. She was in a living nightmare.

Before Payton had fought her captor, he was eerily calm, ignoring her as he placed his torture tools onto the counter. As if he'd done it a hundred times. His expression remained neutral, almost bored, even as he'd started to chain her to the wall.

Then, she'd fought him and everything had changed in an instant. The moment she'd head butted his nose, fire flared from him.

Excitement.

And then it began.

With the first burn, he'd started trembling with excitement, his chest heaving with blood lust.

That was an hour ago.

"You're stronger than the others. Ready to become your lead story, Payton Chase?" He pushed to a stance.

She wanted to ask him why, ask where they were. She wanted to get as much information from him as she could so when she made it out of here...

He positioned the camera, clicked it on, then returned with a knife she was one-hundred percent certain sliced Mary Freeman's wrists.

It was his grand finale.

She closed her eyes.

"No, keep them open."

His words were a buzz in her ears.

"If you won't, I'll do it for you."

Her eyes drifted open to him raising two needles. She frantically shook her head.

No, no, please don't pin them open like the others...

Eli skidded to a stop in front of her house.

Please be here, please be here...

It was the only place he could think to look before he hit the panic button. Maybe her father had arrived and given her a ride home to take a nap. Maybe that's why she had called him.

Why the *fuck* hadn't he answered?

He jumped out and sprinted to the front door.

Bang, bang, bang.

When there was no answer, he cupped his hands and looked through the window into the dark house.

He knocked again, then popped the lock and pushed inside.

The air was still, stagnant, with no sign of Payton.

Something was wrong. Something was definitely wrong.

He jogged to the kitchen and looked into the backyard as his phone rang—Ethan.

"Hey, listen—"

"Glad I caught you. I spoke with Dustin Bisset's manager. He worked both nights Mary Freeman and Jane Doe were murdered. Closed the restaurant down until after midnight. He's not our guy."

Fuck.

"Listen, I think CK's got Payton." Eli's eyes darted around her kitchen. "We were supposed to meet for lunch, I... I..." he stuttered, unable to conceal his panic any longer. "She wasn't at the hospital, and she's not at home. Ethan, *fuck,* I think he's got her. I shouldn't have fucking left her."

"Okay, calm down, man. Have you tried her cell?"

"It's in my fucking hand! I found it underneath a picnic table outside the hospital." He paused, inhaled, trying to calm the freight train running through his head. "I need you to check the hospital's security system, see if they have cameras out back, by the delivery dock."

He heard keys clicking in the background, and his eyes landed on Payton's laptop sitting on the counter.

"Okay, give me a minute..." Ethan said as he did his magic.

As he waited, Eli opened the computer, and the screen lit—no password. He clicked on the browser—bank log-in, a website on LaRouche, another on criminal profilers, one on a log-in screen that looked very ominous, and the last, *Luxe Trade.* Payton's smiling face filled the corner of the screen above the username *Hurtin_for_a_Birkin.* He wasn't sure what a Birkin was, but he assumed it cost a lot of money. He clicked on her friends, all attractive with rows of luxury bags listed.

Pretty, rich females.

His stomach tickled the way it did when he was onto something.

"Hey, Ethan..."

"Almost there."

"Wait. Stop. I need you to tell me if our other victims have a profile on a website called *Luxe Trade.*

"You want me to stop what I'm doing?"

"Yes."

"Okay, Luxe Trade... hang on."

He closed his eyes and blew out a breath trying to rein in his impatience.

"Holy shit..." Ethan muttered. "Yes, Courtney Howard, Pam Robertson, Mary Freeman and Valerie Walsh all have profiles. And, Eli, it's not just bags, this site sells and trades expensive art, too."

"Check to see if there's any LaRouche."

A moment ticked by. "Yeah, dude, there're prints of his paintings, and a ton of freaky-ass masks with blackened eyes."

"Are there copies of the *Sans Couer* painting?"

"Hold on... *Yes.*"

Eli scanned the women—each profile had a picture and state attached to their username. And if he had to guess, addresses and credit card information was also collected. "Who owns the site? Can you look that up?"

"Okay, hang on... ... okay, it belongs to an LLC... Davis Ventures, LLC."

Davis. He didn't know a Davis, but why did that name sound vaguely familiar?

"Where is it registered?"

"Whoa. Right here in Berry Springs."

"It's our guy, Ethan." He closed the computer and jogged out the front door. "I need the name of who it's registered to."

"Okay, hang on, this might take a second."

He jumped in his truck and peeled out of the driveway.

His mind raced... *Davis, Davis, Davis...*

Suddenly, an image as clear as day popped into his head. The patio of Frank's Bar... Payton standing underneath a golden string of lights... a drunk asshole hitting on her.

Ted Davis.

24

"*I* NEED YOU to get me everything you have on Ted Davis. Hell, fuck that, I need you to get me his location right now."

"You really think this is our guy?"

"No doubt in my fucking mind. He finds his victims on his website—each resemble the *Sans Couer* painting he's obsessed with—picks them out and stalks them. It's him, Ethan, and he's fucking got her."

"Okay, let me see if I can get his cell phone information..."

Ethan's voice trailed off as Eli skidded on a patch of loose dirt.

"...if I can get that, I can ping his cell phone and get his exact location. Assuming he doesn't have a burner, of course."

"This guy doesn't have a burner. He runs a business. He's got a fucking cell phone."

"I'm on it." Keys clicking rapidly in the background. "Where're you going?"

"The woods around Summit Mountain." It was the only place he knew to go. He needed to call backup. "Call me as soon as you've got him. Ethan, hurry."

"Will do."

Eli's heart raced as he pressed the gas and clicked through his cell.

"Colson here."

"Quinn, I need everyone you've got out at Summit mountain. We've got him. His name is Ted Davis—

"*Ted Davis?*"

"Yes."

"The drunk that hangs out a Frank's?"

"Yes. He's got Payton. Ethan's tracing his cell. Get your ass out here."

"Where, exactly?"

Good question. "Just be ready. Be close. When we get his location, I'll need backup."

"I'm there, man."

Eli clicked off the phone and flew down the pitted dirt road. Dense forest flew past his windows. He hung a left onto a barely visible road with ruts made from hunters' tire tracks. If memory served him correctly, this was the path they took to get to Mary Freeman's location, which was less than a half-mile from Jane Doe's.

He frowned—they'd searched this area for tire tracks. Was there a road he didn't know about?

He picked up his phone.

"Hello?"

"Mr. Powell, this is Eli Archer."

A moment of silence ticked by, which was better than he expected. Silence was always better than profanity laced rants.

"I need a favor."

"Well, well, well," Gary's gruff voice chuckled on the other end of the phone, and Eli guessed the land owner was already drunk.

"You said you saw the truck with the camper on your land, right?"

"That's right. Crossing through."

"Do you remember where exactly? What road specifically he was on?"

"It's not even a road, just tracks that kids take to go off the grid. It crosses Shadow creek and then splits off in three different directions."

"I need you to tell me the shortest way to get there."

There was a pause, and Eli knew the man deciding on whether or not to help him.

"You think you've found the guy?" Gary asked.

"Unless I lose him because you're wasting damn time trying to decide whether to help me out or not. Tell me how to get to the fucking short-cut, Gary."

Another pause, then, "I appreciate you looking the other way about my little side-business. So, you scratch my back, I scratch yours."

As Gary rattled off the directions to the shortcut, Eli rolled the windows down and wound his way through the woods, his car bottoming-out more times than he could count. He kept his eyes peeled for a red truck towing a camper trailer, or any vehicle for that matter.

It was almost noon, the sun like a ball of fire above him, with flames of light shooting through the canopy of trees like fingers pointing him toward doom. The air was still, not even a breeze to rustle the leaves.

Quiet.

Sweltering.

Most people thought of night—darkness—as the time when the demons came to play, but Eli had seen plenty of malevolence happen in the shadows of broad daylight.

The time of day didn't matter.

Evil was evil, and it was on-call twenty-four hours a day.

A flash caught his eye, sunlight reflecting off something silver through the trees. His back straightened like a rod and he slowed, craning his neck to see through the dense forest.

Something was out there, just beyond a thicket of trees.

He rolled to a stop, turned off the engine and got out.

The back of his neck prickled.

No birds were singing, no squirrels jumping around the trees. Stillness—evil—engulfed him.

He was close, he felt it in every fiber of his being.

He quickly radioed his location, pulled the keys from the ignition, but left the car door open to avoid being heard.

His heart started to pound as he drew his gun.

She was close. He actually *felt* Payton.

And she was in pain.

He moved stealthily through the thick underbrush, slipping from tree to tree. As he drew closer, he became more and more certain the object hidden behind a thicket of bushes was a camper. Panic, urgency, threatened to cloud his judgment and the cool-headedness that was mandatory in these situations. He wasn't used to this—he wasn't used to emotions interfering with cases.

He inhaled deeply through his nose, exhaled, moving swiftly.

Finally, a silver camper, hooked to an old, red Ford came into view—and his heart sank.

Shadow.

The name of the camper was etched in cursive down the side.

Shadow.

He clenched his jaw. Pam Robertson had seen the word printed on the camper as he dragged her into it. That's what she was trying to tell Eli moments before she died.

This was it. *The Shadow.*

Careful to stay out of sight, he peered between two trees — the curtains inside were drawn, no movement.

And then he heard it—a muffled scream so intense it made the hair on his arms stand up.

Payton.

He lunged out of the trees and rushed the camper, his finger sliding over the trigger as he tried the sliver door handle—locked.

Fuck. He hunkered down and circled the camper, checking for another point of entry, but found nothing.

Another scream, and then his training, years of experience dealing with serial killers—it all went out the window as the sheer terror of losing Payton overcame anything else.

"FBI!" He yelled as he raised his gun and ran back to the door. "Open the door!"

Adrenaline vibrated through his body, a fear greater than he'd ever felt gripped him. And it was that moment he realized Payton Chase was the first victim to have that kind of control over him.

She wasn't just another victim.

She was someone he'd fallen madly in love with.

He *felt.*

He took a step back, narrowed his sights and pulled the trigger.

Pop, pop, pop!

The door lock exploded, the handle clattering to the ground.

There was no thinking, no time to remind himself he wasn't wearing a Kevlar vest, no considering his hostage negotiation training. He stormed the camper and was met with a rain of bullets. He dove forward, his body slamming onto the tiled floor. He flipped onto to his back and raised his gun—*pop, pop!*

A terrifying-looking masked Ted Davis dove to the side, his gun flying from his hands, allowing Eli a chance to get his bearings. His gaze landed on Payton, chained, bloody and unconscious in the corner.

Bam!

Pain exploded in his jaw from a solid right-hook.

Distraction—it had cost many agents their lives.

Fury rose inside him as he lunged forward, tackling Ted, the mask sliding off his face. They tumbled to the floor, the close quarters making for an interesting fight. Knives, tools, lighters tumbled off the counter onto them, moments before Eli received another punch to the nose—the blood pouring from his face. He was pinned against a bench seat, but managed to land two back-to-back punches of his own, followed by a kick to Ted's ribcage, allowing Eli a second to scramble backwards toward the gun in the corner.

Ted grabbed his ankle, threw his body over Eli and pressed a knife to his throat.

Eli froze, and stared into the wild, feral eyes of a crazed man. Blood smeared Ted's contorted face, dripping onto Eli's cheek.

He had two choices, stay still or fight and risk getting sliced open from ear to ear.

The cloying scent of blood filled his nose—not just his, not just Ted's, but Payton's blood.

Payton.

Rage surged as he slammed his fist into Ted's kidney, kneed him in the groin then shifted out from under him, but not before the blade ran across his skin.

Eli straddled the Couer Killer, pounding his face until the body went limp under his.

Then, he lunged for Payton.

25

Thirty-one hours later...

BALANCING AN ARMFUL, Eli carefully got out of his rental car and kicked the door closed with his foot. Dusk was settling behind the mountains, the buzz of cicadas ramping up for the evening to come. Stars were beginning to twinkle, high above the deep orange and red blanketing the mountainside. He made a mental note to water the begonias as he made his way up the mani-cured walkway to Payton's front porch. He silently opened the front door and stepped inside. The air conditioner that had been set to blast cooled his hot skin, slicked with sweat. The relentless heat wave continued, and so did the media circus covering the Couer Killer. Along with an evidence response team, and every single member of BSPD, Eli had searched Ted Davis's house, uncovering not only a shrine of LaRouche paintings, but hundreds of his own. As Eli's profile had suggested, Ted was an avid painter, a secret he kept close to his chest along with his drug use and lifelong battle with depression. Ted identified with the pain rumored to consume LaRouche's life, and particularly with the haunting *Sans Couer* painting. He fixated on, stalked, and murdered the "woman in the painting." Ted's love of art extended into sales and trading, where he'd set up a popular website years earlier to buy, sell, and trade art, along with pricy shoes, bags, and jewelry. He'd made a solid chunk of change for himself over the last few years. Courtney Howard's auburn-haired profile picture caught his attention, beginning the year-long streak that will be forever remembered as the Couer Killings. But perhaps the most insight into the man's mind came from Ted's girlfriend who gave a glimpse into a life of domestic abuse—that went unreported of course—drugs, and obsession.

A tortured soul.

Arnie Miller was awaiting his release from prison, and as expected, the story was all over the news. Payton, and her help in tracking a serial killer had made national news. A media circus.

It had been a day and a half of interviews, phone calls, paperwork, with no end in sight. And now, it was almost seven-thirty in the evening and although he had plenty left to do, the last few days had shuffled his priorities in a way that had shaken him to his very core.

The warm scent of vanilla filled his nose, accompanied with silence—No TV, no radio, nothing. That was good; Payton needed her rest.

"You must be Eli."

He jerked his attention to a man stepping out from the shadows and immediately kicked himself for not leaving his right-hand free. *Always have your gun-hand free, idiot.* What was it about this woman that made him lose all common sense?

Love, he thought.

He looked the tall man over, dark circles under his eyes suggesting lack of sleep, pale, gaunt skin suggesting physical and emotional exhaustion.

"Mr. Chase," Eli said.

"Please, call me Arthur." Arthur's flight had been delayed overseas, setting his arrival back a full day. Mona had agreed to stay with Payton while Eli went into town to tie up loose ends.

"Here," Payton's father reached forward and took the crock pot and flowers from Eli's hands. "Let me guess, chicken noodle soup?" A small smile crossed his face.

"It's a cure-all," Eli said as he followed him into the kitchen, hoping Arthur wasn't going to ask where he got it. He didn't want to explain that he'd spent an hour in the kitchen at the B&B whipping up a batch of his grandmother's famous soup, when he really should have been working. Eli used to love to cook, but he hadn't done it in a decade. He'd hadn't cooked for a woman in his entire life. It brought back a joy, a relaxation he'd forgotten about, back into his life.

"I've heard about you, Agent Archer. The best criminal profiler in the FBI."

Eli said nothing—he was never good with compliments.

Arthur continued, "But all that pales in comparison to saving my daughter's life." Tears welled in the man's eyes, but he quickly blinked them away. "And I hear that you haven't left her side since the... incident."

"Only to do what I needed to do to make sure Ted Davis never sees the light of day again."

Arthur nodded, looked down and ran his fingers

through his thinning hair. "They've requested interviews from me as well, but I told them not until I saw my daughter first." He glanced at the clock. "I'm supposed to be at the station in twenty minutes." He looked at Eli with a plea in his eyes. Although the threat was gone, Payton's father still wanted his daughter looked after, protected, if only to give himself peace of mind.

"I'll be here."

"Good, thank you." Arthur blew out a breath. "I... I don't know what Payton has told you, but I haven't been the best father since... since her mother passed. Losing someone you love..." he looked at Eli with an intensity that had him steeling, "changes the very core of who you are. But, not anymore." He squared his broad shoulders. "This was the slap in the face I needed. Things are going to change now. They already have." He looked around the kitchen. "Do you know I've never even been here? To my own daughter's house?" He shook his head. "Anyway, I don't know why I tell you this other than that I have a feeling you're going to be around a while. Payton's going to need you through this— the media firestorm that's already knocking down her door, the backlash from Charmaine, the divorce, everything." He paused and stared at a small nick in the marble counter for a few seconds. "She's scarred." His voice cracked. "The son of a bitch scarred her."

Eli's jaw clenched as the unrelenting anger that has been clawing at him the last two days gripped hold again.

"She's going to need you, Eli."

Eli nodded, and matching the man's intensity said, "I give you my word, sir, nothing will happen to your daughter ever again."

A lone tear slid down Arthur's face as he nodded. He inhaled, then waved his hand in the air as if to wave the emotion away. "I look forward to getting to know you, Eli. Hell, I look forward to getting to know my daughter again."

"I'm sure she looks forward to that, too."

"Good, good." Another deep breath. "Okay, I'm going to head into town. Not sure how long I'll be—"

"I'll be here."

"Thank you. Mona's going back and forth between here and my house to help look after Charmaine." His face dropped as he said the name of the woman who'd betrayed him in so many ways. "But you'll be here, so I won't worry." He grabbed his keys and started for the door, but paused and turned back. "My wife betrayed me, my best friend betrayed me, but at the end of the day, it's my fault. It's my fault for closing myself off to them after losing my wife. If I'd have given more, been more open, who knows if we'd be here right now." He narrowed his eyes. "Don't let bad experiences, fear, depression, darkness to define you, Eli. Allow the light in."

The words hit him like a sledgehammer.

Darkness.

He stood in the foyer for a solid minute after Arthur walked out the door.

Let the light in.

He grabbed the vase from the counter and walked down the hall, pausing at the doorway of Payton's bedroom before tip-toeing inside.

A sliver of light shone through the slit in the curtains, beaming across the bed. Her auburn hair fanned across the white pillow, a few strands running along her cheek.

A lump caught in his throat as he looked down at her. Emotions swirled inside him, anger at what had been done to her, guilt that he hadn't gotten there sooner, gratitude that he'd gotten there before it was too late, fear that he could lose her again... fear that he could lose the only woman to crack open his shriveled heart.

She was so beautiful.

As if sensing him, she stirred, and he quickly took a step back, freezing like a statue.

She rolled to her back and opened her eyes, her gaze meeting his.

A soft smile crossed her lips.

His heart swelled "Hi."

"Hi." Her smile widened. "You brought me lavender."

"Supposed to be relaxing, or so the lady at the farmer's market told me."

She started to sit up, and he quickly slid the vase onto the end table. "Careful, now, here." He helped her forward and stacked pillows behind her. She leaned back and nestled in. After making sure she was comfortable, he sat on the bed and lightly stroked the top of her head. "How are you feeling?"

"Better. Didn't even take a pain pill this morning."

"Good." He made an effort to not allow his eyes to drift to her bruising, or her scars. "Do you need anything right now?"

"For my phone to stop ringing."

"Well, that's an easy fix." He picked up her pink phone and clicked it off.

"I kept it on in case you called."

"I'm sorry I had to leave you."

"No, no, don't say that. I know you had to go in."

He did have to go in. He wasn't going to sit back and rely on anyone else to ensure Ted Davis got everything he deserved.

"I just met your dad."

Her eyebrows popped up. "Did you?"

He nodded.

"How'd that go?"

"He cares about you, Payton. Wants a relationship with you."

She nodded and began picking at the edge of the comforter. "He got here a few hours ago. We had a good talk." Her eyes met his. "He's leaving her, you know."

Eli nodded.

"He's not pressing charges, do you know that?"

He'd been informed that at the station. Arthur Chase offered not to press charges as long as Charmaine waived her right to his fortune after the divorce was finalized. She had no choice—jail, or freedom. Charmaine accepted freedom and along with her signature, Arthur wrote her a five-hundred-thousand-dollar check to leave town and start her life over somewhere else. It was a shocking move to everyone, but having met the man now, Eli wasn't so surprised. The man carried a mountain of guilt on his shoulders and the money was a sense of closure to release a bit of that weight. Charmaine would be out of Payton's life forever and if Eli had to guess, out of the country within the next few days.

"And Mateo?" She asked.

"Charged with attempted first-degree murder."

Payton nodded, took a deep breath, and he could see the next question brewing in her eyes.

"He's gone too, Pay." Eli leaned forward, stroking her head. "They're pushing for the death penalty."

A heavy moment slid by. Tears filled her eyes as she turned to him.

"I'm scarred, Eli."

His heart shattered in a million pieces.

He ran his finger over the scabby welts along her

jawline. "You're beautiful, Payton. The most beautiful woman I've ever seen in my life." His voice cracked and, overcome with emotions, he pushed off the bed and walked to the window.

Let the light in.

He drew back the curtains, and the room filled with the bright, golden light of sunset. He sat on the edge of the bed and grabbed her hand.

"This is just a part of your story, Payton. A small part in a life that's going to be filled with joy and happiness. I promise you that. I promise I will never let anything happen to you again. You have your dad, again, and me, now. Forever." He swiped a tear from her cheek while fighting his own. "We've both lived our lives in darkness, in shadows, but no more." He leaned inches from her face. "I love you Payton. More than I've ever loved anything in my life. You've brought me back to life. Reminded me of the man I used to be." He traced his finger along the stitches on his neck, then down hers. "These scars have nothing on us."

She sniffed, smiled. "Matching scars."

"I guess that makes us partners for life." He dipped down and kissed her, slow, soft, steady.

"I love you, Payton," he whispered, allowing a tear to drop. "'I love you."

"I love you, too, Eli."

～

SNEAK PEEK

THE CAVE (A BERRY SPRINGS NOVEL)

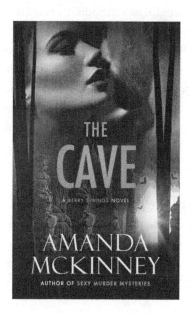

After getting trapped in a remote cave, two strangers

must work together to survive while being hunted by a ruthless killer...

Life is full of surprises, rescue swimmer Owen Grayson knows that better than anyone, especially when he's forced to take an indefinite military leave and return home to pick up the pieces of his dad's latest mistake. As Owen struggles to settle back into his roots, he is called to a remote cave where he's pulled into a mystery that hits a little too close to home. As the clues begin to unravel, it becomes apparent that the cave is hiding secrets worth killing for... and everyone on site has a target on their back.

Coming off a bad break up and an even worse few days, Forensic Anthropologist Dr. Sadie Hart is brought in to excavate human remains found deep in the treacherous mountains of Berry Springs, in a cave rumored to be haunted, nonetheless. When her team stumbles upon a dead body before they even reach the cave, Sadie quickly realizes this is going to be no ordinary job—especially when she meets a particularly charming Adonis who's hellbent on becoming her next mistake.

A storm hits, trapping Sadie and Owen inside the cave with nothing but a flashlight and a small backpack with provisions... and someone who wants them dead. As the odds stack up against them, Sadie begins to fear she and Owen will become the next pile of bones found deep in the catacombs of Crypts Cavern...

THE CAVE is a standalone romantic suspense novel.

∽

CHAPTER ONE

SHE WAS BEAUTIFUL. Alluring, magical. A commanding force who had a way of reminding you how little and vulnerable human life was. How she could chew you up and spit you out without so much as a happy ending. She was powerful, relentless, unforgiving, and tonight, she was in one hell of a mood.

Owen knew her well. He loved her, respected her, and had found a home with her even though she'd take everything from him in a moment's notice, then build him back up, only to destroy him again. She was addictive, an adrenaline rush second only to jumping out of a MH-60 Jayhawk at a hundred feet, then getting pelted with a 120-knot rotor blast. He'd seen the bodies she'd devoured in her wake, watched the friends and families cry. But the truth was, he'd be nothing without her. She'd made him into the man he was today. For better or worse.

She was a bitch of a mistress, and Owen's gut told him they were in for a helluva fight tonight.

Owen buckled the waist belt, giving it a quick tug before moving onto the chest straps. The helicopter dipped, dropped, then lifted again causing him to glance up at the pilot, Lieutenant Potts, who was laser focused on the controls glowing through the dark night. A flash of lightning streaked the sky in the distance, sparkling off the rain-streaked windshield. Up ahead, the lights of a capsized sailboat—the only light in the black, swirling water—swaying back and forth on its side, at the mercy of her angry waves.

Yeah, she was in one hell of a mood tonight.

Petty Officer Williams handed him a dive mask, and Owen pretended not to notice the tremble in the rookie's hand.

From the flight deck, Potts's voice crackled through the radio. "We've got a second round of storms coming in at one-hundred twenty kilos. Need to get a move on this, boss."

"Almost ready. What've we got?" Owen strapped on his gloves.

"Surface winds of fifty-two, nine foot swells. I'm as low as I can go in this wind."

Owen cast a side-long glance at the rookie's rounded eyes. "Another walk in the park, kid." He winked as the prominent Adam's apple in the rook's throat bobbed.

Lieutenant Foster, a two-thirty tank of muscle with an attitude to match, pushed past the rook, shoving him to the side. His steely eyes met Owen's, and after a quick shake of his head, he checked Owen's gear one last time. The helo dipped again, sending the rookie stumbling. Owen caught him by the arm and yanked the kid to him.

"I need you to pull it together, Williams. You've trained for this, kid. We're search and rescue swimmers. This is it, *this* is what we do. Grab your fucking balls. You've got this."

Williams blinked, then steeled himself and nodded. "Sorry, boss."

Owen turned toward Foster, who was in charge of operating the hoist. "I'll bring the kid up first, then the mom, then the dad."

Foster nodded—*I'm ready.*

"When you are, Potts."

"10-4. Target is directly below us. Remember, names, Gary, Beverly, Timmy McCarver. One yellow lifejacket in the water, next to the boat."

"One?"

"One."

One lifejacket for a family of three didn't bode well.

Owen removed his radio, pulled the wet suit over his

head, and secured his mask. The door opened, sending a freight train of whirling wind and rain inside.

It was go time.

Owen looked down at the black water swirling twenty-five feet below, only visible by the white caps of the crashing waves. He scanned the water, looking for the family who'd been tossed overboard. The spotlight from the helicopter illuminated a wide circle over the water but through the slanted rain, visibility was shit. He'd just have to trust his team.

Just another walk in the park, his own words echoed in his head as Foster counted off on his fingers—*one, two, three.*

Owen shimmied to the edge, and after a quick inhale, dropped off the platform, plunging into the water below. The wind was strong, relentless, the bitch of all bitches. After a thumbs-up to the crew, the helo rose, taking most of the rotor spray with it.

Owen zeroed in on the capsized sailboat circled with a yellow spotlight. A four-year-old boy, his mother, and father had made the poor decision to ignore weather warnings and take the boat out for the evening. They'd drifted further than expected, and, to no one's surprise, got caught in the storm. The Coast Guard received a mayday twenty minutes earlier, before the boat had capsized. Owen wondered if this would still be a rescue mission, or body retrieval at this point... assuming the other bodies were even found.

A massive wave roared toward him, and he dove under, waiting for it to pass as it crashed down on him, tossing him like he was nothing—a small speck in the middle of an endless black sea. After years of training, years of leading rescue missions, the force of the ocean never ceased to amaze Owen. And for a man who liked control, the irony wasn't lost on him. He'd fallen in love with a force stronger than him, bigger than him. The only thing he could count on was that she was unpredictable. Like most women in his life.

Like this mission.

Owen came up for air, fighting the churning water around him, then dove again pushing through water that felt like thick molasses, twisting and turning him with each stroke. Finally, he reached the boat.

"Help!" The shrill scream carried though the howling wind like a beacon.

Through the sheets of rain, a man waved wildly from his death-grip on the mast, his bright yellow life jacket reflecting in the spotlight. Owen dipped under again, careful to stay away from floating debris.

"Mr. McCarver, I'm US Coast Guard Search and Rescue," Owen shouted over the crashing waves once he reached the mast. "Where is your wife and son?"

Eye's wide with shock, McCarver's face was pale, panicked, wild. The man opened his mouth, but shut it when they rose with a wave and were splashed by buckets of water. But, by the look on the man's face, Owen knew what was coming before he even said it.

"She's..." he spat out ocean water. "He... Timmy, my boy, he slipped off, into the water... she dove in after him. I tried to stop her! I *tried—*"

Shit.

Owen turned and scanned the dark water, catching a glint of reflective material a few yards out.

Child first.

"I'm going to get your wife and boy, first. I'll be back for you. Keep the life jacket on, stay on the mast. I'll be back."

As he turned to go under, a wave crashed over them, a

Mack truck barreling across the sea. Owen breached—
McCarver was gone.

Shit, shit, shit.

He dove under, gripped the man under the shoulders
and pulled him up. Coughing, spitting, gasping for air,
McCarver swatted, grabbed and pulled at Owen. "I'm
drowning," he gasped. "I'm drowning."

McCarver had at least thirty pounds on Owen but when
survival instinct mixed with adrenaline, it felt more like an
eight-hundred pound grizzly bear wrapping around him.

"You're not drowning. *Gary,* I've got you."

With every second that ticked by with Gary McCarver
trying to crawl onto him like a damn life boat, the storm was
getting worse and Owen was losing time searching for the
rest of the family. So, he made the snap decision to save the
father first, then go after the family.

"Sir," he slipped behind and wrapped his arm around
the writhing panic attack, "I've *got* you."

He looked up at another wave about to barrel onto them.
Owen clenched his jaw as he gripped the yellow life jacket a
split-second before the wave hit. They both went under,
then bobbed back up.

"I'm going to take you to the basket and pull you up." He
yelled as he turned, kicking his fins wildly against the whipping current. The rain had picked up, reminding him of
Potts's warning about the lightning. The helo hovered
above, swaying in the storm as the ocean swayed in the
opposite direction. McCarver continued to pull him under
despite Owen's repeated warnings not to. It took three tries
to get ahold of the rescue basket, before Owen could even
secure the man into it. Water pelted them like shards of
glass hurling through the darkness. Owen gave the signal
moments before the basket began to rise.

One down, two to go.

As he started to turn away, a light from the helicopter cabin caught his attention—a bright red light waving back and forth.

Kill the mission.

His gaze shifted to a flash of lightning piercing the sky, closer now.

Kill the mission.

Just then—a distant scream.

All or none, he thought as he turned and dove back under allowing his instinct, his sixth sense, to guide him knowing that every second longer he spent in the water put his crew's life on the line.

A mother and child.

Adrenaline flooded his veins as he fought through the storm, the waves, and the fatigue numbing his legs.

"*US Coast Guard. Where are you?*" He yelled over the wind, the helo spotlight scanning the water, nowhere close to his location. The lights from the sailboat barely illuminated the radius of the boat itself.

A second passed...

"*Over here!*"

Owen would never forget the sound of the woman's scream for the rest of his life. It wasn't only panic... it was a wild, primal tone, a terror he'd never heard before...

And then he found out why.

With one arm wrapped around a life preserver, a mother gripped her four-year-old boy, dangling lifelessly over her other arm.

"He's *dead!*" Her eyes met his across the black churning water. "*He's dead!*"

The boy's skin was pale, lips blue, eyes closed as his head bobbed against the water.

And then... the world went black. A pitch-black inky dark. A darkness only being out in the middle of the ocean could provide. The capsized boat had finally lost electricity, and with no light to guide him, he had a nice little problem on his hands. One shift of location, one big wave, and that boat could crash down on top of them, killing them in seconds flat. He looked up at the spotlight shooting out of the helo, scanning the ocean for him.

They were a good twenty yards off.

Fuck.

Owen swam toward the hysterical screams.

"*Ma'am!* I'm here, I'm going to get you out of here." Kicking, he reached forward until—*finally*—he made contact.

Frantic arms swatted at him. "He's dead! *He's dead! My boy is dead.*"

Eclipsing the father's panic, this woman was hysterical, which was obstacle number one. The second obstacle was that if the child was dead, there was no way in hell she was leaving the boy's body. Obstacle three—about ten more minutes and they'd all be at the bottom of the Atlantic Ocean.

"Keep hold onto the life preserver, and onto me, Mrs. McCarver," he said as he felt the thin arm of the limp body next to him. "I need you to let go of your son. I've got him."

"He's dead!" She continued to scream, but a well-timed wave knocked her grip just enough for Owen to pull the boy to him. Owen wrapped his arms around the little, cold body, fisted his hands and shoved them into the child's sternum. Again, again, using each kick under the water as leverage with each thrust of his fist.

Another wave, another force under the water.

He shifted the boy and blew five rescue breaths into his mouth, then turned him again.

His brain was screaming at him to get back to the helo *and* out of the path of the sailboat.

One more, Owen. One more fucking try.

As his fist bored into the tiny chest, the spotlight found them just as water spewed from the child's lips.

"My *baby!*" She screamed as the child wailed like an infant.

For a split-second the world froze around him as he looked into the boy's eyes, now full of life. A wave pulled him back to the moment and his determination switched to tactical—he had to get the fuck out of there.

"I've got your son—"

"Is he alive?" She squeaked.

"Yes, ma'am," he yelled over the rain and screaming child. "I've got him. You have to trust me."

"I have to—"

He locked eyes on her. "You have to trust me. Do you trust me?"

She stared at him with round eyes, helpless, exhausted, fatigued... but *hopeful*—another moment he would never forget.

"Yes." She nodded. "Yes."

"Good. Let's go."

Owen looked in the direction of the sailboat—total blackness—called a Hail Mary and with one arm hooked around the child and gripping the life preserver with the mother, they swam to the rescue basket dangling a few yards away.

Two more waves crashed over them until he finally gripped the basket. Thankfully, the mom was a tiny thing and Owen was able to allow her and her son to ride up together. He watched from the churning water as the mother gripped onto her baby boy, swaying in the wind.

Alive.

Once they were safely inside the helo, Owen was hoisted inside. It took both Williams and Foster to get him into the cabin.

Owen ripped off his mask, his gaze darting around the cabin until he spotted the boy—he was okay.

He looked around at his team, tending to the family—they were okay.

Okay, Owen, okay.

Extreme exhaustion waved over him like an unstoppable force. He fell to the cabin floor, chest heaving.

Williams kneeled down beside him with a grin the size of Texas. "Holy shit, man," he yelled as the door closed and the helicopter lifted.

Holy shit was right.

"Hell of a way to go out, man. A fucking legendary last mission." He patted Owen's forehead before taking his seat in the front.

Legendary last mission.

His *last* mission.

Owen's gut clenched—not because of the near-death experience he'd just had, or because of the adrenaline crash, but because he was about to walk away from the only thing he'd ever loved.

Owen rolled down the windows as he bumped along the pitted dirt road. The mild, autumn breeze whipped around the cab of the truck, the spicy scent of fall triggering memories—some good, some bad. He mindlessly swerved around a pothole—the same one that had given him multiple flat tires growing up. He looked around the dense woods that surrounded him, the last of the day's sun spearing through the thick canopy of trees. The Ozark Mountains were a canvas of yellow, orange, and red leaves, each desperately hanging on to the past, before their time was up.

Like his was.

He turned up the radio in an attempt to distract the nerves threatening to grab ahold of him. Nerves make you messy, and if there was anything Owen wasn't, it was messy.

He inhaled deeply—what a cluster fuck.

It had been two weeks since he'd saved the McCarver family from the Louisiana coast. Two weeks since he'd signed the papers that released him on indefinite military leave. Two weeks since he'd received a call that his dad had been arrested for his third fucking DWI, and after a short stint in jail, was being forced by the judge—his father's old high school buddy—to enter a sixty-day rehab program.

His *dad*... in *rehab*. His mess of a father who after his mom walked out on him, went into a deep liquor-induced depression throwing away everything and anything positive in his life. The man had given up on everything except booze.

Lester Grayson had spent his life serving his country in the Navy, just like his father—Owen's grandfather—did. Owen was born between his father's deployments, to a nineteen-year-old girl who'd decided it would be fun to go home with a sailor after a few too many whiskey shots at the local bar. That single decision turned into a baby boy they'd named Owen. Despite the birth of his first and only son, Les continued his career in the military, but only after deciding it was probably best to marry Sheila—he had knocked her up, anyway—in jeans and T-shirts at the county courthouse. And so began a tumultuous relationship of a man who put his country above all else and a woman who never wanted his baby in the first place.

Owen spent his childhood roaming the mountains of

Berry Springs, doing everything he could to avoid being home where arguing was as common as empty whiskey bottles. The woods, the mountains, were his home... until his uncle, Ray Grayson, taught him to swim in the lake just below their small cabin.

At seventy miles long and including over five-hundred miles of shoreline, Otter Lake was one of the main tourist attractions in the small, southern town. Splitting off into dozens of rivers and creeks that wound through the treacherous mountains, the lake was speckled with soaring bluffs, deep valleys and miles of caves.

Before school, Owen would swim four miles every morning, despite the temperature. He taught himself how to fish and eventually bought a small fishing boat, where he spent most of his evenings. The water was his peace, his solitude, his escape from the chaos of his house.

Owen found his new home in the water, so it was no surprise that the day after graduating high school, he enlisted in the Coast Guard, spending the next fifteen years of his life as a rescue swimmer on an elite Search and Rescue team stationed in Louisiana.

He'd found his one true love in the ocean, and he'd found his family in his teammates, and despite several trips home to bail his father out of jail or to attend funerals, Owen had vowed never to return to the Ozark Mountains. For good, anyway.

That was until he'd received the call about his dad's latest fuck up, and was informed that his father had not only spent the last year of his life drinking himself to death, but also barely paying his debt to the bank, stopping payments altogether over the last few months. Owen was at risk of losing his family home and the family business while his dad went away.

"Let him lose everything, Grayson. It's his fuck up, not yours," his Coast Guard buddies had told him. *"Maybe this is what he needs to finally wake up,"* they'd said.

But just like the times he'd made the ten hour drive from his base in New Orleans to bail his dad out, or just like the times he'd wired money when the man couldn't make ends meet, Owen couldn't turn a shoulder to his dad. Never had been able to. Because the truth was, Owen knew what serving decades in the military did to a man. Owen knew the sacrifice and respected it. Owen knew the weight of seeing dead bodies, watching men die in your arms, and making life or death decisions in the blink of an eye. It fucked with a man's psyche. Some men were stronger than others, but they were all bonded by a common thread— serving their country.

Commitment.

Honor.

Respect.

That's why he'd come back.

Owen shook the thoughts away as he braked next to a rusted mailbox with more dents in it than his Chevy.

L. Grayson

The damn lid didn't even close. He pulled out the stacks of mail, noting more than one red envelope.

Nothing good ever came from a red envelope.

After taking a second to jimmy the lid closed, then adding a new mailbox to the running shopping list in his head, he stared at the narrow dirt driveway that led to his family home.

Tall oak trees grew like a tunnel over the drive, swaying in the autumn breeze. Dead leaves covered the ground. The underbrush was thick, with snarled bushes, rotting logs and tree limbs. A massive tree had fallen inches from the ditch, probably during the last ice storm, he guessed.

Owen tossed the mail on the passenger seat and turned into the driveway. It had been five months since he'd been home last, and based on the mailbox and landscaping, he couldn't wait to see what condition the house was in.

He descended the long driveway with one elbow hanging out the window, and memories of his childhood racing through his head. He passed the pine tree where he'd carved his initials, a mound of moss-covered boulders where he used to play cops and robbers—with himself, of course. A hundred-year-old oak tree that he used to climb and nestle himself in-between the branches with a Coca-Cola and a Hardy Boys book that he'd read a thousand times. So many memories, yet, as he drove down the dirt road, he realized they were all lonely memories. No family trips, no brothers, or sisters. Not many friends' parents were willing to drive that far into the woods just for a playdate. Hell, Owen had felt alone his whole life.

Just like he did now.

As he descended deeper into the valley, he eyed the old barbed wire fence that ran along the sides of the road, and hit the brakes.

I'll be a son of a bitch, he thought as he peered out the window at the long, black hair caught in the wire, and just beyond that, two massive bite marks on the tree. The black bears had moved in... which meant two things—his dad apparently didn't make it past the liquor cabinet when he was home, and two, the Ozark Mountain ecosystem was thriving.

Of all the times Owen had played in the woods as a child, he'd only seen a bear one time... and that was nothing compared to the mountain lion he'd come across one morning while hiking. It was all part of what made the woods magical to him—you never knew what you'd find.

Bears, elk, white-tailed deer, coyotes, were just a handful of the creatures that roamed the mountains. And although his home turf was the opposite of his address on the ocean, the woods were just as beautiful. Well... they *would be* after he spent weeks of back-breaking work getting the land up and running again.

He pressed on, driving deeper into the woods, when finally, the musty scent of lakeshore filled his nose.

Home.

A steep dip in the terrain, then a sharp corner, and the woods opened up to a small clearing speckled with maple and pine trees. Old, wooden fencing ran along the yard of his childhood home—the small cabin he stood to inherit one day.

Shaded by tree cover, the two bedroom, two bathroom log cabin was nestled in a small cove just above the lake. A pebbled walkway in the back led down to a dock, complete with a humble fishing boat.

Home.

Owen parked next to the single-car standalone garage, which was packed with boxes, old furniture, and whatever else his dad didn't have room for, and got out of the truck.

The woods were still, quiet.

The sound of the water lapping against the dock in the distance pulled him back in time—a familiar song of his past. A breeze swept past his skin, rustling the trees above as he fisted his hands on his hips and gazed at the decrepit house.

Rotted planks ran throughout the wraparound porch, the front window was cracked from God knows what, and there were dozens of shingles missing around a rock chimney. Leaves scattered the front porch, piling on the crooked porch swing that, apparently, his dad never used.

Owen grabbed his camo backpack from the bed of the truck, slung it over his shoulder, and walked up the aged wooden steps that led to the front porch. He kicked the pine needles and cigarette butts away from the front door as he slid the key inside.

With a deep breath he pushed through the heavy wooden door.

Stale, humid air hit him like a brick wall. Musty, dirty, was his first thought—his second was *holy shit.* The house he'd grown up in was an absolute wreck. Newspapers, beer cans, and magazines covered the leather couches that sat in front of floor-to-ceiling windows that looked out to the lake. Dust particles danced in the dimming sunlight spilling in through the smudged, dirty glass. The back deck was in the same shape as the front. A kitchen that hadn't seen a sponge or a can of Comet in months sat to the right, and beyond the massive rock fireplace to the left were two bedrooms—and based on the clutter he could see on the floor, also hadn't been cleaned in months.

He dropped his bag onto the dusty floor and blew out a breath. His father had given up. What man just gives up on life? Hell, his father had raised him to get up after every fall. No kissing or coddling, just wipe yourself off, and get back up.

What the hell happened to his dad?

Owen looked around the house, recalling their last conversation at the funeral, months earlier.

He knew. Owen knew exactly what had happened to his dad... and that thought brought a surprising pang of guilt. Maybe if he had stayed around after everything had happened. Maybe if he had never left in the first place...

Owen pushed the thought aside. *One thing at a time... one thing at a time.*

He made his way to the kitchen, set the stack of mail on the counter, killed a line of ants, then yanked open the fridge. Beer, more beer, boxed wine, wine coolers, and hot dogs. Owen grabbed a Shiner, popped the top and stepped outside onto the back deck.

A camping chair lay on its side next to an empty beer bottle filled with cigarette butts.

He walked to the middle of the deck, to a spot where he could see the lake through a break in the trees. After taking a sip, he leaned his forearms on the railing and gazed out to the water, sparkling under the setting sun.

He could not believe he was back here.

He could not believe the twist his life had taken.

He could not believe the knots in his stomach.

One thing at a time, Owen...

And with that thought, he ignored the unease coursing through his body and began making the long list of things he needed to get done.

THE CAVE

ABOUT THE AUTHOR

Amanda McKinney is the bestselling and multi-award-winning author of more than twenty romantic suspense and mystery novels. Her book, Rattlesnake Road, was named one of *POPSUGAR's 12 Best Romance Books,* and was featured on the *Today Show.* The fifth book in her Steele Shadows series was recently nominated for the prestigious *Daphne du Maurier Award for Excellence in Mystery/Suspense.* Amanda's books have received over fifteen literary awards and nominations.

Text **AMANDABOOKS to 66866** to sign up for Amanda's

Newsletter and get the latest on new releases, promos, and freebies!

www.amandamckinneyauthor.com

If you enjoyed The Shadow, please write a review!

Made in the USA
Monee, IL
05 April 2025

15230262R00163